IN SEARCH OF
DEATH

IN SEARCH OF
DEATH

CRAIG R. E. KROHN

IN SEARCH OF DEATH

iUniverse books may be ordered through booksellers or by contacting:

iUniverse
1663 Liberty Drive
Bloomington, IN 47403
www.iuniverse.com
1-800-Authors (1-800-288-4677)

ISBN: 978-1-4917-3841-2 (sc)
ISBN: 978-1-4917-3840-5 (e)

Library of Congress Control Number: 2014911455

Printed in the United States of America.

iUniverse rev. date: 07/14/2014

For my lifelong friend David, who reads my books and gently tells me how to improve my work. Also for Emily, who courageously braves the peril of living with a writer.

CONTENTS

It is said that there are no atheists in foxholes.

THE REPORTER

THERE WAS AN OLD MAN sitting on the edge of a bed and staring at his feet. He wore no shoes or socks, as these things were placed by the foot of the bed with great care. There was nothing remarkable about the man. He was clean shaven with short gray hair and otherwise would have blended in with a crowd of five people. His face held with it a certain wisdom that can only be granted by old age. He breathed evenly and confidently with a warm smile resting on his face.

The dull gray room was sparse with only one crude bed, a wooden chair, a small wooden table, a washbasin, and a hole in the floor for a toilet. The only decorations were pencil drawings of angels that were hung on the walls. There was a tiny opening in the wall to the outside with bars on it; it was too small to be called a window and too large to call a hole.

When the iron doors to the room opened, the distinct metal-on-metal sound broke the silence. The old man's ear twitched slightly, but he never averted his gaze from his feet. A younger man came in, and the door was closed behind him with a metallic clang as a heavy lock clicked into place. "Thank you," the younger man said over his shoulder.

The young man stopped and stared at the old man for a moment and then removed his hat and took a chair that was leaning up against the wall and moved it closer to the bed. He took off his coat and placed it neatly over the chair. He rubbed his wrists, which were red and irritated, before he rummaged through a pocket and produced a leather-bound book. He sat down on the old wooden chair.

For a long moment, no words were spoken. The old man kept looking at his feet and rubbing at them, and the younger man sat in anticipation. The younger man cleared his throat and held out a brass cigarette case with several cigarettes in it. The old man looked up. His brown eyes danced a bit in the dim light as he raised a hand in protest.

The young man closed the cigarette case without taking one out and tucked it back into a pocket in his suit jacket. He pulled at his shirt as if he were still wearing a tie and fiddled with his notepad. "I have been studying your case. It is very … unique. Did they tell you I would be here?"

The old man smiled and nodded; he went back to rubbing his feet.

The younger man continued, "It would seem that everyone thinks you're crazy."

The old man shrugged. "You can't believe everything you hear."

After taking a deep breath, the younger man said, "Well, I've seen the reports, and I was at the trial. You weren't exactly shy during your testimony. You made it quite plain that you think an angel told you to do the things that you did. You even said that you had a magical sword from the last crusade. The doctors all believed you to be insane, as did the jury. All of your claims do indeed sound crazy, wouldn't you agree?"

The old man laughed, and a smile came to him, but he returned his gaze back to his feet. "Do you always start conversations this way?"

The young man tilted his head to one side. "No. I was just anxious to get started, and I know we have limited time. I'm sorry. I'm Erich Kunze. I've been assigned to write a story about you. I'm a journalist for the local newspaper in town." Erich reached out with his hand open.

The old man looked at the journalist's hand for a moment and then clasped it in a firm handshake. "What makes you think I have a story to tell? Not many young people wish to hear the ramblings of old men."

"Well, I was intrigued by the talk of angels, magic, and other fanciful things. I wanted to hear more about these stories. It's sort of an interest of mine." The young man paused and put the leather-bound book in his lap.

The old man looked back at the reporter. "People will try to make sense of their world in the only ways they know how. We can't fault them for that, now can we?"

The reporter cleared his throat. "So, are you?"

"Am I insane?" The old man shook his head. "No. But when there's no proof—what does it matter? I might as well be insane then. That would be a shorter and easier tale to tell. And I think it would look nice in newsprint, wouldn't you agree?"

The younger man tilted his head to one side. "Well, this matters to me, and it certainly should matter to you."

The old man took a long, easy breath as if he were smelling fresh roses. "Oh, it matters to me, but in a way that is difficult to explain. I don't care to be remembered as a crazy person, but that's how it just might have to be for now."

Erich folded his arms once and then unfolded them. "Well, that's why I'm here: to put clarity to this … situation. You were very sure of yourself in the trial that you spoke to angels."

The old man considered the other for a moment and then said, "Those sound like crazy words, don't they? Who would believe that if presented with such a story?"

The young man cleared his throat again. "Well, as a reporter, I am just supposed to talk about the facts. I'm not supposed to put any judgment on these things."

The old man smiled. "Ah, and that's the rub, isn't it? It's difficult not to put your own bias into anything, now isn't it?"

"That may certainly be true, but we endeavor to do the best that we can. Do you believe that you were helped by angels?" the reporter asked, looking into the eyes of the old man.

The old man harrumphed. "'Believe'? Your choice of words is telling. You have already decided upon the outcome of this story, have you not?"

The young man broke his gaze, opened up his book, and took out a pencil. "Please forgive me. I'm rather new to all of this. I didn't mean to offend you."

The old man straightened out his left leg and rubbed his knee. "You cannot offend me. No harm done. Can a squirrel offend a bear?"

The reporter laughed. "Am I the squirrel in this analogy?"

"I don't know. Are you? A man is what he thinks he is. If you want to be a squirrel, you can be a squirrel. If you want to be a titan, that is also your right. Wouldn't you agree?"

"I think I'm a bit lost." The reporter tapped his pencil to his notebook.

"Mm, yes," the old man said, now rubbing his leg.

Leaning forward, Erich said, "I would like to hear your story. I would like to know if you had a magical sword."

The old man looked at the younger man; his eyes scanned him head to toe. He pulled his cane closer to him. "And what would you do with this story should I be the one who tells it to you?"

The young man straightened himself up in his chair. "I would take your story to the people so that they would know exactly what happened here."

"Ah. And what people would that be? The people of this country? The people of the world?"

"Well, anyone that's interested in knowing the truth."

The old man harrumphed, but a smile was still present on his face. "The truth? And what is that exactly? The truth is manufactured by the historians."

Erich sighed. "I just was curious. This seemed like something so fantastic I had to come here to find out for myself."

The old man tapped a finger to his forehead and then absentmindedly placed his cane in his lap. "Now we are getting closer to the truth. Thank you for your candor. To answer your question, yes, I have seen angels, and I have wielded a magical sword."

"How did you first see an angel?"

"How do you know that anyone is an angel or not?" the old man said.

The reporter tapped his pencil to his notebook several times before asking, "Can you tell me about this sword?"

The old man looked at his hands and rubbed them together. "I could, but you would not believe me. All you need to know is that it was a sword. It was a gift, and it was the single best thing that anyone had ever done for me."

"So it was magical, then?" Erich asked.

The old man shrugged. "I don't know, but it had wondrous power."

"You can tell me your story. I will believe you."

The old man looked up at Erich, and the reporter shrunk back somewhat. "In a very short time, I will be gone, and this story will be forgotten."

"All the more reason to relate your story—so that it will not be forgotten," Erich said.

The old man smiled again. "You will not believe me, and you may call me a liar or simply insane. I can tell you that I am neither, but you will likely dismiss this as fiction, anyway. I'm not interested in convincing you of who I really am or why I did what I did. All I know is that I saved someone very important to me, and I traveled forward and backward in time in order to do it. This is enough for me and for my conscience."

"You traveled through time?"

The old man nodded. "Yes, that's the heart of the story and perhaps the hardest thing to swallow."

The reporter looked down at his notepad and scribbled some notes. He didn't look up when he asked, "Is that why you did not mention it at the trial? You mentioned angels and magic swords but never time travel."

The old man shrugged, and there was a moment's pause.

Erich then asked, "Aren't you afraid of what happens tomorrow?"

After shaking his head, the old man said, "No. Why should I be? I'm an old man. I've lived a long life. I've done many things, and I've traveled the world and met fantastic people. What meets me outside of this door is irrelevant now. I've completed my life's mission. I've done my duty, and I've never felt this type of joy and freedom in my entire life. With each breath, I feel the world and my heart mending. I know that my mother and my father would both be proud, as would my wife, my children, and my children's children. I know now a peace that I've never felt before."

The old man paused to point at the iron bars. "No cage can hold me now. Not these bars and not this body."

The young man looked up from his notebook. His scribbling stopped. "I'm not sure why you feel such peace, because what you did was horrifying. Can't you see that?"

The old man smiled and touched the other man's arm. "And yet you are sitting so close to me. You are exceptionally brave, disbelieving, or incredibly stupid."

The young man swallowed and smiled. "My mother would say a bit of all three, I'm afraid."

The old man removed his hand from the reporter. "Sounds like a good mother. What I did was necessary. If you understood my world ..." He paused. "I can honestly say I have no regrets."

Erich bit the end of his pencil. "There's one thing that bothers me, so I'm going to come out and ask. You are to be executed. If you could really travel through time, why did you stay? Why are you staying now?"

The old man leaned in again and squinted at the reporter. "I have no reason to leave. Not yet, at least."

"How did you travel through time? Was it the magic of the sword?"

The old man leaned back and rested his head on the wall behind him. "I don't know that. I suppose one could think of it as magic, but I didn't. Like I said to the others, I didn't make the sword, I only wielded it."

"You didn't try to escape."

The old man shrugged. "Escape what?"

"You stayed where the crime was committed until you were caught. The report said you stayed there for a few hours. Why didn't you flee? Certainly there was time."

The old man took a deep breath and exhaled as he looked up at the ceiling. "You will never know the liberating feeling of completing your life's mission until you have achieved it. All my life was in search of Death, though I may not have thought of it this way at first. But once the deed was done, I was free for eternity."

Pausing only briefly to turn pages in his book or look up momentarily to make eye contact, Erich said, "Can you tell me why you did it?"

"Sure. How much time do you have?" the old man said through a laugh.

The reporter tapped his pencil on his notebook for emphasis. "All the time you need."

The old man cocked his head to one side and closed one eye. "It would take all night to explain it."

Erich folded his arms once again but then unfolded them soon afterward. "The guards told me I could stay in here as long as I like."

The old man grunted. "It may seem like a tall tale to your ears. Are you sure you are up for my ramblings?"

"I'm sure. I like tall tales. Tell me the entire story. I will make sure to not leave a single detail out. The people want to know who you are."

The old man watched as the reporter scribbled notes. "You are new to journalism, aren't you?"

The reporter did not look up. "Yes. But I've already written a book. Well, I haven't written the ending yet. I'm still stuck on it. But it's mostly done."

The old man harrumphed and looked out of the window. "I used to be a journalist a long time ago, but that might be jumping ahead too far."

The young man turned to a fresh page. "I'm ready when you are."

The old man squinted and looked up and down at the reporter. "Do you believe in angels, Erich?"

"Are you asking me if I am Christian? Yes, I believe in God."

"That wasn't my question. Do you believe in angels?"

Erich shrugged. "I suppose I do. They're in the scriptures, after all."

"Once I tell you this story, I will ask you this question again, because the crux of my story hinges upon this belief." The old man was silent for a moment and then said, "I will retell this tale but only on one condition. I ask that you save your bias and your questions for the end of my story. I don't like being interrupted, as I can often lose my train of thought. I'm very single-minded, and I can't multitask well. Can you do that for me?"

The reporter nodded and adjusted himself in his seat. "I can do that, but I'm not sure of the phrase 'multitask.'"

The old man grunted. "It's irrelevant. Well, at least for a few more decades. You will have many questions like this; know that I will answer them in time."

Erich smiled. "I know when to keep my mouth shut. My mother raised a good boy."

The old man scrunched his face and tapped a finger to his lips. "Where should I begin, then?"

The young man looked up from his notepad, his face blank. "Where all stories begin, sir. At the beginning."

The old man rested his head against the wall, let out a deep breath, and looked about the room; his eyes hovered for a moment at the iron bars. A smile grew about his face. "I was born in June of 1929."

"That's almost thirty years from now," Erich said.

The old man made sucking sounds as if he were playing with a bit of food that was stuck in his teeth. "Do you want to hear my tale, or would you rather sit here and smile at each other?"

The reporter waved his hands in protest. "I'm sorry. It won't happen again. Please go on. I will refrain from any more outbursts."

The old man waved away the reporter's comment. "I'm old. I get lost easily in a story. I will try to stay on track. Like I was saying …"

THE STORY OF JOSEPH

I WAS BORN IN 1929 in a rural part of Washington State in the United States, near a town called Spokane. It was a town like any other in the west, cold winters and hot summers but not as extreme as, say, Chicago. It was mostly a quiet place and wasn't all that large to attract too much negative attention. It was a town born from a farming community and a link with the railway; most people traveling through Spokane were simply on their way to Seattle and the coast.

My father owned a farm on the outskirts of town, but we weren't exactly farmers. He inherited it from his father, who was too weak at the time to tend to it in the right manner. It then fell to my father's care. My father, however, worked in town as an accountant for a bank, and so the farm responsibilities went to my mother, who stayed home and fed the cows and chickens and tended to our gardens and our small orchard.

Our farm was outside of the city, along some winding, hilly roads that would often get overrun by snow in the winter and filled with rattlesnakes in the summer. Our nearest neighbors were two miles away in either direction of the road.

All in all, it was a pretty great place to live; I had a really good childhood, except for normal growing pains. I belonged there with the pine trees, the open fields, and the fresh air that would wash over you like sacred incense.

This story really shouldn't begin with me, because I was simply one witness upon a grand adventure that would consume my whole life. The story really begins with my older brother, Joseph, whom I admired greatly, even before he became a hero and even before he wore a uniform. It was Joseph who ultimately led me to my true mission in life, though I would not recognize this for many years to come. He highlighted something that was so intriguing and so unbelievable that it would haunt me for a lifetime.

Joseph was eight years older than I, and for as long as I could remember, he was everything I wanted to be. People simply liked Joseph. Girls liked Joseph because he was handsome, and he had a smile that attracted them from several counties away. This got him into and out of all sorts of trouble. Guys liked Joseph because he was strong, independent, and fiercely loyal. He wouldn't mind settling any dispute with his wit or with his fists. If you were a friend of Joseph, you had an army at your side. He would protect his friends and family with his life. Even the family dog was put under his direct protection.

Our neighbor's son, Tommy, and his friends Brian and Matt, who were the same age as Joseph, came to learn a lesson the hard way. One day, these three clowns came by our farm, which was on the way to Tommy's place, when our dog ran out to them in the road. Tommy played the tough guy and ended up kicking our dog, Patches. When Joseph heard about this, he marched right over to the neighbor's house and demanded an explanation. Tommy simply folded his hands and blocked my brother from coming inside their home.

"Yeah, I kicked your dog, so what? He was in the middle of the road. You should be more careful."

"That's no reason to kick him," Joseph said.

Tommy rolled his eyes. "Your dog stinks!" A drop of spittle came from his mouth when he talked.

This seemed to enrage Joseph, and he kicked Tommy in the shin so hard that Tommy went down to the floor. "If you kick my dog, you might as well kick me!" Joseph kicked Tommy once more in the same shin. Tommy rolled over onto his back and grabbed his shin, screaming. Joseph raised his fist over Tommy, and the boy cowered away, holding both his hands over his head to protect himself. Tommy began crying immediately.

"Help!" Tommy cried to his father.

When Tommy's father, Mr. Alexander, came over, both Joseph and I backed up, thinking Mr. Alexander would take a swing at us. Mr. Alexander was a tough older man who was brought up on a farm and had working man's hands. He rarely smiled, and he rarely added much to pleasant conversation. I was afraid of him as long as I could remember. He never hit me, but sometimes I wondered whether he thought about it. He didn't like children much, and more still, he didn't like the voices of children. At this time, he really was on board with the whole "children should be seen and not heard" mantra.

To our surprise, Mr. Alexander said to us politely, "Thank you for bringing this cowardice to our attention, boys. I'm sorry my son did you wrong."

Joseph's fists relaxed. "I'm sorry to have struck your son, sir. I understand if you need to tell my dad."

Mr. Alexander shook his head. He turned to Tommy and said, "You see that, Tommy? That's how a real man solves his problems. He goes to the source and stands up for what's right. Look at you. Still on the floor. What's wrong with you?" Mr. Alexander then turned his attention back to us. "I'm sorry you two had to see this. I will have the missus send over some cupcakes later. She just put a batch in. Please accept that as an apology."

Joseph nodded and said, "Sorry for the disruption, sir. Please send our best regards to your wife."

Mr. Alexander grumbled something and then returned to his normal demeanor, and his face went blank. He nodded and headed back into the house, closing the door behind him. We heard shouts coming from behind the closed door.

Joseph and I walked back to our house like heroes. I felt good even though I had nothing to do with that act of bravery. I felt stronger than

I ever did before, and I owe that surge of confidence to my brother. This fortitude would be the center of the man I was to become and gave fuel to my mission later on in life.

Patches even came running to us on the road, running circles and barking at both of us. It seemed he too understood the victory that day and danced with joy with the two of us. If I had loved my brother before, he was forever my hero after that day.

#

When I was ten years old, Joseph joined the army. Joseph was a very driven person, and he had to be the best at everything, and so it wasn't long before he became a part of an elite unit of the army called the Rangers. He appeared ten feet tall and had wide shoulders. He made a fine soldier. He made that army uniform look great, and I remember him proudly coming into the living room with it on for the first time. My mother insisted upon a picture. She was all smiles, and she pinched his cheeks and hugged him often. But my father wore a concerned look that I didn't quite understand. He fiddled with the camera longer than he should have, pretending perhaps that the film was not loading properly. My father wore the look of a parent who realized he no longer had any control over his children.

After basic training at Fort Lewis, Joseph was transferred to Camp Forrest, Tennessee, where he officially joined the Fifth Ranger Battalion. Later, he was shipped off to England, where he received more training. We never saw him off; we corresponded by mail, of course, but I wished I could have seen him on the start of his adventure. Maybe then I could have helped with what was to come.

Once overseas, Joseph continued to send us letters—one each week—but he couldn't give many details of his activities, as these things were classified. Sometimes he would send us pictures with signs in the background that let us know exactly where he was; somehow these got past the censors. His letters warmed our hearts, and we would read them after dinnertime around the table. Even though the letters were seldom sad, my mother would end up crying, so my father would take over reading the letters. He would put his glasses on the edge of his nose, and he didn't read as well as my mother. In fact, sometimes he would have to stop and reread a sentence because he either couldn't read a word or it was not clear by context what Joseph meant. However, it got the point across.

After Joseph's training, he was promoted to corporal, and we were really excited for him. Mother made cookies in the shape of chevrons, and she even made me real chevrons, which she stitched to one of my jackets. I loved that jacket, and it reminded me of not only my brother but the vast adventure he embarked upon. I was so proud of him, and I wanted very much to go with him. When I first put on that jacket, I marched straight outside and pretended to be a real soldier.

I would often spend my nights in the woods outside of our home fighting invisible enemy soldiers and throwing rocks, pretending that they were grenades. I had a rifle, but it was only a .22-caliber single-shot squirrel gun. I would take that gun out and pretend it was a real Ranger's weapon. I didn't bring ammunition when I played with it, not unless my father was around. He was always worried that I would accidentally shoot myself. There had been a death in his family from such a firearm, and I heard the story each time he saw me pick up the rifle.

While I was playing soldier in my backyard, my brother was living the soldier life, and eventually, on June 6, 1944, he landed in Normandy in what became known later as Omaha Beach. He was part of the D-Day invasion of a war that would later be called World War II, in one of the bloodiest battles of all time—a battle that would echo through time as being one of history's turning points. He was there: facing the guns and bombs of a foreign people. What he may have witnessed, I can only guess at from what I've seen in movies and old photographs as a child.

He fought long and hard throughout Europe. His generation was later to be known as the greatest generation for the sacrifices that they made. As months droned on, his letters began to become shorter, more chaotic, and more desperate sounding. He tried to hide this and tried to be positive, but even the handwriting was different. There were jagged edges and short sentences, as though he were worried that there were enemies close by or that he might be blown up before there was time to finish the letter. We never mentioned this in the letters we sent back to him, and we always wrote a great deal. Well, my mother wrote the most, and my father and I added a paragraph or two at the end. We hoped that he appreciated our support, as much as we could have given him halfway around the world. We ended each letter saying that we loved him and missed him at the farm.

As it turned out, the war dragged on, and a swift victory was not easily seen. The enemy launched a strong counterattack, which tore through the Allied lines and caused a lot of casualties. My mother would listen to the radio and read the paper, looking for his name, but she never said anything. She became increasingly worried, and I would catch her up late at night, staring out the window with a drink in her hand. I'm not sure if she was expecting my brother back or some military official to let us know that Joseph was dead.

I grew up not only with Joseph but also with my two cousins, Ryan and Roger, who were the sons of my mother's sister. I liked my cousins very much, but they were closer to my brother's age, and they paid very little attention to me. Since I always hung around my brother during our cousins' visits, they would torture me the only way family can do. It was terrible. They tied me up in the pigpen, marooned me in the chicken coop, or they threatened to put me in with the bull.

They even once stuffed my pants with crab apples and made me walk around like that all day. One time, they forgot to take me out of the pigpen, and my father found me tied up there. I never saw him so mad before. I thought he was mad at me, and he simply snatched me up after cutting my bonds and marched into the house with me over his shoulder. He passed me like a sack of potatoes to my mother and then gave my brother and my cousins an earful. This was the first time I saw my father strike my brother—or my cousins, for that matter. He slapped them all about the face—with an open hand, mind you—but it was enough to send them down to the ground, crying.

I began to cry too, but I was very young. I didn't understand what was happening or why my father was so mad. I thought I was next to be hit, and I was very afraid. My mother rocked me gently in her arms as I apologized for everything.

"It's not your fault, dear," my mother said. "Those boys tied you up. It's not your fault."

I didn't listen to this, and I kept apologizing, and I made a promise to my mother that I was going to be the best son she ever had.

Unfortunately for both of us, I was to break that promise many years later.

The war was difficult not only for my brother but also for our extended family. The same war claimed the lives of both of my cousins, Ryan and Roger. My cousins were both in the navy, but they did not serve on the same ship or even in the same theater.

Sadly, having my cousins on separate ships did absolutely nothing to keep them safe. Even though they were thousands of miles apart, they both were killed at sea within a week of each other. Their bodies were never recovered. They were simply blown up in severe ship-to-ship bombardments. I was too young to really understand what an artillery attack would mean, but I remember being bewildered by it. In my mind, soldiers and navy seamen died only from grenades and from gunfire. I knew about artillery, but for a common soldier, I didn't think this was much of a threat. Not nearly as bad as machine guns or rifles. I couldn't help but feel bad for my cousins, not just because they died but because they didn't die from enemy bullets. They were killed in the most random, meaningless, arbitrary sort of way. For all we knew, those artillery shells could have been our own guns, firing upon the wrong boat.

Since both Ryan and Roger were killed within a week and the notices of their deaths came a day apart, their memorial services were combined. Their funeral was the first funeral that I ever attended. I remember that day well because of how very surreal it was. I wore a tie around my neck that kept choking me, and my wool coat scratched at my body something fierce. I remained quiet, though, as the eyes of my uncle and my aunt would often find me. Both of them would come up to me, rub my head, pinch my cheeks, or pick me up like I was a cat. I didn't understand why, but I suppose they saw their boys in me. After all, we were very similar in appearance. My aunt in particular would give me bits of advice and fix my hair, all while wiping tears from her eyes, which smeared her makeup; her breath smelled of cigarettes and wine. I found that odor repulsive because my parents didn't smoke, which was unusual for the time, because quite frankly everyone else did.

JOSEPH'S RETURN HOME

JOSEPH'S JOURNEY HOME AFTER THE war was a protracted one. He took boats, planes, trains, and buses to get back to Spokane. It was a long trip by any standards and terrible for anyone who was homesick. We all knew he would be coming that day, and we hoped he would arrive early. I looked out of the window every ten minutes, and with each passing car that came down the road, I asked my mother, "Is that him?"

This started to wear at my father, and he shouted, "Get outside! Get out and enjoy the air!"

This was startling, as my father rarely yelled, so I wasted no time and obeyed. I still feared my father, though he never did lay a hand to me. It was a healthy fear, though; I knew my father's limits, and if I were to cross those lines, I would pay dearly for it.

My brother survived the war. That is to say, he lived through the war and returned home. What came next was a struggle that no one saw coming, and I was too young to wrap my head around it. I saw war films, and I saw the propaganda—soldiers were heroes, saviors, and even celebrated in the streets for their victory. They were almost above reproach. However, there was another side to the war that didn't make the headlines and didn't get shown in the theaters. It was the damaged people who returned from the hell that they endured, forever scarred by the things they had witnessed.

I think there is a general understanding of what happens in war. People shoot each other, bombs explode, and people die, but this in an intellectualization of something that cannot be reasoned through. It is an emotional nightmare that doesn't stop when the guns stop. I first came to know this fact through the trials that my brother went through following his return.

My brother came back home to the farm after three long years in Europe, fighting for our freedom. There was no denying that he was a hero, regardless of any role that he may have played there. We were happy to have him back and excited to see him, and we wanted to hear about all of his conquests. When he arrived, he looked weary and much older than I remembered him. Even though his uniform was pressed, cleaned, and sparkled with new medals, he didn't seem to fit it, like the clothes were wearing him instead.

The moment I saw Joseph, I knew that he was not the same person who left. In that time, his condition was known as shell shock. This was later called *posttraumatic stress disorder*, and even later still, this was also mixed with the term *survivor guilt*. Whatever you may call it, it was like being handed a shadow of my brother. His eyes were haunted. His frame was lessened, and he did not smile much, and when he did, it was very forced.

His eyes were distant, and the love of life that was once in them was filled with a sorrow instead. There were dark circles under his eyes, something that I had only seen on old people. Not even our parents had that shade of purple on them. I noticed too the creases in his face. He squinted constantly now, like a semi smile, but all this did was create wrinkles on his face like a road map, particularly by his eyes. Joseph's smile was not the same; it was a smile that was not genuine and was something done in response rather than come from joy within. I was pretty sure that the happiness that was supposed to be there was now missing.

His body was visibly smaller. His shoulders used to be broad and thick with muscles, but he looked as though he were starving. He even carried himself differently; he moved with a slight hunch. You might not see it if you didn't know Joseph, but I saw it, and I'm sure my parents saw it too. The hunch would get worse sometimes, particularly if he was left alone.

Often, when I would ask him a question, he would stare off into space for a moment before answering even a simple question like "How are you?" His mind was clearly elsewhere, fighting whatever demons he came across during the war.

One of the first things Joseph said when he returned is that he wanted to be called Joe. His friends in the war called him Joe, and no one called him Joseph anymore. We thought this was odd, but once my father nodded in acceptance, this was now the new law.

It was only later that I thought that Joseph had died in the war and whatever returned was now called Joe. The loving, carefree, and fearless man that I knew was gone. What was left was a shell of a person, riddled with fear and anxiety and poisoned by haunting images that would come to him in the night.

Joe took his old bedroom while he adjusted himself to civilian life. My mother loved having him back at home and made sure that all his laundry was done and that his room was clean. My father, however, would often open conversations about what Joe's plan was for work now that he was back.

This, of course, caused some arguments between him and my mother, with my mother usually winning.

"Don't listen to him," my mother would say. "You have all the time in the world to get back on your feet. We are here for you, and you are safe with us."

This was the first time that I saw a genuine smile from Joe since he returned, but it was soon replaced by another look that I didn't understand. He put his face down and rubbed his eyes briefly and didn't say another word that entire meal.

Joe got tired easily. Conversations were cut short, and he had a difficult time following many people talking. He clearly tuned things out, especially when company was over, and he would often excuse himself from the dinner table so he could be alone.

There were times I would go looking for Joe, even though I knew he wanted to be alone. I would catch him having a drink or a cigarette behind the barn. I wouldn't say anything; I would just come up and sit down next to him. Sometimes he would look at me. Sometimes he wouldn't. But this didn't matter; I just wanted him to know that I was there for him, even though I didn't have the slightest clue about how to go about doing that.

#

At night, my brother would scream. I would often find him under his bed. Since my bedroom was next to his, I was the first one on the scene during one of his night terrors. Sometimes he would be scrambling to find his weapon. Other times he would be holding his ears and crying. I'd never seen a man cry like that before. My father never cried, and certainly my grandfathers never cried, either. At least never that I had seen.

On one fateful night, during one of my brother's fights with the enemy from underneath his bed, he said something. Something so peculiar, so odd, that I just stood there and stared at him.

"Please get me out of here," he said. "Please dance me out of here." He was looking just past me over my right shoulder. I looked to where his eyes were oriented, but I saw nothing.

It was the word "dance" that I had found odd. My brother was good with the ladies, but he was no dancer. As I recall, he was nowhere near any dance floor that I could ever remember.

This, of course, could have been a figure of speech or a euphemism that I didn't understand, except for what came next.

"Do I need a top hat and cane too?" he asked me in all earnestness. "Where do I get a top hat out here? How is it that you dodge bullets?"

I stood there and shrugged while he wiped tears from his eyes and cried at my feet.

My mother was swiftly into the room that time and shooed me away like a cat that jumped onto the table. Her eyes told me that there was no argument. "This is none of your concern."

The door closed, but the cries continued. When I turned around, my father was there, and for a moment, I thought I was going to get a beating. But his eyes were softer and wetter than I had ever seen in him before. He touched me on the shoulder.

My father nodded to me. "It's all right," he said. "War makes men see things. This will pass."

Although I was sixteen, I was still scared of getting a smack from my father, so I said nothing. My father looked at me seriously and nodded again, adding another pat on my shoulder. I thought he was going to tell me he loved me, but he never did. It seemed as though he was about to give me a hug too, but that never happened. Instead we stood there, looking stupid and listening to the painful cries of my brother in the next room.

I touched his hand, and my father's eyes got wetter, but his mood swiftly changed, and I was redirected to my own room with a light push.

My footsteps creaked on floorboards. I turned around one more time to see my father's face in his hands.

MANY LANGUAGES

ERICH STRETCHED AND YAWNED. "I'm sorry to interrupt, but I have a simple question. I know you didn't want to be interrupted, but this is really bothering me."

The old man sighed and rubbed his left knee. "Go ahead. What is it?"

"Why do you keep switching languages?" Erich asked.

The old man cleared his throat and looked at Erich carefully. "Excuse me?"

"There. You did it again. Why don't you pick your native tongue and use that? I happen to understand most of the languages you use, but I don't understand why you insist on switching between languages."

"What languages am I speaking?" the old man asked.

"Right now? French."

"I'm speaking French?" the old man asked.

"No. You just switched to Italian. I'm not sure why you are doing this. Are you trying to confuse me? If you are, it's working."

The old man stood up and paced around the room. "I'm sorry. I don't realize that I'm doing this. Can you understand me okay?" the old man asked.

Erich nodded and played with his eyebrows; there was an unusually long hair there that he tried unsuccessfully to remove. "Sure. I speak five languages, and for whatever reason, you have been speaking only those five. I grew up in a town that spoke French and German. My mother was Italian and British."

"Five? I can speak five languages?" the old man asked as his face contorted into a look of bewilderment.

Erich raised both of his hands up and pointed at the old man with his hands open. "You just said that in German."

"I did? How is that possible?"

Erich shrugged. "I don't know. I was very confused by it. I was hoping you knew why."

The old man rubbed his chin. "Oh. Well, it is not my intention to confuse you. I grew up only speaking English. I've learned a bit of Korean and Vietnamese, but I've forgotten most of that now."

"I thought you might have been testing me," Erich said, trying to pluck his long eyebrow. His eyes darted around the room for a bit.

The old man waved a hand in protest. "Testing you? No. Not even remotely. I've never learned these languages before."

"Well, you are fluent in all of them. Your transitions are fluid too. You speak Spanish and Italian better than I do, though. I can't even hear an accent."

"Well, that's amazing. It's a miracle." The old man straightened himself up and took a deep breath.

Erich shrugged. "Seeing as I don't know for sure if you ever learned these languages in the past, it is hard to prove that this was a miracle or not."

The old man nodded, and his smile faded somewhat. "Well, in my head, I'm speaking to you in English. I'm sorry for the confusion. I'll try not to do it, but I'm not sure that I can control it."

Erich took a deep breath. "You were right; this is quite the tall tale."

The old man shrugged and rubbed his left knee a bit. "I didn't say it would be an easy pill to swallow. That's why I had to tell you everything. Otherwise, skipping to the part where the angel showed me the sword of Michael would be a bit foolish. You would have simply dismissed this story as fantasy, called me a liar, and gone about your day."

Erich stretched his hand and sharpened a new pencil. "I have a lot here, but there are a lot of details missing … including your name."

The old man smirked. "My name is irrelevant. The only thing that means anything is how this story ends. Don't you agree?"

Erich raised his hands and took a deep breath. "Sorry to interrupt. Please continue."

The old man rubbed his hands together and closed his eyes. "Where was I …"

#

My mother was glad to have Joe at home, of course, glad to take care of him, even though he was a grown man by this time. She washed his clothes and cleaned his room, and when he would come out of the shower, she would hug him and kiss him on the forehead.

I have to admit, I felt like I was invisible at this time. I know my mother and my father cared about me a great deal, but it was like I wasn't even there. Sometimes I would ask a question, only to be met with silence. I understood that it was a big deal to have Joseph home, but the boy in me was very jealous.

Joe helped out on the farm like he had done before the war; he began looking for jobs, but there was something very wrong with him. It was as though he lost the will to live. Every action he took was arduous. Every word he spoke took more energy than normally required, and every step he took was heavy and laden with something I could not understand. Sometimes, in the farm field or in the barn, I would catch him staring at something—mesmerized. He would stand motionless for minutes and just be lost in thought or something. I tried not to bother him when he got like this, and I tried not to notice, but it happened so much sometimes that it was simply hard to avoid.

I was sixteen when the war ended. I was jealous of Joseph for many reasons, but mostly because he got to go to war and save the world, while I went to high school and fed the chickens on the farm. I know that may seem petty, but that's how I felt. He was a hero, and I was just the little brother.

I'd just gotten my driver's license, and my father let me drive our 1940 Ford Deluxe sedan. I drove tractors and other farm equipment, of course, but the car represented a freedom that was unlike anything else. No longer would I have to walk ten miles to town or beg for a ride from my father. I could go anywhere I wanted at any time.

I didn't go out as much as I would have or should have. Joseph would sometimes disappear all day, only to return late at night. I wanted to be there for Joe, even though he secluded himself. When he was around, he was always polite, but he grew increasingly distant. At night, I would catch him drinking.

When Joe was drunk, he was even less company than he was when he was sober. He was more removed and more unreachable, even though he was relaxed and calm. He wasn't a mean drunk by any means, and he wasn't the drunk who told everyone how much he loved them. He just shut down and would pass out. Many times I would have to drag him back home from the barn, his usual drinking spot, and into his bed.

This, of course, would wake my mother, but she wouldn't lecture. After all, Joe was a full-grown man now. Mother never said anything about me being out late, but next to the problem with Joe, her mind was clearly elsewhere.

One evening, it was really late, and I came through the back door with Joe wrapped around my shoulder. I could barely see the walkway, and the porch light was out. I nearly dropped Joe crossing the threshold, and he woke up and started giggling. This was the first time I had heard him laugh, and I didn't want to discourage that laugh, but at the same time, we needed to be quiet. The worst thing in the world would have been to wake up my father. He wasn't keen on losing precious sleep.

It was our mother who woke, and she was standing in the hallway with her full-length white nightgown. Her arms were crossed, and she kept her right hand locked around the two sides of her robe to keep them closed. She looked older in the dim light, and a look of disapproval washed over her face, and I couldn't help but feel shame.

"Get him to bed. And fetch him some water, or he will feel even worse in the morning. Mind his shoes. I don't want that barn filth all over this house. Do you know how long it takes to clean up this place?" my mother asked.

I averted my mother's eyes. "Joe's okay. I will take him to bed. He's fine."

My mother gave me a long, hard look. "Don't wake your father. You know how he can get at night," she whispered.

My mother then petted Joe's head and tried to straighten his hair but failed even after several attempts. A tear came down her cheek, and she kissed the top of his head. Then she kissed my head too. "Now go. And be quiet about it."

Getting Joe up three steps into the house proved to be harder than previous nights. Joe had been giggling and didn't want to move. Using his jacket for hand holds, I dragged him by the shoulders with his butt scraping on the ground. This created an effect that I didn't see coming— Joe started shouting. The more I pulled him in this manner, the louder he would scream.

This, of course, drew the immediate attention of my parents. My mother was back on the scene, and she reached down to grab Joe, perhaps to quiet him.

"*Incoming!*" Joe yelled. He then scrambled drunkenly to all fours and crawled under the dining room table, knocking over a few chairs in the process.

This brought my mother immediately to tears, and she held on to her face as if to keep the tears at bay. When my father came in the room, he blinked several times and just stood in the doorway. He looked to my mother and then back again at Joe; his eyes washed right over me like I wasn't even there.

I was still on the floor. Joe was under the table with his hands over his ears, screaming. Mother was shaking and crying uncontrollably, and when she reached under the table to touch Joe, he swatted at her.

My mother recoiled and matched my brother scream for scream.

"Get your own foxhole. You fuckers shit in mine. *Fuck you!*" He then kicked at the table, which caused a vase to fall and crash to the ground. This intensified the shouting.

As if seeing me for the first time, my father reached down and pulled me off the floor. He pushed me through the hallway and into my room. He grabbed me so forcibly that I was bruised under the arm.

"We've got it from here, son," he said to me. "This isn't something you should be seeing." He then closed my door.

Although I was sixteen and almost a man, I knew better than to disobey my father. At the same time, I thought he did me a favor by putting me in my room. The screams continued for a great length of time, and I sat on my bed and cried. Hearing my big brother like this was not easy on anyone, especially me. My brother was the bravest man I have ever known; he fought in the greatest war that our nation ever participated in. He was reduced, however, to a drunkard who was completely broken, and this is why I cried. I cried for him because he lost his way. I cried for my mother, who had no power to help her son, and I cried for my father, who was too strong and too stubborn to cry.

Looking back, we did not know how to help Joe cope with being home. We did not understand what exactly it was that he needed. We did not grasp the gravity of what was happening. We believed that if we just simply surrounded Joe with love and attention that he would get better and that he—the Joseph whom we loved—would come back to us.

My father believed that Joe simply needed a job to occupy his mind and bring him back to earth. My mother wanted to surround him with kisses like he was a little baby. And I just wanted to hang out on the farm with him like we used to. What we didn't know was that all of us were wrong and that none of us had the tools necessary to bring him out of that hole. Joe didn't want any of these things. I don't know if he knew what he wanted or if he just needed time and space.

JOE'S CONFESSION

ONE NIGHT, JOE EXCUSED HIMSELF early from the dinner
table, a habit he would lean on for a few months. I followed
him out to the other end of the barn, where he lit a cigarette
and took a swig of rum from a bottle that was stashed in a bale of hay.
He offered me both. I declined the cigarette, but I took a sip of rum. I
remember I almost choked, and it burned all the way down my throat.
There must have been a scowl on my face.

Joe patted me on the back. "Easy, bro. You don't want to catch fire."

I passed him back the bottle and wiped my lips. I swallowed twice
before I could talk. "Thanks," I said in a raspy voice.

We stood out there and watched the sunset. For a long time, we
didn't say anything. The sounds of the chickens and the cows were our
only company.

Then Joe said something, which surprised me, so I looked up. He
handed me the bottle, and I took another smaller and more manageable
sip. I held on to the bottle.

"There were times in France when the sun set in the valleys when the
skies were clear, and you could see for miles. It was so beautiful there,
and I remember looking up at the orange-and-pink sky that stretched out
to the heavens. Sometimes the setting sun would mix with the burning

of towns or tanks, and it appeared that the sky and the ground were actually connected."

I leaned in closer. This was the first time Joe had talked about the war, and I didn't want to miss a thing. I took another sip of rum and passed it back to Joe.

Joe took a long sip and didn't wince. "It was the smell that ruined it. Had bodies not been rotting or burning nearby, I would have said that was the most beautiful thing I had ever seen. It was always a mix over there. It was never just one thing."

I squinted. "What do you mean?"

Joe took a deep breath. "Well, you might be lucky to find a cup of coffee, only to realize you had nothing to eat that day. Or you may find that you had a perfect night's sleep, only to realize your friend died of exposure during the night. That's the mix. It was never all good or all bad. It was a mash of crap mixed in your stew. You couldn't separate the crap from the stew, so you just had to eat it. Or die from starvation. That was the choice, you see."

I cleared my throat. "I'm glad you are home."

Joe nodded. "It's still crap and stew, though, isn't it?"

I shrugged. I tried to say something funny. "I don't know. I thought it was a pretty good dinner."

Joe actually laughed, which made me feel good. He took another swig of rum and passed me the bottle again.

And then the question I wanted to ask suddenly came out, and I ruined everything. "So … what was it like?"

I saw the happiness drain out of Joe's face like blood from a chicken that was beheaded and hung upside down. "I'm not sure what the worst part was. The anticipation of going to war, the fighting, or the waiting for the next round of fighting."

I realized my mistake, and I tried to make up for it. "I'm sorry, Joe. I'm just glad you are here. I missed you like crazy. It just wasn't the same without you here."

Joe took another swig of rum and handed me the bottle. By this time, I was feeling the liquor, so I only took a tiny sip.

Joe said, "There were periods where I didn't sleep for days. I didn't think that was possible, but it is. Everything is a fog, you know. After a time, you are so tired; your body just does things for you. When you hear artillery overhead, you would hit the dirt and not even realize you were doing it. With the slightest sound at night, you would snap to attention, and your rifle would be in your hands without you having to reach for it. It was constant. The mind would shut off, and the body would just do what it needed to do. When I first joined the army and even the Rangers, I could barely take a dump in the latrine. In fact, I would go once every four days, and I would time it so that fewer people were present when I did. But after a few weeks in the field, you could squat anywhere and in front of anyone. It just didn't matter anymore. That's weird, isn't it?"

I shrugged. I didn't want to say anything to interfere with his flow of conversation. This was the most he said in a very long time. "I can't go if someone is standing outside the door."

Joe didn't seem to hear me. He kept talking. "I was in my foxhole with Henry once. We had been drinking, and we both fell asleep. It was a cold night. Snow on the ground, and we threw a canvas tarp over our hole to keep warm. But since the ground was frozen, you could never really get comfortable. There was always something digging in your back, your side, or your stomach. My fingers and toes were constantly numb," Joe said, pausing to look at his hands. He swayed a bit. "The gloves we had weren't very good, and you constantly had to breathe into your hands to make sure you wouldn't lose fingers to frostbite."

Joe's face contorted into a grimace, and he looked toward the horizon. "The only thing to keep us warm was a fire, but we could never build them too big. We couldn't afford being spotted by the Krauts. You don't want to be a beacon for mortar fire. We made do, of course. That's what grunts do best. But it was this constant drain. That was the worst part. The drain. My stomach was always in knots out there."

Joe paused to take another sip of rum. "I wake up one night. My rifle is in my hands. I'm not really thinking. I'm drunk; I'm cold, tired, and scared. I hear something next to our hole, and I'm awake, and I can feel my heart racing. Like when you ride in a car and lose control over the wheel for a second, and you swerve and you feel the car about to tip over. That was me. Always on edge and about to tip over.

"I get out of my foxhole, and I spring to my feet quick. Standing there, maybe from here to the barn, are two Germans. There was no mistaking them. Their uniforms and their distinct helmets. They're armed with the K98 Mausers. I shoot the first guy in the face. It takes his jaw clear off. Like it was just slapped from his face by a bear. Then I hear something that I don't expect, and that's the pinging sound of my clip flying in the air. I make the rookie mistake of not topping off my ammo the last time we had to shoot. But that was the thing. It had been days since I fired a shot. I assumed that I had a fully loaded gun, but I just had that one shot. I had no time to get more ammo, so I didn't. The other German is yelling something. He looks scared. He's young, like you. And he's yelling at me. I thought his rifle was in his hands, but it's over one of his shoulders. He takes his rifle, and I charge him. All the while he's yelling something at me. I hit him with my rifle. I hit him hard, and he goes down.

"While he's on the ground, he says something to me. I think he's reaching for his gun. I hit him again and again. I hit him until he stops moving. Blood splatters a lot when you hit a man like this. It's all over my pants and even my face. It's like I'm wearing death mask of gore and blood.

"By this time, others had awoken and come to my aid. We're looking in the fog and the trees but can't see anything else. We don't know if this is just a small recon unit or if there are more of them out there hiding. Sometimes we would find a leading edge of a front, and then we'd have a real fight on our hands. Our lines were so stretched out that this tended to happen a lot.

"It is a few minutes later that I realize that the guy that I shot is still alive. Henry shoots him in the face with his pistol. We wait there, but nothing happens. Karl comes by and is laughing. Karl is from a town in New Hampshire. I guess it's close to Boston or something. Well, Karl is an asshole. He's laughing and pointing at the Germans on the ground.

"'What the fuck is wrong with you?' I ask.

"Karl is still laughing. He points to the man I shot. 'This one said, "We are here to surrender!"' He then points to the other one and says, 'This one said, "Please don't kill me." Then he cried for this mother while you beat him to death. He cried for his mother!'"

Joe turned toward me, and he passed me the bottle of rum. He was crying now. But I said nothing. I took a sip and waited for him to say something. Joe looked into my eyes. "He looked like you. His voice sounded like yours. I know he was a Kraut. I know he was our enemy, but he looked like you. He was young, like you. Clean, smooth face. How did I know what he was saying? It didn't make sense to me. How was I supposed to know? I didn't know they were trying to surrender. They were just as scared as I was. They were just as lonely and wanting to go home as I was. Because of me, they won't be going home. They won't be able to hug their brothers or kiss their mothers. I did that; me, the big war hero."

I tried to reach out to Joe, but he moved away. He didn't exactly swat at me, but he made it clear that he didn't want to be touched. Joe leaned on the fence, and I did likewise. I never saw my brother cry before the war. He was always the tough one. He could weather any storm and brave any mountain. He was stronger than my father, and yet, here he was, crying. I started to weep too. I cried for my brother, who clearly was still suffering, even though he was far removed from any battlefield.

Joe drank the last remains of the bottle and then threw it out into the woods and walked away. I started to follow him, but then I went in the opposite direction. I went and found the bottle, and I hid it where I hid Joe's other bottles: in a junk pile under a lot of boxes. I was shocked to see just how many bottles there were. When I returned to the barn, Joe found another bottle and handed it to me, but I only pretended to take a sip. I was already drunk, and I was afraid that I was going to throw up, so it was certainly enough for me. Joe, of course, had easily three times as much rum as I did. I often wondered why he didn't throw up or pass out in the barn.

We were hanging out near one of our pigpens. We didn't have many pigs, but for some reason, we found ourselves there. I desperately wanted to ask him more questions about the war, but I didn't want to scare him away. It was good enough for me to have him close by and look at me. No one else seemed to notice me, only him.

"I should have been dead," Joe said.

I was listening carefully. I wanted to ask what he meant, but I didn't want him to stop talking. I handed him the bottle of rum, and he took a sip.

"I saw some weird shit out there. I'm not talking about normal war things." Joe paused to look at me. He swayed a bit and caught his balance. He passed me the bottle.

I remained silent and took a tiny sip.

"I saw Death," Joe said, pointing a finger at me.

There was a long silence. I knew Joe was on the verge of saying something to me, and I was just going to listen.

Joe shook his head, which made him stumble. "I'm not talking about the bodies or the blood. That was enough to make the strongest guy sick. Don't get me wrong. I was completely unprepared for that. I knew there was going to be shooting. I knew there was going to be bombs. But ... but not like that. That whole beach was blood. There were pieces of meat everywhere. It was like a butcher shop scattered on the sands. I wiped off some goo from my face. I think it was a piece of fat or internal organ or something. I didn't look at it; I just wiped it away."

I took another tiny sip of the bottle of rum, leaned on the pigpen, and handed Joe the bottle. "I'm sorry that happened to you," I said, not knowing what else to say.

"I watched them die, you know. Fuck me! Each time I saw them die, I couldn't help but thank God it wasn't me. I thanked God." Joe gritted his teeth, and his face went red.

I put my hand on Joe's shoulder, half expecting him to recoil, but this time, he didn't.

"I saw Death there. I tried to ignore him. He was trying to get my attention. He was dancing, waving his cane and his top hat. I tried to look away, but every time I looked up, he was there. He was coming for me. I thought he was there to take me away."

"I'm not sure what you mean," I whispered.

Joe either didn't hear me or ignored my question. "He kept dancing. He kept stepping on the dead. Bullets passed clean through him, and no one else could see him. That's how I knew I was supposed to die there. I saw him, and he saw me. When Death looks at you, you know it is your time."

"I hear people can see a lot of things during stress," I said.

Again, Joe was spacing out, wavering. He said nothing for a time and simply continued. "He left me there. I thought he was leading me to heaven. He just left me there. Everyone else passed on, everyone else got to go to heaven. He just left me there."

"Who was he?" I asked.

Joe shrugged. "It was Death, though he didn't carry a scythe. He carried a black cane, and he wore a tuxedo. But he was the Angel of Death." Joe was pointing at me again with a bony finger.

I started to say something, but I choked and cleared my throat.

Joe continued. "He told me to stay there. So I did. I thought he would come back for me, but he didn't. I don't know why he let me live. So many of the guys I knew were killed or really fucked up. I didn't have a scratch on me. Bullets and bombs moved around Death and me. We were ghosts, and bullets were as dangerous as snowflakes to us. Does that sound crazy?"

It did sound crazy, and I was beginning to get scared. Even still, I shook my head. "No, not at all. He saved you, and I'm glad he did."

Joe harrumphed. "One thing I don't understand. Why me?"

There was a long pause, and I knew I should say something, so I tried my best to sound reassuring. "Why not you? You have a family that loves you, and you have your whole life ahead of you. Maybe you were meant to do something. Maybe you were meant to do something great."

Joe harrumphed again. He kicked the pigpen and scared some pigs nearby into a squealing frenzy. When I handed him the bottle, he took a swig that would have knocked me unconscious. I grimaced when I thought how that would taste.

"Yep. I'm home. So many others aren't. Look at all the great things I'm doing."

MEETING THE WIFE

E
VEN THOUGH MY BROTHER TOLD me these things, I still wanted to go to war; I still wanted to be a hero. I was young and naive. I was also going through a lot of changes myself, and I was becoming a man of my own. As much as I loved my brother, and as much as I tried to be there for him, I was still a teenager, and I was still filled with hormones and fiery emotions. I kissed plenty of girls before I was sixteen, but when I truly locked eyes with the girl I knew I would have as my wife, my world was turned upside down.

Like most people of my generation, I met the woman of my dreams at church. This isn't surprising, really, because I spent a lot of time at church doing activities and events outside of Sunday services. When Pastor Jacob was available, I would always hound him with questions about angels, demons, faith, and the afterlife. He was always there for me and always showed an enthusiasm that could not be faked or forced. For this, I truly appreciate his teachings. He was sincere and was always willing to lend a helping hand when I needed him.

When I met Lorraine, I was not prepared for the onslaught of emotions that overcame me. Lorraine was pretty, but not overtly so like women in the magazines would be thought of as beautiful. She moved in a way that mesmerized me; she made me dizzy and my heart stutter as though I were having a heart attack. In short, Lorraine made me crazy.

I made sure to try to be around her as much as possible. Lorraine was active in the church as well, and she was around for many years, but it was like I didn't care to notice her then. That all changed one day when she smiled at me. I'm sure she didn't mean to enchant me the way she did, but her smile made me feel as though I had been hit by a truck. I held the door open for her once, and she curtsied and said, "Thank you."

I knew she was a year younger than I, but I didn't know much else about her. So I asked around and found out little things here and there: what type of flowers she liked, what type of music she listened to.

Lorraine had curly, light brown hair that bounced like springs when she walked. She wore bows in her hair, usually pink ones, and her smile was the thing that got me up early on Sundays to make sure I brushed my teeth, bathed, and combed my hair.

My mother was the first one to notice this new behavior in me.

"Planning on seeing someone today?" she asked, raising her eyebrows, a huge smirk on her face.

My cheeks must have flushed bloodred; I couldn't hide anything from my mother. I washed my face again to ignore the question. She gave me a quick pat on the back and went about her way.

My mother and I were always ready for church, but my father always lingered. This never bothered me before; in fact, I used to like it when my father stalled. It meant less time at church. But now that I was infatuated with Lorraine, every moment my father spent not driving us to church was painful. Of course, at this time, I could already drive, and I would offer to drive us. But my father refused. He didn't want me behind the wheel, and he was in charge of his family's safety, not me.

My mother and I were waiting in the car. I wanted to reach out and honk the horn, but I knew that this would have severe consequences for me, so I refrained. With each passing moment, my anxiety grew. I was sweating, and it wasn't even a warm day out.

"What's her name?" my mother asked.

I think I was blushing again. I couldn't tell because I was so warm already. "Who? What?" I asked, trying to dodge this whole embarrassing discussion.

My mother shrugged. "I've just never seen you get ready for church before, let alone comb your hair. I thought either that you have decided to become a clergy member or that you fancy someone in our congregation."

I put my face in my hands. I wasn't going to dodge this one. "Her name is Lorraine."

"Oh, the cute curly haired girl? She's very pretty. I know her mother. I can have a chat with her if you like."

I grabbed onto my mother's shoulders before I realized I was doing so. "Please, please don't do anything. This is hard enough. Here comes Dad." I let go of my mother and sat back down and hid my face with one hand.

My father was bumbling toward the car, and he was doing his usual routine of checking to see if he had his wallet and keys. Patting himself down several times, adjusting his hat twice, only to take it off once he was in the car. It was infuriating, but I kept this to myself, lest it cost us even more time in explaining my situation with him.

It felt like four hours later when he finally got himself into the car. Then, of course, he drove slowly. He even passed a neighbor with whom he had to stop and chat for a while, leaning out of the driver's-side window. I think my mother sensed my aggravation, and she tapped my father on the shoulder. She apologized to my neighbor but then said, "We will be late for church, and God doesn't help those who are idle."

My neighbor nodded and smiled. He tipped his hat to my mother and said, "Sorry to keep you waiting, ma'am."

My father sighed, and we were back on the road to the church. By the time we got there, most of the congregation was already seated. When we walked into the room, all eyes were on us; I was mortified. I suppose people thought we were Pastor Jacob coming in to give us his sermon.

There was an overwhelming disapproval with our late arrival. Many faces turned as we entered the room, and there were whispers here and there; I felt the eyes of the Lord on me as well. We sat down in such a hurry that I didn't even notice that Lorraine and her family were only a few rows ahead of us. With my face still flush and my brow with a thin film of sweat on it, Lorraine looked over her shoulder and smiled at me. This immediately drained all of my earthly worries and concerns. This melted my heart, and I could think of nothing but her.

Pastor Jacob came out and gave his sermon, but if pressed, I would not have been able to repeat even one word of what was said. I was so fixated on her curly hair that I missed my cues to stand up and sing hymns several times. My father didn't notice, but my mother would tug at my sleeve, and I would shoot straight out of my seat and stand at attention.

After the sermon was over, the whole church became chaos like usual. People moved at a snail's pace toward the exit, and the whole place was filled with conversation. I tried to pull away from my parents, but my father wanted to make a quick getaway. This plan was folly, because the line up to chat with Pastor Jacob was far too great to get beyond. We were stuck. My father wanted to take the back exit, but I wanted to stall, so I excused myself to use the restroom.

I didn't have to go to the bathroom; I just used that as a means to escape my parents. I spotted Lorraine deep in the crowd, and I skillfully maneuvered like a fish upstream toward her. I didn't see her parents anywhere.

When I got next to her, she was looking the other way. I hoped she would turn to face me, but she didn't. Time was running short. I tapped her gently on the shoulder. My head began to spin, and my knees weakened. My courage was failing, and I wanted to duck or turn the other way. But I didn't do that. I stood there, and she turned around to look at me.

"Hello," I said in a tone that was much higher than I anticipated. I cleared my throat.

Lorraine turned around and smiled. "Well, look who it is."

I nodded. I felt very awkward and said nothing.

Lorraine squinted at me. "Are you okay? You look rather feverish."

She reached out and placed the back of her hand at my forehead. Her touch was electrifying.

"Oh, I'm fine. Just a bit warm. This collar is a little bit too tight for my liking."

Lorraine reached in and adjusted my tie. The gesture was very intimate, like we were already lovers. When our eyes met, my heart calmed down.

"Thank you. I was about to be choked to death."

"We wouldn't want that," she said. She then touched my shoulders to straighten my shirt out. "There, better?"

"Much better." There was another awkward silence, and it was our turn to move up in line. I almost lost my spot next to her but managed to remain by her side. I couldn't see my parents or her parents anywhere.

"Lorraine," I began. When she turned around, I lost my thought, and there was another moment of silence.

I wanted to leave. I thought about escape. I wanted to get into our car and drive far away, but something told me to stand there and to have patience, because I was on the precipice of something grand. I pretended that I was my brother Joe—not the new Joe, certainly, but the Joe that was unstoppable. I pretended that I had his strength and courage.

I cleared my throat. "I was wondering if you … if you and I …"

Lorraine smiled. "Um … There's a dance next Saturday here in the basement …"

I was shocked. I swallowed. I didn't know anything about any dance, and I was very active in the church. This didn't stop me from asking, "Lorraine, would you do me the honor of being my date for the dance?"

Lorraine smiled. "I would be delighted. You can pick me up at my house and meet my parents."

I nodded, but because I stood still, I lost my place in line, and Lorraine made her way up to Pastor Jacob and shook his hand. She said some words to him that I did not hear, and she looked back at me and smiled.

THE BIG DANCE

O N THE NIGHT OF THE big dance, I must have bathed three times. My father smiled and laughed at me when he saw me finally emerge from the bathroom.

My mother pinched my cheeks and gave me unsolicited advice. "Now, dear, you don't have to be nervous. There's nothing to worry about. You both will have a fantastic time."

I groaned. "Mom, I'm not a boy anymore. I'll be fine."

My father barked from the living room, "Let him be. He's a man now, and he can take care of business. If he ever gets out of that bathroom, of course."

I combed my hair many times, changed clothes twice, and was out the door way earlier than I should have gone. I was about to get into my father's car, but my mother came out of the house holding something in her hands.

"Wait," she said. My mother came over to the driver's side of the car and handed me a handful of flowers. "You need to take these. There is one for you and one for her."

I grabbed the flowers and placed them on the seat next to me. When I turned around to face my mother, she planted a kiss on my cheek. "That one over there is your boutonniere. The other one there is her corsage."

I looked at the flowers, but I couldn't tell them apart. "Okay."

My mother took a deep breath. "Oh, let me get that for you. Hand me that one, will you? I will pin it to you."

I was about to refuse, but I knew how pointless that would have been. I grabbed the flowers my mother was pointing to, and she pinned them to my suit.

"Okay. There you go," she said.

I tried to smile, but I was more worried that I would have lipstick on my face than anything else. My mother stood there in the driveway and watched me leave; I waved to her several times and drove away.

I arrived early to Lorraine's house. I stopped the car and made sure to wipe the lipstick off of my cheek. I triple-checked to see if I missed any, and I even looked up my nose to make sure I didn't have any unwelcome visitors there.

I got out of the car, and my legs were shaking, and I held the flowers, which were shaking too. I knocked on the door, expecting to see Lorraine, but instead I saw her father.

He was a smaller man, but he wore a mean disposition, and he looked me up and down as if to set me on fire with his eyes. "What do you want?" he asked.

I cleared my throat. "Hello, Mr. Abbot. I'm here to see Lorraine. Is she here?"

The man scowled. "Of course she's here. Where else would she be? She lives here. What do you want with her?"

I swallowed. I was not ready for such an interrogation; certainly not on their porch. I tried to look past her father and up the stairs to the second floor. I wanted to see Lorraine so that she could rescue me from this torture. "What do I want with her?"

"Yeah, boy, you deaf?" Mr. Abbot asked.

I shook my head. "No, sir."

"Well, answer the question, then."

I tried to stand still, but I was moving from side to side. "I've come to take Lorraine to the dance. That is all, sir."

Just then, a woman who I recognized to be Lorraine's mother came to the door. She shoved her husband aside. "I'm sorry. Please excuse my husband. He lost his manners many years ago, and we've been trying to find them since. Please come in."

Lorraine's father harrumphed and moved into the living room; Lorraine's mother gently ushered me to follow.

"Thank you, ma'am," I said.

"Lorraine will be down shortly. She's still preparing her hair."

I nodded. "I'm sorry; I may be a little early."

"An hour early. Now what the hell are we to do? Stare at each other?" Lorraine's father grunted from a comfortable chair.

I tried to ignore the comment. I instead focused my attention on Lorraine's mother. "My mother always taught me it was rude to be late, so I've taken a habit of always being early."

Lorraine's mother smiled. "Your mother is a wonderful woman. I just love the cake she made last September. If you have a chance, please ask her for the recipe."

I wiped the sweat from my hands onto my pants. "That's mighty kind of you, ma'am. She's often said very nice things about you and your husband."

"Yeah, like what?" Lorraine's father asked.

Mrs. Abbot picked up a tissue that was on the table and threw it at her husband. She missed, but the sentiment was clear. "Henry, honestly. Treat our guest politely, or you won't have steak tomorrow."

Henry grumbled something and then got up and turned on the radio. I was glad for this for many reasons, mostly because I no longer wanted to be interrogated.

I waited there in the living room, making small talk with Mrs. Abbot for over an hour and a half. I kept clutching the corsage that my mother made. My hands were getting cold and clammy, and my feet wanted to jump out of my socks. Every so often, I would take a glance up the hallway whenever I heard a noise.

Usually, this was Lorraine's younger sister, Michelle, who would peek around the corner and spy on us adults. Whenever I caught her looking at me, she would dart away, and I could hear her little feet run upstairs.

"Oh, that's just Michelle. She's a shy sort, you know. Doesn't talk much. She didn't talk until she was three, either. We were scared that she was retarded or something. But she just has her own way about her, and no one is going to stop her."

"Ha!" Henry said. It was not immediately clear if he was laughing at us or the radio play that was going on at the moment. "Just like her sister!" he later added, which made it clear.

"Listen to your show, Henry!" Lorraine's mother shouted but then put a hand to her lips. "Oh dear, I'm sorry for shouting like that."

I smiled. The relationship reminded me of my mother and father. "I don't mind, ma'am. It feels like home."

Mrs. Abbot placed her hands on her hips. "Well, isn't that a nice thing to say. Aren't you a charmer."

Our conversation ended when Lorraine entered the room. I leaped out of my seat and fumbled the flowers, but I managed to catch them before they fell.

Lorraine's mother beat me to Lorraine, however, and she kissed her on the forehead. Lorraine muttered something that I couldn't hear.

Mrs. Abbot's face was beaming with a bright smile. "Oh. Absolutely lovely. Henry, where's your camera? I told you to get your camera."

Lorraine's father groaned and didn't look in our direction. "Why do we need my camera?"

Lorraine's mother's eyebrows shot upward. "Oh, for heaven's sake, Henry. I'll get it myself. Where did you put it?"

"How should I know? You put it away!" Henry shouted.

I took this moment to close the distance to Lorraine; I could smell her perfume from where I was. I was staring at her. She looked like an angel; her flowing dress moved like wings, and I wondered for a moment if she would take me away into the heavens with her. I handed her the flowers that my mother had made.

"You look absolutely stunning," I said. "But you usually do. My mother made this for you. They're flowers from our garden."

Lorraine smiled and glided over to me. "Thank you. That was very thoughtful." She smelled the flowers and then said, "Could you help me put it on?"

I swallowed. I wasn't exactly sure how to do that. There was a pin in the corsage, but I didn't want to stab her with it. Likewise, I was extremely uncomfortable touching her in front of her parents, but I had to try. I took the pin out and tried to think of the best way to pin it. My first two attempts failed, which made Lorraine giggle a bit. I came in closer this time in order to see where the pin was going, and I felt her lips touch my neck.

I paused. Lorraine was blushing, and I must have been too. I tried to ignore what just happened and successfully pinned the corsage.

By this time, Lorraine's mother came out with camera. "Okay, you two. Scoot together so I can get you both in. Oh dear, you have something on your neck. Let me help you." Mrs. Abbot came closer and wiped my neck with a handkerchief; she studied it briefly but said nothing. "Oh, don't be shy. Put your hands together."

Holding Lorraine's hand, I was surprised to feel that her fingers were just as cold as mine were. Mrs. Abbot must have taken twelve pictures. We held our smiles for so long that my face ached.

Lorraine rolled her eyes. "Okay, thank you, Mother. We'll be home soon."

"That's right," mumbled Mr. Abbot from the other room.

Mrs. Abbot kissed me on the cheek and gave Lorraine another quick hug before we left. We left the porch in a hurry, and I opened the car door for Lorraine. After waving to Mrs. Abbot, we were free from the confining hands of her parents.

"I thought we would never get out of there," Lorraine said. She scooted closer to me in the car and kissed me on the cheek.

It might be noted that in later years, a kiss on the cheek would have been a very innocent thing to do, but in 1946, this was a very bold move for a lady. Some may have even called her derogatory names for being so bold, but I liked it. I didn't want the burden of trying to figure a woman out. I'd kissed girls before, of course, but it was always awkward; girls wanted me to be able to read their minds. This wasn't the way it was with Lorraine; she knew exactly what I wanted and when I wanted it.

Our minds combined to create a new mind. We clicked very well right from the start, and I knew the moment her lips touched my cheek that tonight would be a very good night. At least this is what I thought.

#

I wasn't exactly a great dancer, but I must admit I was better than my brother. What my brother had in looks, I made up for in style. I knew from a young age that there was no way that I could woo a woman by my looks alone. I wasn't a hideous thing, just plain. My brother would stand out in a crowd of a thousand people, and I would disappear and be forgotten. I'd danced with my mother before, and I'd gone to other dances, so I'd proven to myself that I could do it.

It wasn't that I liked dancing. On the contrary, I would simply rather not dance if given the choice. However, on the dance floor is where the ladies were. If you wanted a lady, you needed to get up and dance.

And so it was. I knew Lorraine was excited for the dance, and I made sure to get us on the dance floor almost immediately. There was only one couple dancing when we first started, but I didn't care. I was fueled by a courage that I never knew until that night. Her kiss gave me a sense of bravery that I never saw coming. I grabbed her hand and pulled her onto the dance floor.

The band wasn't the best that I've ever heard, but they certainly weren't the worst. Some of their transitions to other songs were slower than what professional bands would do, but this gave Lorraine and me a chance to have a few words.

"You are a great dancer," Lorraine said to me as her eyes sparkled.

I smiled and touched her hand. "I can only be as good as my partner."

"Oh, so we are partners now?" Lorraine asked.

"I certainly hope so."

The next song came on, and we took to our feet again.

"Me too," she said.

Lorraine and I did not take any breaks: we simply danced to every song that the band played. Others would sit down often and take bathroom or smoke breaks. Some of the guys would go out back for a quick drink, but we did not bother with such things.

It was the best night of my life. My heart was racing, I was full of sweat, but neither I nor Lorraine cared. Several times, I managed to hold her close to me, albeit briefly. I remember her perfume and her curls tickling my nose.

Things, however, went from amazing to terrible in a heartbeat.

There was some commotion outside, and many of the people left to go see what was the matter. I was successful in ignoring this until my friend David ran up to Lorraine and me and said, "Hey, man, you need to come outside." His face told me it was urgent.

I gave David a harsh look, but I said in a tone so Lorraine wouldn't hear, "Not now. I'm busy."

David shook his head, which messed up his hair. "No, you need to come outside right now. It's Joseph. He's fighting both Randy and Paul."

"What? I didn't even know he was here," I said.

David was moving to the door when he said, "Are you coming or what? He's really drunk."

I held Lorraine close. "I need to help my brother. I will be outside. I'm sorry."

"What's going on?" Lorraine asked.

I stood up. I didn't want to let go of Lorraine's hand. "I don't know. You should stay here to be safe."

"I'm not made out of glass, you know. I'm coming too."

David and I made it to the door to the outside. It was lightly drizzling out, and the whole back courtyard of the church was filled with people. It was chaos, and I couldn't see exactly what was going on, but I did see four men fighting.

When I moved in closer, someone put his hand on my chest and said, "Let them fight it out."

I could see that Joe was there, his clothes in disarray, and his face was wet with blood and rain. The other three men were equally bloodied. Currently, they were all wrapped up and punching each other.

"Air force faggots!" Joe yelled, punching Paul in the face and stomach.

Another man grabbed Joe from behind; this gave Randy a chance to hit Joe again.

Joe, however, could not be pinned down for long. He broke the grip and, with blinding speed, let out a flurry of blows, some of them hitting, others not. But he managed to strike all three men down. He then stumbled a bit and fell to his knees.

I took this opportunity to close the distance to him. "Everyone back off," I said. "I think everyone's had enough." I looked at my brother. "What the hell are you doing?"

Joe looked up at me, his eyes half-shut. "Oh, hey, bro. Just thought I'd stop by for the dance."

I gritted my teeth. "Joe, you are drunk. I'm taking you home."

Joe's eyes went wild as he looked around. "Who's drunk? Oh. That's me. I don't want to go home."

I grabbed him by the shirt. "Too bad. That's where I'm taking you before someone calls the police." I then looked at the others that were all around. "Is everyone okay?" I asked.

Paul, Randy, and the other man I didn't know were back on their feet and wiping blood from their faces.

"Take that drunk home!" Paul yelled.

"Ranger homo," Randy said.

The other man made his way toward Joe, and I stood in the way. "Don't you think you've had enough?"

"Who the fuck are you?" the man asked.

I felt like a mama bear with a bear cub. "I'm his brother. What's it to you?"

This answer made the man back down in a hurry. He took a step away from me, spit, and said, "Get him out of here, then."

I reached down and picked Joe up. When I turned around, Lorraine was there helping me.

"I thought I told you to stay inside. It's not safe for a lady out here."

"It's not safe for you out here, either," Lorraine said.

We walked over to the car, and Joe got very heavy in our hands. So heavy, in fact, we dropped him several times. We plopped Joe in the backseat, and we got in the car. Joe passed out, so we had to squish his feet in an awkward position so that we wouldn't close the door on his legs.

When we closed the doors, Lorraine started laughing. I looked around; I wasn't sure what was so funny.

Between laughs, Lorraine managed to say, "This is not how I imagined our date would go."

I smiled, and Lorraine's laughter was infectious, so I too began to laugh. "Could be worse, I suppose."

Lorraine pulled at her dress. There were mud stains all over it. "I'm pretty sure this is ruined."

I suddenly felt sick. How was I going to explain this to Lorraine's parents?

"I'm so sorry." I leaned in to see if there was anything I could do about the stains. "My mother could maybe fix it. She's really good with this sort of thing. She raised two boys."

"Don't worry about it. It'll be fine."

Lorraine moved a lock of my hair so that it was out of my eyes.

I'm not sure exactly how we started kissing, but there we were in our church parking lot, with my drunk, passed-out brother in the backseat. We kissed for a very long time. So long, in fact, that the windows had fogged up, and my lips actually began to ache. By this time, my brother roused, and he sat up briefly looked at us both.

"This is my bro," Joe said, pointing to me. "I love this guy. He's the best." He leaned in toward Lorraine and almost head butted her. "Oopsie! You … you should be honored to have a man like my bro here."

Lorraine smiled. "Yes, I know."

"Okay, Joe, thanks. Time for bed. Lie down. I don't want you to get sick in Dad's car."

Joe's face lengthened. "You stole Dad's car?"

I shook my head. "No. I borrowed it. Now lie down," I said. I wasn't really worried about Joe getting sick. I was worried he would have a flashback and that he would start acting crazy. I didn't want Lorraine to see that.

I started the car and began driving to my farm, but then I changed my mind and drove to Lorraine's house instead. I figured if I needed an excuse, I would have my brother to show for it.

Pulling up to Lorraine's house was perhaps the boldest and bravest thing I had done in my life up to that point. When I stopped the car, I let out a big sigh. "Your father is going to kill me. He's going to think I did that to you."

"Oh, no, he's not. He's a big softy. I've been coming home with dirty clothes for years."

I blinked. I wasn't sure what that meant.

Lorraine's eyes bulged when she realized what she just said. "I mean I was a tomboy when I was a kid. Not anymore, of course, but when I was younger, I fell down a fair bit. It won't be too shocking. I can assure you."

I was relieved. "Okay. You ready?"

Lorraine shook her head. I wasn't sure what that meant at first, but my gut told me she wanted another kiss. I leaned in and kissed her. However, my eyes were open this time. The last thing I needed to have was her father standing there with a shotgun.

The kiss ended abruptly.

"Okay. Now I'm ready," Lorraine said as she quickly got out of the car.

I followed her up the stairs to her porch. To my relief, it was her mother who answered the door.

Lorraine talked quickly and to my surprise handled the situation better than I could ever have. She explained how Joe had gotten drunk and gotten into a fight with some air force brats. She then explained that I heroically protected my brother from further harm and how I protected her honor by making sure no one would lay a hand on her.

I, of course, added to the story, but I wasn't a talker like Lorraine and her mother were. In mere minutes, a near-catastrophic blunder was turned around into an unparalleled success. Somehow, Lorraine made me look better.

Mrs. Abbot checked me for wounds to make sure I was okay. She gave me a quick hug and opened the car door to take a look at Joe. "He's a mess. We should get him inside and clean him up. Your mother will not be happy if he comes home looking like this."

We brought Joe up to Lorraine's house. Mrs. Abbot was insistent, and there was no arguing with her. We took my brother to the upstairs bathroom, where we washed him up. I made Joe take a quick bath, and when he was done, I helped him get dressed. Mrs. Abbot provided a clean shirt and some pants from Mr. Abbot. The shirt didn't fit, as it was too tight, but it was certainly good enough. And it was certainly nicer than the bloodied shirt he was wearing. Mrs. Abbot did a thorough job cleaning up Joe's hair and cleaning his wounds; it was like the fight almost never happened.

While the two ladies put the final touches on Joe, I headed downstairs. I thought I should talk to Mr. Abbot, and I wanted to do this without Lorraine present, just in case I made a fool of myself.

I sat on a couch and watched Mr. Abbot read a book. I didn't say much, and I picked lint off my shirt every so often to amuse myself.

"Don't worry. Mrs. Abbot will clean him up nicely," Mr. Abbot said.

"I wasn't worried," I said.

Mr. Abbot looked at me from over his book. "Hrm. He's been through a lot. Saving the world isn't an easy thing, you know. Just make sure you are there for him. Okay?"

I nodded. "Yes, sir. I'm sorry to disturb your night like this."

"Are you kidding? I never get a chance to read. Mrs. Abbot hates to see me read. She's always on me. It's good for her to have a project to do."

This made me smile. "I'd like to ask you one more thing, and then I will leave you alone to read."

Mr. Abbot squinted and looked me up and down. "What is it?"

I cleared my throat. "May I come see Lorraine again? I will make sure there isn't this sort of drama again."

Mr. Abbot stared at me for a long time. No words were spoken, and the clock ticked in the background, and we just stared at each other like two dogs not wanting to back down.

Finally, Mr. Abbot grunted. "I like that you don't talk much and that you get straight to the point."

"Thank you, sir."

Mr. Abbot turned his attention back to his book. "If Lorraine wants to see you again after this, I suppose it would be all right with me."

"Thank you, sir. I will let you read now."

I sat and watched Mr. Abbot read for another half hour before Mrs. Abbot and Lorraine came downstairs.

RELEVANCE OF STORY

E RICH STRETCHED AND YAWNED. "THIS is all very touching and all, but I don't see how any of this story is relevant. I don't think the people really want to hear about how you fell in love. I'm sorry; it's just not that interesting, and more importantly, they don't really want to remember you like that. You are the monster. You are the one that did those horrible crimes. They want to hear about how it was that you became so evil. They don't want to identify with you, and they certainly don't want to like you."

The old man took a deep breath, but if he was annoyed, he wasn't showing it. "For this tale to be understood, you must look at every facet."

Erich sighed and shook his head. "Skip to the crime. That is what the people want to hear about. The rest of the stuff isn't that relevant." Erich shifted in his wooden chair.

The old man looked away and rubbed his face. "Everything in life is relevant. So long as there is air in our lungs, we can make choices. While this part of the tale may not seem directly relevant, it very much is. Lorraine would be the backbone of our relationship. Lorraine would give me the courage to do the things I had to do. Lorraine would be my guardian angel and my guiding light."

"You mention angels a lot. Lorraine was an angel, then?" Erich asked.

The old man shook his head. "No. Not that kind of angel. Lorraine was my world. She gave me fuel to fire my dreams. She was the driving force for my life's mission. To that end, I think she deserves an introduction, don't you think?"

Erich bit his lip and looked at his watch. "I suppose, but I'd much rather get back on track. I'd much rather hear about why you butchered those people, why you are here today, and why you are about to be executed. I think the world wants to hear that story, not the story of you having a happy life in some small town no one knows about. We are running out of time. You are running out of time. You will likely want some sleep tonight, so that doesn't leave us with much of anything."

The old man waved his hand. "Patience. I will get to all of that soon enough. Don't you worry. You will see how all of these things are connected. But in order to understand where I went and how I got there, you must see where I was coming from. Like any good road map, you need to know where you are and where you are going. Otherwise, the map is useless without points of reference."

Erich nodded. "Okay. But can we speed things up? You will need to get some sleep."

The old man grimaced. "Sleep?"

Erich's eyes widened for emphasis. "Yes, of course. I don't want to keep you up all night, and we have a lot of story to cover before I go home for the night."

The old man started to laugh. The reporter looked uncomfortable but started laughing, anyway.

"What is it?" Erich asked.

The old man wiped some tears out of his eyes. "My time here is over. I have all the time in the world to rest. I don't need sleep if you don't."

Erich tilted his head to one side. It was clear he never thought about this. "So you will tell me your story all night, then?"

"If that is what it takes," the old man said.

Erich nodded. "Okay. My wife will understand. I just wanted to get to the heart of the story; you can't fault me for that, can you?"

The old man shook his head. "Of course not, but to get there, you must understand the root of all the causes; otherwise, the end will simply stump you. And I'd rather have you leave here with a full understanding of what happened."

"I'll just have to tell the guard the next time we see him," Erich said, flipping over a page in his notebook. I'm ready when you are." He rubbed the rash at his wrists and cracked a few of his fingers.

The old man raised his eyebrows. "What time I do have, I will give it to you."

Erich blinked and lowered his head. He bit his lip and nodded.

The old man took a deep breath and squinted.

#

I know you are getting anxious for me to begin with the real journey of my tale, so I will get down to it. I will tell you the day that my life changed forever and the day I truly understood my purpose in the world.

I remember the first day my true life began. I'm neither talking about the day that I was born nor the day that I met my wife. While these things are important to the story, it was not the point in time that I am referring to. I'm talking about the day that God gave me a mission. I didn't know God gave me this mission at this time. It was only upon closer reflection much later in life that I knew this to be true. But the date was forever burned into my memory.

It was November 7, 1946. It was a stormy night, and there was a lot of snow on the ground. When I woke up that morning to get ready for school, I stared in disbelief at how much snow there was in the yard, covering everything. I remember the joy I felt that I was granted a snow day. I remember the relief that I would not have to listen to boring lessons in math, biology, and English. There was a test scheduled in physics that day, and I wasn't exactly prepared for it as I should have been. Math was not my strong point. I was always more interested in books, in words, and things that were more real.

Math seemed so devoid of emotion and removed from all the things that made life great that I detested it. My math teacher, Mr. Peters, said, "Everything is math. Even English is math. Don't believe me? There are twenty-six letters in the alphabet. How is that not math? Even poetry uses math. Each line is counted for syllables and is balanced for symmetry. To understand math is to understand the world."

I didn't want to understand the world in this fashion. Reason and logic can get you from point *a* to point *b*, but imagination can get you anywhere. At least that is what Einstein once said, and I think we can all agree that he was a pretty smart guy.

I started that day the way I started any other day. I drew a bath, washed up, and got dressed. By the time I arrived in the kitchen, I could already smell the bacon and eggs cooking. I hugged my mother and asked where father was. My mom pointed outside, and I could see my father frantically shoveling snow. I quickly grabbed my coat and joined him outside. My father jumped into his truck with a plow and began to plow the driveway, leaving me to clean up the edges. While my father plowed the driveway with one of our trucks, I ran along beside with a shovel and got the remnants that he couldn't get with the plow's blade. The truck was old, but it still ran, and it was perfect for clearing snow, which was what we usually used it for.

I got a pretty good sweat going, and we cleared the walkways and the driveway of snow. Being a farm road, we had a really long driveway, but the plow made quick work of this. Even still, this would make us seriously late for breakfast, but I didn't want to disappoint my father. I think he was under the illusion that he would still be able to make it to the office.

The main road leading into town was impassable. My father would likely clear some of it for the neighbors, but for now, he resigned himself to get some breakfast.

When we opened the door to the house, the beautiful smell of cooking was replaced with the smell of burned toast, burned eggs, and burned bacon. My father and I rushed to the kitchen to discover a small fire on the stove. My father took care of the fire in a heartbeat, while I tried to pry a frozen window open for some fresh air. I finally gave up, and I propped the back door open instead. The cloud of smoke was slowly reaching out for the opening and escaping outside.

My father went off to find out what happened to my mother, and then something odd happened. The whole house fell ghostly silent. I was poking around the bacon, trying to salvage what was there, and I wore grease all over my hands and face. I tried to find my family.

"Hello?" I called out, licking my fingertips. I walked out of the kitchen to the hallway. I walked past my room and found my father and mother in my brother's room. My mother was collapsed upon the floor. I pushed past my father and kneeled down by my mother. I thought she'd had a heart attack or something. Her face was pale, there were tears in her eyes, and she was not responsive. I shook her by the shoulders.

"Mom, what's wrong? Are you okay?" I asked.

She said nothing, but she pointed to the closet. My eyes lifted up, and my world collapsed. I almost dropped my mother in my fright and in my haste to understand what was happening to me. I felt the blood drain out of my face and my hands, and I felt my heart stop for a moment. I felt this strange gasp for breath as I realized that I had been holding my breath this entire time.

There, gently swaying back and forth, was Joe, suspended by his neck by one of the neckties I had given him for Christmas one year. His neck was at an odd angle, and the tie about his neck was stiff and dug in deeply into his neck. A small chair lay upon its side underneath him.

I gently let my mother go, and I grabbed Joe by the waist, trying to lift him up, to let the pressure off his neck. Joe was a big man, and I was smaller than he was by my age.

"Help me!" I cried in vain, but no help was given to me. I was thin and relatively weak. I couldn't support his weight. I struggled and accidentally kicked the chair across the room; it almost hit my mother. I cried out for help again, but none came to me. My father stood in the doorway, staring at us, and my mother lay upon the floor, her mouth still agape, spit pooling about her on the floor, and tears streamed silently out of her eyes. I never saw her more completely broken or so lost.

Looking for my father for help, I received none. He was lost in a world I could only guess at. His eyes would go to me and back to my mother. He stood there like a soldier waiting for orders. He stood on guard to fight an enemy that would never appear. He was like a tool that had no use, and he knew it. He stood there and stared and did nothing.

I gave up my attempt to hold Joseph up by myself. I reached into my pocket and got the pocket knife my father had given me on my birthday years ago, and I cut him down. Joe's head had hit the wall even though I tried my best to catch him. But it was far too late. It was clear to me now that Joe had been dead for hours, and there was nothing in my power that I could ever do for him ever again.

I would never talk to Joe again. I would never hug Joe again. I would never have a drink in the backyard with Joe again. I would never go fishing with him the way we used to, and I would never chat with him about girls or about school. My brother was dead, and my life was forever changed.

#

We didn't have breakfast that day … or lunch or dinner. I set Joe in his bed, took off the makeshift noose from his neck, and closed his eyes. His skin was cold to the touch, and I knew his soul was gone. I pretended that he was simply sleeping, which stalled the tears and sorrow that were welling inside of me; there was a deep ache in my soul and the clawing pain at my center.

By this time, my mother tucked him into bed, and for a brief moment it looked as though Joe had just been resting or passed out from too much rum. The odd stillness of his body, though, only accentuated the fact that he was no longer with us.

My father spent a good deal of time on the phone while my mother and I sat with Joe. The lines were very busy, with the snowstorm and all, and it was some time before he could reach the appropriate emergency services to help with our situation. And again due to the snow, no one came for the entire day and the entire night. This left me and my mother a lot of time to kneel at the side of Joe's bed. We cried together, and I would often look over my shoulder to make sure my father wouldn't catch me with a tear in my eye. I knew that men didn't cry, and I didn't want to look weak in front of my father. But in front of my mother, I could be as weak as I wanted to be. And she was far too destroyed in spirit to say otherwise. We held each other like two monkeys in the zoo. We would have periods of calm accentuated by periods of her crying uncontrollably. I did my best to hold her tight, not knowing what else to do.

My father, in the meantime, did the only thing that he could think of doing—getting into the truck and plowing the roads. He cleared the road in front of our house first, and then he cleared a path to the neighbors on either side. He then continued down the street, clearing a path for the emergency vehicles to come to get his dead son.

When my father left for the truck, I did not know whether I should follow him or stay with my mother, who refused to leave Joe's side and would stroke his hair and talk to him as though he were still with us.

I was ashamed to cry, but it was all I could do. So I sat there with my mother, holding her and listening to her while we both wept.

Joe had left a note with my name on it, and I put it in my pocket before anyone could see it. I think my parents were in too much shock to look for such a thing. Later on in life, I studied a bit about suicide, and I learned that it was not usual to find notes on suicide victims. And so I appreciated the words that my brother left to me.

I first read the note in the bathroom of my home, with my father outside busy plowing the streets and my mother busy tending to my dead brother. I must have read that note a million times over the years, because I wanted to know why my brother chose death over life.

The note was accompanied by a poem written in the previous world war, "Before Action."

The note read thus:

To my bro:

I had thought that God had something planned for me in the war, that I was to save someone, to help someone. But I did nothing of the kind. I marched, I followed orders, and I destroyed life. I came home, and people called me a hero.

Even Death in a tuxedo wasn't interested in me. I know there is nothing I can say. So I'll just say I'm sorry.

Joe

PASTOR JACOB

I GREW UP IN A Christian family, so by default, that made me religious, though we were not crazy devotees. My brother and I were both named after biblical characters. We went to church, as did everyone at the time, and my mother made sure that we never missed the holidays, such as Easter and Christmas.

We didn't talk about religion much at home, and we didn't say grace every night at dinner. Religion was almost just something to do rather than a mission in life. I grew to accept it as part of our routine and part of our lives. I didn't question faith, because there was really nothing to question; it was just something we did. I knew at a young age what was right and what was wrong. I was shown by my parents the difference between what makes a good person and what makes a bad person, but after my brother's death, my whole world was turned upside down.

It was this turning point, then, that led me on a path that would forever change my life. A few weeks after that painful incident, I went to see Pastor Jacob at our church. Pastor Jacob was a kind and gentle man who had a big bushy beard and a warm smile on his face every time I saw him. When we would go to church, he would be standing at the door welcoming people in and shaking their hands. He was forever happy and forever in a state of peace and tranquility. In fact, I'd never seen him in a bad mood ever, which always made me wonder what his secret was.

Even the way Pastor Jacob walked and moved seemed holy to me. Each step was deliberate, and each gesture was one that showed kindness and love. He moved in a slow and deliberate way that created an immediate calming effect. I saw this echoed in his congregation, who subconsciously mimicked his behavior. As a result, the people in our community were very happy and calm people; it was a nice place to grow up.

The day I mustered the courage to talk to Pastor Jacob was on a Sunday. I drove myself to church, and my mother stayed home with my father, who was sick with the flu. I waited until the entire congregation departed; I stood in the doorway to his study for about two minutes before he noticed me. His head was down, peering into a book, with his back toward me. I didn't want to disturb him, so I just stood there like an idiot, hoping he would take notice. The moment I decided to give up and to walk away was the moment that Pastor Jacob looked up from his work and called out my name. I turned around, but I couldn't look at him in the eye. Instead, I pretended to pick lint off of my shirt.

"My poor child," he said, though I was seventeen and no longer a kid. "Come in, please. Have a seat."

I came in with my head held low and my hat in my hands. I became acutely aware of the water that was dripping off of my boots and onto his hardwood floor.

"I should have taken off my boots," I said. "I'm sorry. I should go."

Pastor Jacob dismissed my statement with a wave of his hand. "Forget your boots, and just sit. Water can be cleaned up, but matters of the heart require extra attention. Would you care for a cookie? One of the ladies in our Bible study baked them last night. They are wonderful." Pastor Jacob pointed to a plateful of cookies on the end of his wooden desk.

I took a cookie off the plate, but I didn't take a bite. I didn't think I would be able to chew it even if I were hungry—there was a lump in my throat, and I couldn't shake it. I feared that I might start crying. And my father used to say that men should always be strong, and only wimps cry. I needed to be strong not only for myself but for my family.

Pastor Jacob walked over to his study door and shut it. Instead of going back to his desk, he grabbed my head and placed it in his belly—sort of a head hug. He said a prayer then, but I did not hear it. I grabbed him by the waist, and I cried into his chubby belly, wiping the snot and tears from my eyes onto his prayer robes. Pastor Jacob knew our family well, and he knew about what happened to Joseph, of course, because he was the one who presided over the funeral.

I don't know how long I cried, but Pastor Jacob held me there and continued his prayers until I regained the use of language.

"Do you believe in angels?" I asked after a considerable time of putting the words together.

Pastor Jacob was rocking me slightly, like my mother did when I was young. "Of course I do. Angels surround us and protect us at all times. Have you ever thought about doing something bad, only to change your mind? I believe that is an angel whispering in our ears to steer us back on course."

"What do they look like?" I asked, wiping some slobber from my face.

"Well …" Pastor Jacob moved over to some books and opened up a page with a picture of a typical angel on it. It had wings and a halo and was surrounded by white light. One picture displayed an angel wearing armor and carrying a sword, and the angel was stepping on the face of the devil. He spun the book around so that I could see the images and pointed to the one on the left, who was looking up into the heavens. His wings were spread wide.

"Are there any angels that wear tuxedoes and top hats?" I asked.

Pastor Jacob looked at me quizzically. "I don't know if I understand the question."

I cleared my throat and mustered the courage to talk about what I came there to talk about. "Joe said he saw an angel back during the war. The angel picked him out of the beachhead and pulled him to safety. His whole unit was killed. He survived but only because he was pulled off of that beach. He said the angel was dressed in a black tuxedo."

Pastor Jacob scratched his beard and gave me a kind smile. "Angels can take many forms, and so it is possible your brother saw one dressed like what you are describing. It sounds to me too that he must have felt badly for surviving."

I bit my tongue, because I felt a lump building in my throat again. The death of my brother was still new, and it was still a difficult thing to wrap my head around. "Why did the angel save my brother, then, only to have him die now?"

Pastor Jacob's face grew serious, which was not normal for him. He usually wore a smile, even during difficult times. "War does terrible things to people; you must understand this. One can see many things. I should know; I've been there." I squinted at Pastor Jacob; he was far too old to have been in the war. My face asked the question, because he added, "I fought in the Great War. The war to end all wars. It was there that I realized my mission in life. And from that point forward, I dedicated my life to God."

I was still wiping spit off of my face. The Great War was a terrible thing that ravaged Europe in the early part of the twentieth century, and it saddened me that he was there. "How did you come to that realization? I never knew you were in that war."

Pastor Jacob put his fingertips together and sat back in his chair. There was a clear wet spot on his shirt from my face. "Not many people do. I'm telling you this because I know I can trust you. I don't like to talk about that war, because I left that back in the trenches in Europe. There is no need to carry this pain any longer."

"How did you find God?" I asked.

"In the trenches. In the suffering and in the death. I saw Him there, and He spoke to me."

I straightened up. "You saw Him?"

"Yes. In a manner of speaking. I was cold, afraid, and one night all alone. I had become separated from my line, and I was in what was called no man's land. That was the place between the lines of fighting men. A place of mud, craters and death. I crawled into a large shell hole that had many fallen trees around it. Despite the fact that it was a war zone, it was very good shelter. I slept very well that night. I slept through the bombings and machine gun fire. When I awoke, there was a German soldier there with me.

"I was so surprised to see him there. I grabbed my rifle and held it close to my chest. I didn't point it at him, though, because he wasn't pointing his rifle at me. He made no move to strike me. He certainly could have killed me in my sleep. He looked tired, worn out, as if he had been wounded a dozen times, but he wasn't bleeding. He said something to me, but I couldn't speak German.

"We sat there staring at each other for a while. He took out a chunk of bread from his pack, he tore it in two pieces, and he handed me some. I took the bread; it was a bit stale, but when you are starving, anything tastes good. I felt bad that I had nothing to give him. Instead, I pulled out a picture of my girlfriend, and I showed it to him. He smiled, said something that sounded pleasant, and showed me a picture of his mother and his father and him in uniform. I smiled at him and said some kind words, which I'm sure he didn't understand either.

"We sat there until dawn turned to morning light. Before we parted, I realized that I had a package of cigarettes. I gave these to him. He smiled and nodded to me and left. I gave him a good head start and watched which way he went. I still didn't know which side was ours, and so I crept out of there carefully and went the opposite direction.

"Before I fell asleep that night before, I had asked God to not only come to me but to go through me. I asked that He take over my life and said that I would dedicate my life to Him, if I could just get some sleep. My wish was granted. I got my sleep, and He got His faithful servant."

I nodded and said, "But you didn't actually *see* God, though."

Pastor Jacob wore his usual smile and opened his hands up, which lightened the mood somewhat. "I didn't have to. I felt His presence. I believed that He would save me, and He did. I believed that if I were to continue to show kindness to others, that kindness would be given to me. That soldier also showed me kindness, a kindness I would never forget. He could have done away with me, but he chose not to."

"Do you think that German soldier survived the war? Why do you think he let you live?"

Pastor Jacob chewed his beard for a moment. "That is the great question, isn't it? I may never know the answer to it. But I think the answer is very clear. God showed me something very precious that day. He showed me that the enemy was just as tired, alone, and scared as I was. He showed me that my enemy could show compassion, even though there was absolutely no reason to. This was war, and he could have slit my throat. Or, at the very least, he could have rummaged through my pockets."

My face was almost dry at this point. "How long was he there, do you think?"

Pastor Jacob shrugged. "The soldier? I have no idea. A few hours, I'm guessing. I hope he caught some sleep; he looked dreadful."

"Maybe you could find him somehow. Maybe he's still alive," I said.

Pastor Jacob shrugged. "Or maybe he was an angel showing me what I needed to see. I am happy not knowing. I will meet him again on the other side, anyway, and we will embrace and know each other when we see one another. It would break my heart to find out he died in the war or in the war that followed. That type of kindness is rare, and I'm hoping he lives a long and peaceful life."

I shifted in my chair, still holding my uneaten cookie; I tucked it into a pocket. A thought occurred to me, and I wanted to say it, but it came out in a mumble. "If there are angels that whisper to us, does that mean there are demons that whisper to us?"

Pastor Jacob paused for a moment to consider the question. "You cannot have light without shadow. You cannot have day without night. Yes, I believe there are those out there that mean to do us harm. But one can only be influenced by them if you turn to them. If you actively choose darkness, they will find you. This is why it is important to concentrate upon the good. Don't try to be good. Simply be good. Don't try to suppress the bad, as suppressing the bad will make those demons stronger. If you force down a spring, it will only gain in potential power and will one day shoot out. The way of peace, then, is in acknowledgment of the bad but concentration upon the good in life."

"What do demons look like? Could it have been a demon that Joe saw?" I asked.

Pastor Jacob shook his head. "Demons don't help men out of danger. Also, I know Joseph. He was a good soul, and good souls are not plagued by foul creatures. They are turned away by the goodness and spiritual light that good people bring. You see, the love that we have is distasteful to them, and they can't be too close to it, because it hurts them to do so. Have you ever heard that saying 'Misery loves company'? Well, that is what demons seek: others' misery."

I was confused. "War is misery, though. Wouldn't they be drawn to war?"

Pastor Jacob nodded. "Yes, you are right; they are drawn to war. But war affects people differently. Those that have been holding down the evil spring inside of them burst out and become more evil. Demons are attracted to that sort of person. This does not describe your brother in the slightest. I don't recall him ever holding anything back in Sunday school."

I smiled at this. Joe would always speak his mind and was never shy about pointing out that he or someone he loved had been wronged. He was a true defender of justice and peace. I always thought he would be a great superhero if he possessed superpowers.

There was a deeper question I wanted to ask, but it was taking a while to muster the courage to say it. I placed both my hands on my face, not to stop me from weeping but to prevent my soul from escaping. "But suicide is a sin. Is Joe …"

Pastor Jacob raised his hand. "Your brother was meant to die in the war. An angel saved him. Perhaps he was meant to live long enough to return to you and tell you of his tale. Perhaps Joseph was meant to renew your faith. Your brother is safely in heaven."

"How do you know?" I asked, the tears starting up again.

Pastor Jacob placed his hand on the center of his chest. "Because I know in my heart, and you should know it in your heart too. Your brother was a kind and generous man. He loved you very much."

I looked away to keep the tears at bay, and I dug a fingernail into my left forearm to take my mind off of what was just said. "How is it that you are fine after suffering a war, and my brother was broken?"

Pastor Jacob took a deep breath and stroked his beard. "I was broken too. But I broke during the war. I couldn't sleep for weeks. I could shut my eyes, but I never really slept. I thought I would die at any moment. I thought that I would hear the call for gas too late and that I would fail to put on my mask. I feared sleeping in the trenches, as I felt the shells looming above me. I feared sleeping in the shelters we made, because I've seen many people buried alive in such things."

I looked up. Despite my best efforts to hide my tears, my whole face was wet again. "But you survived. You're fine. You run a church, and everyone loves you. Your life is perfect."

Pastor Jacob smiled. "What you see now is the man that I was transformed into during the war. I changed my life, and God was my guide to making that happen. You are looking at a man at chapter thirty in his life, not chapter one."

I choked on some spit. "But you must have killed people, during the war, I mean. Aren't these things sins?" After I said this, I waved both hands in an apology. "I'm sorry. I shouldn't have said that."

"I honestly don't know if I killed anyone. Most of my time as a soldier was spent dodging artillery shells and digging trenches. I fired my rifle a lot in the early part of the war. I'm sure I hit some people, but I never really saw what I was shooting at. When we crossed over into enemy lines, I was lucky enough to never be in a first wave, so most of the Germans were already dead or dying. I never stuck my bayonet into a dying man. I just couldn't do it. It may have been the merciful thing to do. But I couldn't bring myself to it. There were plenty of other men that could and did. After that night I spent with that German, I never fired at another human being ever again. I didn't want to hit him." Pastor Jacob smiled. "Ha! I never thought of it like that until now. Bless your heart for asking. I had forgotten about that. I didn't want to shoot the man who spared my life. I owed him everything, after all."

My nose became juicy, and I wiped it on my sleeve. "But you are so … normal. You don't dive under tables worrying about artillery."

Pastor Jacob put his hands upon his desk. "Oh, but there you are wrong. For two years, I dove for cover in the middle of the night. It scared my wife something fierce. But when I would wake, I would pray and settle my mind. She too would be by my side, rubbing my back and telling me it was all right. I'm not sure what I would have done without her."

At this point, I began to cry again. Joe didn't have a wife to help him in that manner. I think Joseph was afraid to show his vulnerability to me and my parents. And so he must have felt very alone in his last days. Not having much more to say, our conversation was basically over. I got up and thanked Pastor Jacob. When I was about to leave, he grabbed me gently by the shoulders, spun me around, and gave me a hug.

This was the hug I had been wanting. I didn't know it, but I really wanted to hug my brother, and I wanted to hug my father. But there, in Pastor Jacob's office, I held an embrace that I would never forget. He knew I needed that hug, and he gave it to me. I sobbed in his arms like a baby, and he held me tightly and didn't say a word.

When it was time to go, I noticed that I'd gotten his robes wet and sticky. I tried to pat it dry with a handkerchief, but I made it worse. He only smiled at me, and with his beard, for a moment, he looked like a chubby Jesus. I thanked him and went on my way.

Over the next coming months, I spent a lot of time in our church. I volunteered for various activities, and any moment I could chat with Pastor Jacob, I did. He never said no and never dismissed me, and he never chastised me for telling the same story over and over again. He was very supportive and was another guiding light for me in the years to follow.

In one such conversation with Pastor Jacob, I asked, "If angels are happy, why do most pictures of them have them look neutral? They look as though they are neither happy nor sad. Their faces are simply blank."

Pastor Jacob was always quick with a response. "Well, first of all, these are artists' representations and aren't actually the real things, so keep that in mind. Angels are doing God's work. Perhaps there is some work that they do not wish to do but have to—like doing the dishes, for example. Are you happy or sad when you do the dishes?"

I shrugged. "I don't do the dishes anymore, just the chores outside. I broke an expensive piece of china my mother received on her wedding day, and that was it. I was banned from the kitchen."

Pastor Jacob almost rolled his eyes but didn't. "Well, okay, are you sad or happy when you clean the barn?"

I thought about this for a moment. "Well, neither, I guess. I suppose that makes some sense. But why are angels armed in some pictures? I see them pictured in armor and carrying weapons, such as swords or spears. Why would angels need armor or swords?"

"They don't. These pictures are representations of how we would like them to appear. The armor of any angel is faith. The weapons an angel employs are love and forgiveness. But how do you draw forgiveness? How do you see that good defeats evil through love? This is very hard to draw, but a sword is a thing, and a thing can be drawn. And so many artists take these shortcuts to depict scenes of angels doing God's work."

I looked at my hands, and I suddenly understood a key ingredient that would lead me down a path that I could never turn away from. I decided to arm and armor myself with faith.

DISCOVERING MY PATH

T HERE ARE A LOT OF things that happen to a teenage boy when
he loses a big brother. The first thing I felt was a loss so great
that nothing I could do could ever fill it. This was the obvious
pain, the thing that most people can immediately identify with. The
harsher pain was that I was the remaining son, and I was no longer
invisible. This was both good and bad. It was good to finally be noticed
but bad because I constantly felt like I was being compared to Joe. No
one directly did this to my face, of course. But deep down, I knew that
Joe was the better man. I was just a weak, thin teenager who didn't have
the backbone Joe did.

Joe's death changed my life for the better and for the worse. My
parents paid closer attention to me the months following, which was both
a blessing and a curse. If I needed to do anything remotely dangerous,
even driving a tractor, I was forbidden to do it. I was treated as a child,
and I was protected from the world around me.

This made me crazy, of course, but what was I supposed to do? I
wasn't exactly going to run away, and even if I did, I would have nowhere
to run to.

Joe had told me many strange things about the war, and the night of
his death, I decided what my life's mission was: to find out exactly what

he was talking about. I wanted to see an angel myself, and I wanted to talk to an angel, just as Joe had done in the war. I was holding in a lot of anger in my early days, and I wanted to corner an angel, if I could, and ask it many questions.

I knew that looking for an angel might be a fool's journey; there was no way of really knowing if my brother was just insane. However, I believed him. I also believed in God, and I believed in angels, and so to me, this was not a foolish quest. This was a journey worth fighting for but also a journey I kept hidden from everyone. I never told anyone of my definite chief purpose in life, not even Lorraine. In fact, this is really the first time ever that I have exposed my true purpose in life to anyone. I had other minor purposes, of course. I wanted to get married and have a family, but the overriding arch was fueled by this desire to understand the spiritual world and the supernatural.

Finding out anything I could about angels would dominate my mind all of my life. This was the driving force that compelled me to do things that led me into often dangerous situations or simply buried in books on the couch each evening.

I believed in order to truly understand what happened to Joe, I would have to walk in his footsteps. However, I knew that I would not be a good Ranger. I wasn't strong or agile like Joe, and I didn't have that same drive to win like he did. As a child, I always loved boats, and I had built many model ships, and in the back of my head, I always thought I would join the navy to see the world. However, since both of my cousins were killed on boats, I felt less inclined to do this.

Joe told me that he thought the regular army wasn't very good, though he did believe that the Rangers were fantastic. I asked him what he thought about the marines, and Joe had a lot of respect for them. And so, this is how I came to my decision to wanting to become a marine. If I couldn't become a Ranger, and if I wasn't going to be in the navy, the best solution was to be a marine. So, on my eighteenth birthday, I went to the recruiting office with the intention to join.

It was 1947, I was out of high school, and I was eighteen years old. In my mind, I was going to march into the recruiting office, sit down with a recruiting officer, and sign all the necessary paperwork. This didn't happen, as the first time I went to the recruiting office, it was closed. The second time I went, it was also closed.

By the time I got there when there was anyone there, I was politely told to leave.

I didn't expect to be declined from joining. I looked at the recruiting officer. "Why can't I be a marine?"

The recruiting officer was missing his left hand. This was a bit distracting and made me feel uneasy, but I tried to ignore it, even though he tried to hide it by stuffing it into a pocket. He became very animated when I was insistent on joining.

"No one can join, son. Major cuts to our budget, I'm afraid. You see, the politicians don't believe they need us anymore. After we defeated the Japs and the Krauts and all. Of course, they don't see what I see, the looming force of communism coming our way. If I had it my way, we would be fighting the red bastards right now."

The recruiter's enthusiasm touched the right button in me. "My brother fought on Omaha Beach. He fought his way inland. I wanted to follow in his footsteps. I know the marines weren't there, but I know the marines did landings like this all over the place."

The marine officer sighed. "Omaha, huh? That was a tough fight. Your brother sounds like he was made from steel and whiskey. Wish I could help you, son. The government wants us to fight the commies with one hand tied to our balls. If we don't do something soon, the next war we'll be fighting will be with harsh language."

"I thought all I had to do was come down here and sign up," I said.

The recruiter nodded. "That's when the government was all in a panic when Hitler and Stalin were playing ball. But now, they have been lulled into a false sense of security. Don't you worry none. Something will happen soon. I'm not sure where or when, but they will call on us like they did before. It is coming; trust me. And we will have to pull their sorry asses out of the shit storm they made, and we will bleed for it. But saving our country's ass is something we happen to be good at. So let them flounder. I'm prepared in my mind for what is next."

I stood there, deflated. My hands were by my side, and my shoulders slumped.

The recruiter seemed to notice this and took pity on me. "You might have some luck joining the air force. They need people to help rebuild in Japan and in Germany."

I scowled. I didn't want to join the air force. My brother wasn't fond of the air force because of some poorly dropped bombs that killed Allied soldiers. I wanted to be a marine.

"Fuck that," I said. I surprised myself with my language. I placed a hand over my mouth, and my face went red. "I'm sorry, sir, I'm no fairy air force guy or even an army guy. I feel it in my bones—I'm a marine. I might even be part fish."

To my surprise, the recruiter slapped me on the back with his good hand so hard that I almost choked on my own spit; he was surprisingly strong.

"Goddamn right. You don't look like no lazy army to me, either. Shame I can't take you in today."

I wiped a bit of spittle from my lips. "Do you know when you will be able to?"

The recruiter shook a fist into the air. "Beats the hell out of me. As soon as Congress pulls their collective heads out of their asses. We are taking apart our military while the Russians laugh and continue to build. They are going to sell their arms to neighboring countries and poison the world with all that commie crap!"

"So I'm just supposed to wait, then?" I asked. "What am I supposed to do? This is what I was going to do."

The recruiter put a hand on my shoulder. I was glad it wasn't his severed limb.

"Get some job somewhere. Make your parents happy. Find a girl you like. In a few years, they will come to their senses, and you can join up then."

Disappointment wasn't the right word for what I felt. Utter loss and depression would be more accurate. I walked out of that recruiter's office with my head held low and my shoulders slumped forward. I walked all the way home, because I didn't have my own car at that time. It was a good ten-mile hike to my farm, but I think I needed that time alone to myself. It was a hot afternoon, and it hadn't rained in days. There was a lot of dust along the road, and each car that passed me kicked up more dust. I must have looked rather pathetic, because two people stopped to offer me a lift home. I politely declined.

I felt that with the war over I'd missed my opportunity for heroism that my brother participated in. I know the war broke him, but I also knew that the war didn't break everyone. I wanted to see firsthand what it was all about. I wanted to test my courage, and I wanted to find an angel. And if I did manage to find an angel, I had a ton of questions to ask it.

Since I couldn't join the marines and I didn't want to rebuild Germany or Japan in the army, I had to come up with another solution. I was just out of high school, and I needed to find a job. I didn't exactly know what I wanted to do with my life. I was happy on the farm, but I knew that if I was ever to get married and have a family of my own, I couldn't very well stay at the farm. I wasn't particularly interested in going to college, so I figured I might as well start making money.

Fortunately for me, my father had many connections, and one of his good friends was an executive at the local newspaper. This was how I landed my first official job. I say "official job," because I worked on the farm for many years prior to this real job. I just never got paid for it. Of course, my efforts kept the place running and put food on the table, so I never really asked for anything. I knew we didn't have much, and during the war, everything was in shortage, anyway. It was just how the world worked back then.

As it turned out, working for a newspaper was completely different from life on a farm.

I was very nervous on my first day on the job. I didn't know what to expect or what was expected out of me. I changed my clothes twice, just like it was another big dance, but this dance was different. I wasn't going to kiss any pretty girls. I was just going to do some meaningless job. I didn't want to disappoint my father, and I wanted to get a head start and actually do some work. While I was in school, my parents didn't want me having a real job—not because they didn't want me to have money but because they needed me to feed the chickens, tend to the cows, and tend to the gardens and the apple trees.

"Just remember to be polite and keep quiet. No one likes a blabbermouth," my mom said before I left for my first day. She even adjusted my shirt collar before I left.

My father was reading the paper and didn't remove his eyes from it when he said, "You'll be fine. Just do what they ask and a bit more. Always do a bit more than you are asked. Going the extra mile will make you stand out and get you promoted. You can't ask for more money when you aren't doing more to earn it. See?"

"Thank you," I said to both of them, but I didn't really mean it. I wanted to tell them to shut up and mind their own business, but I was still under their roof, and I had to play nice for the time being.

When I got to the office, it was pure chaos. I didn't know where to go or who to talk to. People were running around like ants that just had their hill kicked over. There were papers everywhere, and it was remarkably noisy. People yelling into phones, people yelling over the noise, and the clanking of typewriters filled the air. There was also a thick blue haze of smoke, enough to choke on, and this took something to get used to, as my parents didn't smoke at all. I felt like a spectator watching something at the state fair. Fortunately, someone spotted my desperate and lost look and came up to me right away.

"Who you looking for, honey?" a middle-aged woman asked me. Her blouse was slightly open, and I could see her cleavage. This stunned me for a second, and I couldn't get any words out. She smiled and pinched my cheeks like I was a toddler.

I rummaged in my pocket and pulled out a piece of paper with the name of the man I was supposed to report to. I handed the paper over to the lady without saying a word. My eyes found her cleavage again, and I could feel my face boil.

She smiled, showing a bit of lipstick on her teeth. "Mr. Thompson is one floor down, hon. Go down the stairs here, take a right, and it is the big door on your left. You can't miss it."

I smiled weakly and tried not to move my eyes downward to see her breasts, even though I wanted to look. "Thank you," I said.

The lady winked at me and went about her way.

I descended the stairs like I was told, and my jaw dropped. If I thought it was busy upstairs, the mail room was a lot worse. I was both stunned by the activity and scared. Part of me wanted to play with all of the machines that were there, and the other part of me wanted to make a run for the door.

Before I could do anything, however, someone grabbed me and pushed me into an office. The man closed the door behind me.

In the office was a man on the phone, smoking a cigarette. He was yelling at someone for something, which made me feel like a troubled student who was being sent into the principal's office. I took off my hat and waited. I tried not to listen to the conversation, but it was quite difficult to ignore, because he was yelling at the man on the other end of the line. The last words I heard were, "I don't give a fuck what your goddamn problem is. You either show up tomorrow, or I'll find some other ass to fill your goddamn spot. Got it?" He then slammed down the phone, which made me jump.

The man turned to me, as if seeing me for the first time. "You aren't stupid, are you?" Mr. Thompson asked.

I was startled by this question. "No. No, sir."

The man waved a hand in the air, which pushed smoke this way and that. "You don't have any sickness, do you? Flu or that kind of thing?"

I shook my head again. "No, sir."

"Do you drink a lot?"

I shook my head again. "Not really, sir."

The man grunted and tapped his hands on his armrests. "You aren't lazy, are you? You aren't fat, so that's a good sign. I don't need any lazy fuckers down here. Things get stupid busy here, and I mean stupid. You don't mind working hard, do you?"

I gripped my hat like a shield. "No, sir. I grew up on a farm, sir."

Mr. Thompson nodded and took a drag off his cigarette. "All right. Get out there. Talk to Mr. Tanner. He'll train you up."

I nearly bowed, but I stopped myself. "Thank you, sir. I really appreciate this opportunity."

Mr. Thompson rolled his eyes. "Yeah, yeah. Get out of here."

I turned to leave and opened the door.

"Oh, one more thing."

I paused and looked back at Mr. Thompson and noticed his bald spot and couldn't help but stare at it.

Mr. Thompson pointed at me with the hand that held his cigarette. "You come to work on time, do a good job, and I won't have to beat you. If you piss me off, if you skip work, you are done. Got it?"

I nodded. "Yes, sir."

I stepped out of Mr. Thompson's office and into chaos. There were so many parts of this machine moving that I simply could not track it all. I was briefly introduced in the mail room, and I promptly forgot every name that was given to me. I was shown several workstations, and I forgot the instructions.

"Is Mr. Thompson always—" I started to say when I was cut off.

Mr. Tanner wore a suit, but his tie was loose, his handkerchief was absent, and the elbows of his jacket were well worn. "An asshole? Nah, but just don't get on his bad side. He'll cut you." Then he started laughing and he reached over and rubbed my belly. "I'm just messing with you, kid."

Working in a mail room anywhere isn't exactly a dream job, but it was a job. I made some friends there, and as long as I was pulling my weight, Mr. Thompson would leave me alone. I saved up as much money as I could, because I knew I would need it to start the life I wanted with Lorraine.

I worked the mail room for six months before I caught a break that I was dreaming about. There were three reporters out of the office one day, and they needed someone to cover a story. It wasn't my department, but I overheard a conversation from a few of the managers who were obviously distraught. I was nervous, and fear crept into my stomach. I almost walked away, but I recognized this as an opportunity, and I knew I should act. Luck is simply where preparation and opportunity meet.

"I can do that, sir," I said to one of the managers.

He looked over at me like I was a cripple or something. "Who the hell are you?" he asked, taking a drag from his cigarette.

I stepped confidently forward. "Sorry to listen in, sir, but I do a bit of writing myself, and I think I could help out. It sounds as though you need someone."

"Well, it ain't a glorious job, kid," the man said, continuously sizing me up. "You work in the mail room, right? You'll have to talk to Mr. Thompson about this. I don't want it coming back to me, understand?"

The man started to walk away. "Does that mean I got the job?" I asked.

The man nodded. "Talk to your boss. Clear it with him. If he says yes, I'll see what you can do. If you disappoint me, we are done."

I smiled and tried to hide my excitement, but I was failing. "I won't let you down, sir. You can count on me."

#

It wasn't a fantastic story and wasn't all that interesting, but this was the break I had been waiting for. I interviewed a lady who owned twenty-five cats. She rescued them from various places and provided them a safe place to live. Her house stunk. I like all animals, but I think that twenty-five was a bit much. At any rate, this was my first story to hit the paper. Of course, it was near the back of the paper—and it was buried—but not only did I get it done, and not only did I take my own pictures, but I got everything to the copy editor early. This impressed people, so I got another assignment. It was another local story about some vandalism that had occurred. I didn't get much sleep that night, and I worked my fingers to the bone. I whipped up a story in record time and handed it in early the next morning.

My story, as boring as it was, was enough to impress the right people, and I soon became a regular reporter, and I never went back to the mail room again. I received a modest increase in pay, though an inordinate amount of stress was added to it. I enjoyed the rush of finding a good story, talking to people, and putting their story to words. I enjoyed the atmosphere at the office, and it fueled my excitement; there was always something big just around the corner. It was like we were all searching for treasure without a map or reason to believe it was out there. Many times, of course, we would fail to find anything; sometimes we would scrape together a simple story and submit it. Other times, we would find a bit of gold, and that was what made everything worthwhile. Just a taste of gold made me want more.

This is important, because the skills I learned as a reporter would one day be the tool I would use to find the Angel of Death. My faith was the driving force and my motivation; my journalism skills were how I applied my faith.

BEGIN ANGEL
INVESTIGATION

To satisfy my curiosity about angels, I started reading a lot of books specifically about angels. If there was a book on angels, I've probably read it. I read the Bible several times, and I pulled out all of the excerpts on angels that I could find. I copied these by hand and kept them in a notebook.

I then went to other translations of the Bible and cross-referenced my findings. After that, I looked at other religious texts like the Quran and other scriptures, looking for pieces of the puzzle.

Of course, my progress was very slow. I worked during the day and had a family to look after, and so I would read late at night or early in the morning when circumstances permitted. This meant sifting through a mountain of material that largely did not aid in my investigation other than give me some sort of starting point and backdrop to understand what I was doing. I read accounts of near-death experiences, and I chatted with some folks who believed they crossed over and then crossed back. None of these accounts or books, however, mentioned anything about a dancing angel in a black tuxedo.

Angels were often completely invisible, glowing white light, or the winged creatures normally depicted in paintings or in churches' stained-glass windows. My search continued, and my interest never wavered. I wasn't finding the things that I wanted to find. It was after doing this for a few years that I realized I was looking in the wrong place. I started chatting with veterans, and I started looking up newspaper stories. This is where I first found something that piqued my interest. A soldier from World War I had seen an angel, and it had been reported in a paper.

I never got to talk to the man myself. However, the man said that, in the heat of battle, an angel of the Lord appeared to him. The article was vague, but there was one thing that caught my attention. He described the angel as if it were dancing. There was no mention of a tuxedo, top hat, or a cane. "I danced away toward my freedom," the man said. "I followed the lead of the angel, and together, we danced toward a new day. A new dawn."

Of course, this man had died after the war, and I was not able to interview him directly. However, his statements sent chills down my spine. I finally felt like I was getting closer to the truth.

#

There is something about working for someone else that dulls the mind and the senses. I liked working, and I liked my job, but my mission in life felt like it was put on hold. I needed money to get a place of my own and a car of my own. I wanted to marry Lorraine, and I couldn't do that without money.

So from 1947 to 1950, I worked a lot for the town paper. I took as many stories as I could get and took many pictures. I put in a lot of hours, and all my free time was being spent with Lorraine. At that time, Lorraine had a job as a secretary for a law firm in town.

We saw each other mostly on the weekends, though sometimes I was forced to cut things short to get some work done. My mother gave me a travel-size typewriter that I took with me everywhere. I loved that thing, but Lorraine didn't as much, because she saw it as taking time away from her.

By 1948, Lorraine and I already decided to be married, but her parents wanted us to wait. And so we did. We snuck around at that time, and I think her parents knew, but I also think they just wanted us to wait to make sure we were doing the right thing. I don't think they cared that we were together. After all, we were very discreet about it and didn't flaunt it too much.

This was fine, as I lived at home and Lorraine did too. We saved up a lot of money, so by the time we did get married on Saturday, June 11, 1949, we bought a house with some help from my father, who also helped set up our home loan.

Our house wasn't huge, but it was ours. It had three bedrooms and one bathroom, and it was in a nice part of town, closer to both of our jobs. The yard was a lot smaller than what I was used to on the farm, but it was more important for me to have a house than a big lawn.

In April of 1950, my first daughter, Angela, was born. I wanted to call her Angel, but Lorraine didn't like that so much, so we agreed upon Angela. I thought that was close enough, and to me, she would always be an angel. Witnessing the miracle of her birth got me thinking again about the promise I made to myself.

I worked at the Spokane newspaper as a reporter for three years. I liked the job, but there was always this nagging thing in my mind telling me that my mission was elsewhere. I still wanted to join the marines, and I still wanted to follow in my brother's footsteps, and I still wanted to find an angel. I knew I wouldn't find one in Spokane, and so I knew that my destiny was elsewhere.

I left my job behind, but before I did, I made an agreement with my boss; I would continue to write for the paper, but I would write about my experiences in the marines and in Korea. He agreed. I wasn't paid much, but I was still paid for two jobs.

Lorraine knew of my dream of becoming a marine, because I spoke of it often. She had mixed feelings about the idea, but she was also incredibly turned on by the fact that I would be a man in uniform.

Growing up during World War II, everyone idolized the soldiers who fought for our country. Boys wanted to be soldiers, and girls wanted to kiss the soldiers. Since we were newlyweds, we agreed that I would only join the reserves and not as a full-time soldier. Of course, this might mean that we would have to move, but she was very supportive of me. We were crazy about each other, and she understood that I needed to do this because of my brother. I think that because we were not in war, Lorraine was much more receptive to this idea. Had she known what was to come, I don't think she would have been so eager to allow me to leave.

I went back to the same recruitment office in Spokane. It was a Friday in mid-1950, just before my twenty-first birthday. I walked in the door, confident, ready, and possessed with desire to see the truth. The same one-handed recruiter was there. He stood up from his desk and smiled.

"I still want to fight the communist bastards. Do you have room for me or not?" I asked.

The recruiter smiled. "I remember you. You have even more fire in your belly now than when I saw you last. Are you sure this is what you want? The marines are not for everyone, you know."

"Is the pope Catholic? I know there is something about to happen in the world. I know things might be heating up in Korea. I figure the marines will be the boys they send in. And I'm going to be on one of those boats," I said.

The recruiter nodded. "Son, if I had twelve of you, I think we could take over China together. Come. Sit. We now have a place for you."

#

That Sunday, Lorraine and I went over to my parents' place for dinner. Mother served us her famous rolls, and the smell of roast was all about the house. My father adored Lorraine, and they got along extremely well.

We went through dinner without mention of what I had done. It was only after dinner that I said anything.

"Mother, I have something to say. I don't know how to say it, so I will just come out and say it. I have joined the marines. I have wanted to follow in the footsteps of Joseph as a soldier and to understand what he went through."

My mother went silent; she did not answer me. She simply got up and went upstairs and saw herself to bed. My father, on the other hand, remained to talk to me. He was wearing his reading glasses, his feet were up on the ottoman, and he was reading a newspaper. Once my mother left the room, he put the paper down and slowly removed his glasses.

Before my father said anything, I said, "I need to do this."

My father took a deep breath, and a sorrow washed over him, draining him of color and expression. He nodded.

"I know. I know what it is like to be young." His body was frailer to me than ever before; it was as though he had given up, and he was resigned to the fact that I too would be a casualty of war.

I leaned in forward toward my father. "I'm doing this for Joseph. I love him, and I miss him. I know he would be proud of me."

My father nodded but refused to meet my gaze. "I know. But I hoped that you would be around to help with the farm. While I'm out at the office, it is hard on your mother, you know. She has a lot of responsibilities here. She does a lot of work."

I nodded. I reached out for my father, but he leaned back in his chair, his eyes still averted.

"I know," I said. "This is just something I need to do. I will be back. I will help with the farm when I return."

My father nodded and fiddled with his glasses. "Okay. Good talk." He grabbed the newspaper in his lap and began to read from it again. I sat there waiting for him to engage me again, but he never did. I looked at Lorraine for support, but she simply shrugged. So I got up and went to my old bedroom, not because I needed to go there but because I needed to get up and move someplace. However, along the way, I stopped at my brother's old bedroom. The door was closed, but I opened it quietly and stole my way inside. Lorraine touched me softly on my back.

"I still see him in my dreams," I said.

Lorraine kissed me on the cheek. "I support you in whatever choice you make. Just come back to me in one piece."

I held Lorraine tightly. "Thank you, and I will."

I looked upon Joseph's room—everything was the way he had left it. My mother had made the bed, washed his clothes, neatly folded them, and put them in his dresser. I opened the closet where Joseph had hung himself. I half expected to see a ghost there, but the only thing in the closet was old clothing. I went through his clothes and touched everything. I'm not sure why I did that, but it made me feel as though he were there. When I got to his Ranger uniform, I pulled it out and laid it on the bed. I touched the brass buttons and traced my hands on the lines.

I jumped when I looked over to see my mother also standing in the room; I didn't hear her come in.

"I'm sorry for walking away earlier," she said. She then passed me a folded-up piece of paper. "I pray to God you do not find anything that Joseph found. Whatever he saw over there hurt him so badly that he never really returned to us, did he? It may be selfish or foolish to think that I could save you boys from yourselves." My mother looked down at the uniform that I placed on the bed and caressed the shoulder of it.

"I'm going to be fine," I said.

My mother looked at me with tears welling in her eyes. She looked as though she were going to say something. Her face was harder than it usually was. She nodded, kissed me on the head, and left the room.

I looked down at the piece of paper she'd given me. When I opened it, I immediately recognized the writing from my brother's hand.

The Angel of Death

The drone of the motor drowns out my thoughts
The weight of my rifle makes me lean forward
I can hear my breath over the gunfire
I can hear my heart over the explosions
I see something to my left
But I dare not look
The boat next to us explodes
I'm soaking wet

Something to my left tells me to take off my pack
I obey. No one notices.
The call is given. The ramp is opened.
Mike and Ted get hit. Their blood is on me.
I dive over the side and into the water
My feet don't touch the ground
Hands grab at me
I ignore them
I swim to the beach with a mouthful of sand
My hands are so cold I can barely hold my rifle
David is hit and goes down in front of me
I move behind a tank trap and huddle next to a body
I watch the beach explode in fire and lead rain
Bodies pinwheel in the air
Pieces of people are floating
My ears are ringing
I can hear shouts but they are meaningless
Our lieutenant was hit
One by one they go, one by one I watch them die
I look to my left
He is here again and taps me with his cane
He dances over to a crater
I follow his lead
He tips his hat and dances to another tank trap
I follow again
He holds out his cane
I grasp the end of it
We dance together briefly toward a concrete barrier
He leaves me there
He tells me that I cannot follow any farther
He smiles and dances off
Today was not my time to die
Where are you going?
To the bridge of tomorrow, over the river of yesterday

THE MARINES

WHEN I JOINED THE MARINES, they sent me to California. There was a base there called Camp Pendleton that was thrown together in haste during World War II. It wasn't as nice as other bases, but at least the weather there was good, and to me, it felt as if it were summer year round. Even cold days were remarkably warm, like spring in Spokane.

I really enjoyed basic training. Oddly, I liked being yelled at, I liked getting a good sweat, and I liked everything about the corps and about being a soldier. I wasn't the best soldier in my unit by any measure, but I wasn't a slouch, either. I got better at everything they taught us. I felt like I was in the right place, and I felt like my life was on track. We would wake up early, but I was already used to this from growing up on a farm. We did a lot of marching and a lot of running. My feet were constantly sore, but I was in the best shape of my life, and I was doing something that I loved.

I made a lot of good friends in the corps. That's the unusual thing about being in a place where everyone wants to be. People are bonded by similar purpose and similar life goals. I doubt that anyone in the First Marine Regiment was looking for angels, but they were looking for a sense of belonging, and they were searching for a higher purpose.

It was this purpose then that bonded me with two very dear friends of mine, George and Andy. George and Andy were both a bit younger than I and probably better soldiers, but we all came together during our basic training, and as time passed, we grew even closer. George was a big man with broad shoulders and thick black hair. Whenever he shaved, he looked like he still had five o'clock shadow. Andy, by comparison, was small, thin, and red haired with a lot of freckles, and he was always about to say something stupid, funny, or both. Andy got us into a lot of trouble, but it was always worth it.

Each day I would wake up, I would imagine that Joe was there with me, pushing me out of bed. When we would march, he would be at my side, and at the range, Joe was lying down next to me as my spotter and calling out my shots. There were times I even called others Joe, especially George or Andy.

The plan was that I was just going to be involved once a month with training. We thought we were going to move to California so that I could be closer to the base. I was going to get a job as a reporter out there, and Lorraine planned to be a stay-at-home mother. This was, at least, what I told Lorraine, which was almost a lie. I knew the politics of what was happening in Korea, because I covered some of the stories for the local paper. I knew there was a good chance we would go to war. I could never tell Lorraine this, of course, and so I kept that from her.

Not surprisingly, the politics in Korea went from bad to worse, and now war was knocking on my door.

We didn't end up moving to California. Lorraine wanted to be closer to her parents so that they could see their granddaughter. This actually gave me great comfort knowing that she was someplace familiar and comfortable.

I found out I was going to be deployed in late July of 1950; I received a letter after only being back home for a week from basic training. I was still a newlywed and a new father, and now I was going to war. I didn't know exactly what was going to happen, but I knew that I was going to see battle firsthand. I was both excited and frightened as I read that letter in our living room. Lorraine was holding little Angela, bouncing her upon her hip, and Lorraine began to cry.

I tried to comfort Lorraine, but my words were not having much of an effect, mostly because I was still in shock myself.

"I knew it. I knew that you were going to be called," Lorraine said.

Still holding her tightly, her hair pressed into my nostrils, I said, "I will be very careful. I am coming home. Don't you worry about me, okay? I received the best training possible. The marines kick ass, and I'll be home in a few months. Korea is just a tiny speck on the map. This isn't World War II, and you will see, this will be over quickly."

I held Lorraine and Angela close. I tried to stop Lorraine from shivering, but I wasn't that powerful.

#

My first taste of combat was in Korea at the Battle of Inchon. I was a part of the First Marine Regiment led by Colonel Puller. Colonel "Chesty" Puller was a man of action with a huge list of battles and decorations. We felt confident that he could lead us to a swift victory.

We did an amphibious assault to start the war, and I landed at a point that was referred to as Blue Beach, which was behind enemy lines. I was terrified. The trip over was awful. The water was so choppy that we drifted off course several times, which made us late in the landings. I half expected to be killed getting off of the boat. Joe's poem of his beach landing was stuck in my head. And so when I exited the landing craft, I fully expected to be shot or blown up.

I remembered pictures of the landings at Normandy during World War II, and I remembered many stories—none of them were positive. I felt myself ducking and not being able to straighten myself out. When the ramp door came crashing on the beach, I scrunched up tight against the walls of the landing craft, as did George and Andy. It was George who actually stepped out first, and for a moment, I imagined him falling to an enemy bullet. I didn't want George to go first—or Andy, either. I suppose one of us had to go first, but I felt protective of them, and because I was older, I thought that if anyone was to die that day, it should be me. As I followed George, I thought I was going to meet a bullet or piece of shrapnel. But that didn't happen, because there were no bullets or explosions anywhere on that beach.

Even still, George, Andy, and I stuck together, and I know they were thinking the same things I was. When one of us would run, the others would find a good position and cover our friend. We made our way up the beach this way.

Fortunately for me, Blue Beach had almost no resistance. In fact, I never even fired a shot. We got on that beach and moved swiftly inland. This calmed me greatly. It felt like victory even though we didn't really do anything. Once the peril was over, Andy was his usual self, cracking jokes and taking our minds off of things.

I was expecting a grinding assault on the beach with machine gun fire, mortars, and bodies flying. I'm not saying I was disappointed. In fact, we were all very relieved that we were all still alive. By the time we moved inland to sync up with the rest of X Corps (that was the name of the combined units), they had already finished their fighting.

That was probably the first time I had ever seen bodies. But I wasn't looking at the bodies; I was looking for angels. I looked in the sand for shoe prints that didn't look like GI footprints. I looked in buildings and in craters, but I didn't see any angels.

"What the hell you looking at?" Andy once asked, standing beside me while I looked off into the distance.

"Just taking it all in," I said as I snapped a photo of him and George. George was taking a swig of whiskey at that precise moment. That picture would become one of my favorites.

It was then that I thought that I would actually have to see action in order to see an angel. I believed I would have to be in some sort of physical danger in order to witness any sort of divine intervention. I told myself that I would have to be brave, and I would have to face incoming fire so that I could witness the angel like my brother had during the Second World War.

I did not have to wait long, and I didn't have to look far, because action would soon enough find me. Our sudden assault had taken the enemy by surprise, and so X Corps, of which the First Marine Regiment was a part, had a very easy time in the beginning. However, for reasons unknown to me, we didn't make a full advance on Seoul, the capital of Korea. It took us eleven days. I think that was right. Eleven days to press some fifteen or twenty miles. This was slow by anyone's standards, and as a result, I got to see a lot of fighting. This delay allowed the Koreans to create a proper defense to repel our attacks. If we'd pushed forward instead of waiting, we might have seen a very different war.

"Why are we standing here with our thumbs up our asses?" George asked as he scratched his face.

"Maybe we like it," Andy said.

"Don't worry. The tidal wave is coming," I said as I snapped more photos of the area we were in.

"You know, I bet Chesty Puller will get promoted from this," George said.

Andy grabbed George's flask and took a swig but winced noticeably. "And he'll get a medal too. Or maybe more."

Of course, I knew it was easy to pass judgment when I wasn't the one responsible for all the lives of everyone in X Corps. I had it relatively easy. All I needed to worry about was keeping my weapon clean and my mind sharp and worry about the man next to me. That was it.

When I knew we were about to get hit by an assault, I would always pray. I would pray not only for my well-being but the well-being of everyone in my unit and for those in command. The first combat I saw, I fired my weapon a lot, and so did Andy, but I don't think we hit much. When you are scared, you tend to pull the trigger too quickly, and easy shots suddenly become very difficult. I don't think I actually killed anyone in those first few days of fighting—not for my lack of trying but because of the fear I was experiencing. In my head, I would have a clear, calm shot of an enemy, and I would line up my sights, take a deep breath, and squeeze the trigger. But the reality was that I was scared, and my hands were not steady. I shot at opponents either real or imagined. I saw movement, and I shot at it. I had no idea if I was hitting what I saw. I understood now what Pastor Jacob was talking about from his stories about the Great War.

Combat wasn't clear like it was in my mind. Most of the time, I couldn't tell where the gunfire was coming from, and if you were to stand up to have a look, you were the only thing visible, and so you would be likely to be shot first. For this reason, I felt bad for George. He was far too tall and far too broad to be a soldier. The Koreans could hide behind a blade of grass, but George was so big that he could rarely find suitable cover.

As a soldier, there was a lot of hiding, crawling, waiting, more waiting, and more hiding. When you saw something moving, sometimes we couldn't tell if it was a civilian, one of our own, or one of the enemy. Sometimes we just shot in the general direction, hoping to make them stop shooting at us. I wasted a lot of ammo early in the war. But so did a lot of others, with the exception of George. He was much calmer than Andy and I; he only pulled the trigger when he meant to. We shot and we shot. But more often than not, we connected with nothing.

Despite this, X Corps was like a rolling ball of fire; nothing could stop us. There was always an aerial bombardment before we pushed our tanks through, and then we followed behind the armor. The bombers and artillery did most of the dirty work for us. We just had to go in and mop up what was remaining. Unfortunately, however, this meant a lot of civilian casualties. Psychologically, that was probably the hardest thing to manage for me. Seeing kids with blood on them or torn to pieces in the streets like forgotten dead dogs. Mothers dead while their babies were by their feet and crying. The whole mess was terrible. This was very upsetting to George, and he broke down and cried several times. He would always leave the group and find a spot, and we knew when he was doing this, so Andy and I made sure that no one bothered him.

After seeing what I saw in Seoul, I realized how a strong man like my brother Joe could break like he did. I believed what we were doing was necessary, but how we went about it was barbaric and savage. Sometimes I would think about how one could accomplish our goals without all of the evil that we were doing. But nothing came to mind. It was all evil, the business of war. I was just a man on the ground, and I didn't have much say or much power to do much of anything except keep on keeping on.

What other choice did I have? If Colonel Puller ordered our regiment forward, we simply went forward. There was no discussion; there was no debate. We just got up and moved our asses.

And that is exactly what we did. As soldiers, you learn quickly to keep moving and keep pressing forward. This is the only thing that really translated for me from basic training. Basic training was always difficult, because there was no slack and no rest. This constant pressure was what war was like for me. We pushed forward regardless of what was happening and regardless of how we felt about it. We were always doing something. We were always on the move, and it was always a crisis.

Our forces pushed the enemy far back, almost to the Chinese border. That's when things went from good to really bad. We were winning for so long, we had assumed that we would all be home in a matter of months and that the war was going to be over. This was not the case.

Korean War and the Account of the Chinese Soldier

T HE OLD MAN TOOK A breath and stretched his neck. He looked at the iron bars for a second and then looked back at the reporter. "I'm sorry my tale is taking a long time to tell. You look bored."

Erich's eyes blinked wide open. "No. I'm just anxious to get to the important part. Your tale is interesting, and I think you are right that these pieces are necessary." Erich then got up, put his notes down, and went to pour a glass of water out of the pitcher. He offered the old man some, but he declined.

The old man looked over at the notebook and picked it up. "This is nice leather. You don't see this type of craftsmanship anymore. At least not in regular stores."

The reporter shrugged. "That old thing? I just picked that up at the general store down the street."

The old man smiled and put the leather book down. "Well, after the seventies and eighties, you couldn't find real leather unless you went hunting for it."

"Are cows extinct or something?" Erich asked.

The old man laughed. "No. They just don't make quality things anymore. Everything is cheap. The benefit is that everyone can afford luxuries, but at the same time, they don't feel as luxurious."

Erich sat back down. "Well, we don't have a problem with luxury here." He sighed and then said, "You speak a lot about wars that haven't happened yet. I'm not sure what to make of all of it, frankly. I don't know what tanks are. And the weapons you describe are also strange. I know you didn't want me asking questions ..."

"Most of it won't matter for the story, so I haven't been bothering to explain it. Machines and devices of war all have the same end results: suffering and death. You may find that there is something more important than these details." The old man turned a page of Erich's notebook, and there was a drawing of an angel on it. Erich reached over and took the notebook.

"I'm sorry," the old man said, holding up both hands. He added, "I was just curious."

Erich was blushing and averting his eyes. "I'm just a bit shy of my work. No harm done. Where were we?"

The old man closed his eyes and took a deep breath, and his face tightened as if he were observing incoming artillery. He raised his left hand as if to shield himself from sunlight that wasn't present. He made a deep groan like an old cat might do if you tried to take its favorite chair.

#

The Korean War. Bloody mess. We found out a great deal of things while fighting that war. This wasn't the triumphant, overwhelming victory that many of us held in our minds. All of us out there heard all the stories about how America helped win World War II, and we simply believed that we would have that same experience in Korea. We thought we would roll through this small country with ease because it was far behind us both militarily and technologically. We thought we were so strong, that nothing could stop us. We thought the war would be over by Christmas and that we would simply go back home to our families and maybe have some sort of parade like the soldiers before us.

We were in for the shock of our lives. We didn't go home that Christmas, and we didn't go home for the next two Christmases, either. We fought out there, in the cold and in the mud.

Another thing that surprised me was the weather; I was surprised that Korea was so cold. In my mind, we were going to be fighting in the tropics, not in the snow. We were high in the mountains, and that snow and blowing wind chilled a man to the bone. You could never be comfortable, and something on you was always freezing. We lost a lot of men out there to the cold alone. Fingers and toes were often amputated, and of course, some men just never woke up in the morning. Many of our casualties were simply frostbite victims, and we had to rotate them out of the front lines and thaw them out. We would sometimes joke that some guys were just too soft and couldn't take it. But the reality was that a lot of people died out there from that chill and not from a bullet or from shrapnel. This was really sad for me, because soldiers weren't meant to die from the elements. They were meant to die facing an enemy, be that from a bullet, a bomb, or a knife but not from the hand of Mother Nature herself.

I was fortunate enough not to lose any body parts, but that doesn't mean that Frosty the Snowman didn't do his damnedest trying. I was used to the cold from Spokane, but I never camped out in the snow for weeks on end, and in the event that I was really cold, I was always allowed the luxury of going inside to warm up. When I was back home playing in the snow, I always got to come in afterward and warm up by the fire with a nice cup of cocoa in my hands. This, of course, didn't happen in Korea. You were parked out in the middle of the wild with only snowdrifts and wind chill for comfort. There was no fire, and there certainly wasn't any cocoa. The only thing to mark our days was by how many times we were shot at.

We had pushed the enemy all the way north to the border of China. But as luck would have it, they pushed back. That was when the war would go from us being on the offensive to everyone fighting for their lives. The Chinese became involved in the conflict, and they threw everything they had at us, and we were stunned by how many of them there were. We were appalled by their apparent disregard for their own lives as they charged our positions and swarmed us like ants marching over hills. Our entire army was like a single exterminator with only boots to kill the oncoming insects.

We set up fire positions with mortars and machine gunned their lines. But they just kept coming, wave after wave after wave. It was pure slaughter and pure insanity. It was here that I learned how to keep calm and how to shoot straight. We couldn't afford to miss. We couldn't afford to throw away bullets in haste or anxiety; each shot had to count. Each shot had to hit home, or none of us would see home ever again.

Some of our ammunition didn't work so well in the cold. The Garands did all right, though you had to watch that the oil or grease didn't gum up the actions. The M1 carbines we had didn't fare so well in the cold and sometimes wouldn't fire at all. I liked the M1 carbine for close fighting in warm weather. It had a larger magazine capacity and lower recoil and was quieter, especially if you had to pull the trigger indoors. Very handy weapon, but on the open field and on the border of China, you really wanted the Garand. It was a true rifle cartridge, and if you hit a man damn near anywhere with it, he would stop moving. The Garand then became our best ally. If you could calm your mind and calm your breathing, you could be sure to stop anyone coming at you. Failure to do these things, of course, meant certain death regardless of what weapon you were using.

Our antitank equipment was terrible and couldn't stop modern tanks. Well, modern for that time. Also, we didn't count on the fact that the enemy was hell-bent on destroying us in the way they were. We thought the days of charging machine gun nests were a thing of the past, but this turned out not to be so.

Part of me wanted to be wounded—not because I wanted to be in a mobile hospital but because I wanted to see if this would bring the Angel of Death to me. It was near China where I first began to have these thoughts. I wanted to go out there, in the line of fire.

I neither had desire to kill people nor did I want to die. I simply wanted to expedite the appearance of an angel, and I was beginning to think that the only way to do this was to step into harm's way.

#

My hopes of ever finding the Angel of Death were dwindling with each day I spent in Korea. With each footfall in snow, with each foxhole I dug, and with each patrol I was on, I felt myself falling further and further away from hope. It was like I was falling down a well and looking upward as I descended; I felt like I was suspended in midair and in time. When I would walk, I would barely pick up my feet to move, barely bring up my hand to my face to take a sip of hot water or terrible-tasting soup. Sometimes we would even have coffee, but I would sit there and hold my cup in my hands until it got cold. I wondered if my soul was cold and if it was trying to steal the warmth from my cup.

I liked coffee, and it was a rare treat to actually have it out in the field, but for whatever reason, I didn't like it in the battlefields of Korea. The smell would remind me of mornings with Lorraine, and I would get this wave of melancholy, which made me think that I would never see her again. Or worse, that I would return to her broken, the way my brother returned to us a broken man. This is something I wanted to avoid, and I wanted to return home victorious both for my country and for my personal mission. It was here that I realized why Joseph looked like he did when he returned from war. I caught my reflection in a cup of coffee, and I saw Joseph there.

I knew my faith was wavering, and the drudgery, the lack of sleep, and the constant fear of death was overwhelming. I was cold all of the time. My hands were numb, my toes were numb, and my mind was numb. It is difficult to get a good night's rest when you think that you might die if you sleep, and a lot of people did too. When we found them the next morning, they always looked so peaceful and calm. It was very easy to want and even wish for such a fate. For the dead, the monotony, the drudgery, and the pain were over. For them, there was no more battle to fight, and the war was over, and they could surrender to whatever was waiting for them.

The first winter in Korea, it was difficult to see past the horrors and put my mind to good work and develop more faith. I went to church services when I could, but out in the field, I felt like I was alone, even though I was surrounded by other marines and my friends, who were just as cold and desperate as I was. We all fought an internal battle, and I feared that we were losing.

It is difficult enough to remain hopeful for your dreams when you can sleep each night in a warm bed and snuggle next to your loved ones. Back home, faith could be pushed aside and forgotten by routine and comfort. Out in Korea, there was absolutely no comfort, only misery, pain, and torturous cold. When I would awaken from whatever little sleep I had, the world would come crashing down upon me. Whatever peace I may have felt in slumber was suddenly replaced with the harsh reality of war.

As a result, I went through a phase where I no longer prayed each morning and each night. I slept when I could, but it wasn't like in civilian life. Sometimes I would only get two hours of sleep to last me through two days. My mind was weakened, and my body was exhausted. All I wanted to do was retreat or even curl up and die like the others.

Most of the other marines looked at pictures of their wives or their children, and that is what kept them going; they found their source of faith in their families. I, of course, did this too, but for me, this only made my heart yearn more for them. For me, I needed something stronger to boost my enthusiasm for survival. It was easy to envy the dead and hope that you would have a quick death to end the suffering.

I kept Joe's poem on me throughout the entire war. On many occasions, I would take that poem out and read it aloud in whispers when the thought struck me, and this would rekindle my faith. I saw many battles, and I saw many strange things, but up until that time, I never saw any Angel of Death. Because of this, I was finally coming to the conclusion that my brother was in fact insane and that there might not be angels at all. He merely saw some sort of hallucination brought on by fear and anxiety—or maybe even drugs. There were a lot of men in my unit who were becoming addicted to morphine. I never tried it, so I didn't know what it actually did to you. But it made me think that Joe might have taken to some sort of drug like this to help him cope with things. In the cold winter of Korea, I finally understood what Joseph had gone through, and I understood him at last. I knew now why he could have broken like he did, because I myself was on the brink of collapse, and I too could feel my grip on reality slowly slip away from me. I felt that I made a poor choice in joining the marines, and I risked losing everything for that choice.

Days became weeks, and weeks became months, and I was beginning to feel even colder and more distant. I stopped writing to Lorraine at this time. I would take my pen and paper out, only to sit there and stare off into space. No words came to me, and I felt my consciousness and maybe even my soul drain from me. I felt so out of touch with the world Lorraine was in, and all that I was capable of seeing was the unending undulating mountains and hills of snow before me. One road looked like the next. One village could have been any other village, and each hill we crossed made me feel like we were walking around in circles.

I was filled with so much despair that I contemplated running through a minefield. I looked at the signpost marking the site. It had a skull and crossbones hastily painted on it and the word "minefield" written as if a child had written it.

I don't know how long I was sitting there exactly, but another unit was coming in with some Chinese prisoners. There was quite the commotion, and this engaged me enough to get up and see what everything was all about.

People were shouting. Several marines kicked the prisoners as they were led into our camp, and there was a lot of spitting, as I recall.

I didn't partake in this—not because I didn't feel the same sort of anger and rage but because I was so demoralized and so weakened from lack of sleep that I no longer cared what was happening around me; it was like I was watching a movie or dream. I probably would have welcomed someone shooting me or stabbing me. But for whatever reason, I followed along with this group like I was a zombie looking for fresh brains to eat.

My feet were just pulling me forward. My eyes were locked on the pair of prisoners who were bound with rope at the wrists and elbows. Their pants were torn at the knees, and they had dirt smeared all over them as though they had been playing in a pigpen. One man held his head low and did not make eye contact with anyone. The other looked me right in the eyes, and I saw something there. It was like seeing someone you knew a long time ago. It was a sort of recognition, but where I knew this person from was a mystery. He shouted something to me but stopped midsentence as a marine hit him with the butt of his rifle. The man jerked away in pain and tried to shield his head by tucking it into his shoulder.

"Just shoot him!" someone yelled.

"Fucking cut them good and then shoot him," another said as he pulled out a knife.

"Shut up—all of you!" our lieutenant yelled as he came out of a tent without his jacket on. He wiped spit from his lips and a thin line of shaving cream from his neck. "What the hell is all this about?"

"We caught these fuckers over the hill, sir," a corporal said, pushing the two prisoners forward. "He's been talking a lot. We thought he could help us figure out a few things."

At this time, one of the Chinese men began to bow and say many things in a very rapid tone; his eyes darted from marine to marine, hoping to find sympathy.

A South Korean translator with a grimace on his face said, "He's just rambling. Something about seeing an angel. He was guided by an angel to us. He thinks God was talking to him."

A few men in the crowd laughed.

"Was this angel dancing?" I asked.

People turned to look at me briefly, as if seeing me standing there for the first time. The translator gave me a quizzical look.

My face went cold, much colder than I had intended. "Just ask him."

The translator turned his attention to the prisoner and said something in Chinese; the prisoner then nodded and looked at me. He smiled and did a little dance. He said something.

The translator scratched his head, which made his helmet tilt to one side. "Yes. The angel was dancing and wore a black coat and a top hat. Like in the American movies. Something about a cane, I'm not sure. I think this one is nuts."

The Chinese man lunged at me with his hands still tied behind his back. I made no effort to dodge, and so he fell face-first into my stomach the way I had pressed my face to Pastor Jacob's belly all those years ago; he looked up deeply into my eyes. He said something to me that I didn't understand.

"What did he say?" I asked the translator.

The translator shoved the man down on the ground. "He told you to go to the bridge of tomorrow. He said something about a line of destiny. That doesn't make much sense. He's just nuts."

It was as though a divine hand reached out from the heavens, picked me up by the back of the neck like a kitten, and gave me a good shake. I was a bear waking up from a long slumber. I nodded to the prisoner, reached out, and touched his shoulder but said nothing else. The prisoner was taken away for further questioning, but I wasn't privy to that conversation. Not that I would have been able to contribute at all; my head was swimming in an ocean of emotions. I was not fully in control of myself, and I took a few steps away from the others to gather the power to stand upright.

Most of the other soldiers dispersed, except for my friend George. He wore a look of concern on his face, and he stood next to me for a moment and leaned in.

"What was that all about?" he asked.

I looked blankly back at him with my mouth slightly open.

"Are you okay? You look like you've seen a ghost or something," George said, spitting on the ground.

I took a deep breath and looked skyward and patted George on the shoulder. "I'm all right. I feel really good, actually."

"That crazy isn't contagious, is it?" George asked through a smile.

I nodded. "I certainly hope so."

George pulled out a flask that was stashed in his coat. "Need a drink?"

I shook my head. "No, thank you."

George shrugged and moved on, leaving me standing there.

I walked away from the crowd and looked upward to the sky again. I didn't see anything in the clouds, of course, but in my mind, our Creator was looking down upon me. I imagined that we shared a secret together and that He was spilling His wisdom onto me, which washed over me in the form of the wind.

This is the way the Lord works, I think—in whispers and not in great fanfare or large, well-lit signs pointing the way. There were no trumpets and no choirs of holy voices singing, and there were no well-lit roads and no candlelight crossroads. At least, not that I could see.

I think some people would call this feeling the Holy Spirit. I don't know what it was or what it should be called, but I called it hope. Isn't that what faith is? Hope of some sort of future achievement? Some sort of benefit for a life of dedicated work?

Maybe my brother was right, and maybe he wasn't crazy, after all. I felt my faith bloom inside me like a rapidly growing flower stretching in the sunshine. A new world was coming, a new dawn, and I was a new person renewed of faith and definiteness of purpose. I could feel this surge at the core of my being, as if I were struck by lightning.

There were angels out there, and I was going to find them for myself.

Of course, the war did its best to crush my spirit and to tarnish my soul. Every friend I carried in a body bag and every shot I fired in anger tried to work its way into my source of faith and enthusiasm. This was no different than before, but now I was the element that was different. I felt like now I possessed the tools needed to push through this sort of resistance, and I knew the recipe for everlasting security.

I gave up drinking. This wasn't a conscious choice, but it was born out of necessity. I wanted to remain focused upon my goal, and I didn't want to be clouded of mind, and I didn't want my decisions to be slowed. I needed to be alert; I needed to have a burning desire of faith. And I did this through constant prayer, day in and day out, a constant dialogue with God, the divine, universal intelligence, or whatever you would call it.

Each time that I awoke and each time I would catch a nap, I would say a prayer of gratitude for all the things that I had and all the things that I would have.

It was during this resurgence that I started writing to my wife again. Hope rekindled my need to reach out and connect to her. I didn't talk about the war much but instead talked about things I wanted to do with her once I got back. I promised to take her on trips to places that she always wanted to go—New York, Savannah, New Orleans, and Oahu for starters. She possessed a keen interest in visiting Europe too, and I made an oath to give her everything that she desired. I imagined us on trips through Paris, Berlin, Athens, and Rome. These weren't just cheap words. These were bonds I made not only to her and to myself but with the Creator himself. I made sure to have this burning desire for those achievements.

The war continued to drone on, but fueled by this newfound enthusiasm, I now tried to find the Angel of Death in the best way I thought possible: by doing stupid, near-suicidal things. This might seem like the opposite course of action, and one might think that this idea was pure lunacy, but there was a method to my madness.

I used my faith as a tool like one would use a hammer or screwdriver. This manifested itself in many ways but mostly as foolhardy, brash, and idiotic decisions that would get a normal person killed. But I didn't think of myself as a normal person. I was a person with a mission, and I truly believed that the only way to complete this mission was to face Death and not run away or hide from it like I was inadvertently doing all this time. I made the conscious decision to meet Death face-to-face in the only way I thought was possible.

ACTS OF STUPIDITY

WE CAME ACROSS A MINEFIELD that we planted earlier in the war to deter the enemy from going through. We never anticipated, however, that we would be blocked by the very device used for our adversaries. While deliberating a way around the minefield, someone noticed a small child playing in one of these fields. There was snow on the ground, and the field looked like any other field. But the warning signs were not posted in Korean—not that a child could read those signs, anyway.

Some of the soldiers started yelling at the child to get out of there. A few spoke Korean and shouted, "Get out of there! You are in danger!"

This confused the child, and instead of coming back the way she came, she turned and fled deeper into the minefield. It was like watching a beloved family pet run into the street. There was this sense of impending doom that one could only feel if he or she had the experience to know how dangerous such a thing was. I felt my stomach tie in knots.

I did not know how I got into that minefield, but I must have run after this child. I found myself trying to run in the child's footprints, but the cadence was all wrong, and I fumbled along and eventually gave up. I heard the CO yell at me to return, but I ignored him. I caught up to the little girl, scooped her up under the arms, and threw her over one shoulder. I expected her to cry, but to my surprise, she giggled with delight and kicked her tiny little feet. Holding her close, I ran immediately back from where I came. I made sure this time to step in my own footfalls in the fresh snow. I made it back in one piece, and so did the child, who by this time was wiggling and laughing more than before.

I earned the nickname "Lucky" that day, and the only reason why my CO didn't charge me with insubordination was that he had a little girl himself waiting for him to come home. He snatched that girl from my arms and held her like she was his own. The girl started to cry, and the lieutenant patted her on the back and rocked her back and forth. I knew I wouldn't catch trouble from this incident, though I didn't hear the end of it from the other marines.

"I can't believe how stupid you are," George remarked.

"I was expecting Swiss cheese to return," Andy said.

"He's the only one of us left with a soul," someone else said.

This comment hushed the crowd. Some marines looked at their feet, others looked away into the field, and several played with the actions on their rifles.

I was still out of breath, more than I should have been for such a short run, but I sat there near a tree stump, looking back at the field I had just crossed.

All the guys thought that I did this for the child, but that wasn't true. I did this for myself. It was a selfish act because I simply wanted to see the Angel of Death, and this was an opportunity to see him. He never showed, however, no matter how hard I stared at that open field. I watched the horizon, I prayed, I looked to the clouds above me, but the Angel of Death never came for me.

I was saddened by this, but I tried not to show it. I felt my faith slump somewhat, but then I thought about something. What if the mines were already gone? Sometimes when bombs fall on minefields, the mines blow up too. That certainly could have happened here. Maybe this was just an empty field and no longer an active minefield. Maybe that's why the Angel of Death never showed that day. Maybe the Angel of Death didn't show up because I was not personally in any sort of danger.

And so I performed many acts of stupidity in order to catch a glimpse of the divine. I did so many stupid things that I have probably forgotten most of them. My nickname "Lucky" was certainly tested and well earned, and for whatever reason, things just worked out for me. I don't know if this was the madness of war and if my mind was broken or if this was true faith or not. Certainly one could argue the point from either side, but for me, it felt like faith. I took many daring risks for reasons which may have appeared to the observer as completely unnecessary.

Our column had been hit by an attack one day, and one of the newer members of the group was fifty yards ahead of us or so and pinned down by fire. He had been hit in the leg and was crying out something fierce. Fortunately for him, he had fallen behind a dead tree and other debris, and the enemy couldn't get a good shot at him, although they certainly tried.

Because the enemy fire was so intense, no one wanted to go out and grab him. No one, of course, except me. By this time, my CO was used to me doing things that were stupid, and he gave up on giving me orders to the contrary. He simply looked at me and said, "Well, Lucky? You gonna go get him or what?"

I tipped my helmet to him and smiled. With each act of stupidity, I felt like I was getting another bite at the apple; I was getting closer to the heavens. There was an explosion nearby, and I didn't really hear what else he said, though I thought I caught enough of it to know.

"Gimme a frag," I said to someone.

"You aren't going out there, are you?" George asked.

I shrugged and checked my rifle; I made sure the safety was on. "I'd go out there for you or anyone else. Do you have a frag or not?"

Andy handed me a frag. I dropped my rifle, pulled the pins out of two grenades, and held the spoons tight in both hands. The grenades would only detonate once the spoons were released. This alone was a stupid idea. If I was wounded and dropped one or both of the grenades, I would pretty much guarantee that I wouldn't be coming out of this stunt alive. And yet, there I was running out there along a road, using the ditch as partial cover.

A machine gun rang out, and bullets whizzed by me and kicked up dirt and threw it all over the place, but I kept running. Some of the older machine guns were harder to maneuver, and so I counted on this to get out of the field of fire by running through it. By all accounts, I should be dead, but I got there.

I rolled to the ground from a dive—something I would never try even in the fluffiest of snow. I could have easily broken my collarbone or something. I still held two live grenades in my hands, and a simple slipup could have cost me dearly. Clearly I didn't think this part of my plan all the way through.

I inched my way up to Gus. "You okay?"

"Hell no, man. They got me in the leg good. I think I'm dying, man!"

I took a peek at his leg. It was bad, but it wasn't necessarily life threatening. "Bah, you are fine. Can you run?"

"Run? I can barely walk. Wait. What the hell are you doing with those grenades? Oh God, are you gonna blow us up?" Gus's face was white like snow.

"What? No. Relax. This is how we are getting out of here. I figure I'd throw these at the machine gun nest, and we can make a run for it." I nudged Gus with an elbow and raised my eyebrows several times.

Gus's teeth gritted together. "I just told you I can't run, man."

I smiled and elbowed Gus again. "Trust me. I'll pick you up. We'll be fine."

"You're crazy, man."

I shrugged, "No, just lucky."

I stood up—something you should never, ever do when someone has a machine gun trained on your position—and I threw my two grenades. When I threw the one in my left hand, I almost dropped it; it didn't go near where I wanted it to, but I think it did the trick. The gunners ducked. I threw my second grenade, and this landed in a better position.

I took this moment to pick up Gus in a fireman's carry, and I got him to the ditch on the other side of the road. That's about the time the grenades went off. I heard a lot of gunfire, but it wasn't coming from the machine gun nest. It was coming from our fellow marines. This really pinned down the Chinese more than my antics.

Even still, there was no way of knowing how many guns were pointed at us, so I kept running. I got to our line and someone yelled for a medic. I put Gus down quickly, and I remember he let out this yelp that sounded like a wounded dog.

#

The old man took a deep breath and looked at the far wall. His jaw was tight, and his eyes became watery.

"What is it?" Erich asked, leaning forward.

The old man grimaced and exhaled. "I haven't thought about Gus in a long time."

Erich shrugged. "Well, you are a hero; you saved him."

The old man shook his head, and his eyes closed for a moment. "Gus died in the van when we were moving him to the hospital. They blew him up—the whole truck. They all died, even the driver. Funny, huh? I save him from one peril only to have him succumb to something else."

Erich straightened himself up. "Well, maybe God had a reason."

The old man looked at the reporter. "That might be true. It might have been Gus's time to go. I don't know. All I know is that my heart was heavy with sorrow that day. It felt as though nothing I could do would wash away the pain I was experiencing."

"You helped in that moment, though. That's all that matters," Erich said.

The old man harrumphed and took a deep breath.

Erich sighed as he looked at his notebook. He flipped over a few pages and then put down his pencil and rubbed his eyes with both hands. "Okay, so you are a war hero. I can't help but feel like you are manipulating me. I feel like you are hiding the truth and that there is no angel, and at the end of this story, all you want is for me to be sympathetic to your cause. Whatever that cause may be. Can you skip to the part where you find the magic sword? I don't see how being a war hero helps this story any. Can you throw me a bone here?"

The old man rocked back and forth. "Have you not heard a thing that I've said? Do you know what bravery is? Do you know what courage is?"

Erich shrugged. "You are going to say something like it is being scared yet doing your duty, anyway."

The old man shook his head. "No. Any idiot can do that. That's not bravery; that's being a sheep and following the herd. Courage is the act of practicing faith. Bravery is believing so much in your faith that you don't *think* you are going to win—you *know* you are going to win. This is what bravery is. This is real courage. It is the discipline of teaching yourself applied faith. Faith without action is just wishful thinking. Faith without moving your feet is simply hope. Applied faith is courage. What I was doing was applying my faith so that I could meet Death. And understanding this transformation in myself is critical for how I actually met the Angel of Death."

Erich rolled his eyes. "Sorry. It's just late, and I'm a bit frustrated is all. I know we are on a deadline here, and I'm anxious to know how this ends. I mean, I know how it ends. You end as a murderer. But how you came to be there is still a mystery. You talk about your wife to make me think that you are a good man. You talk about some war to make me think that you are a good soldier. I know you had children, and I suppose you would like me to believe you were a good father too."

The old man leaned toward the reporter. "Are you a son?"

"What? What does that mean?" Erich's face scrunched up.

"Are you a son?" the old man asked again.

"Of course I'm a son. I have parents just like everyone else."

The old man leaned back on the concrete wall. "Okay. Are you a brother?"

Erich nodded. "I'm failing to see the logic behind this discussion."

"Are you a brother?"

Erich sighed. "Yes. I have a sister. Can we get on with it?"

"Okay, so you are a son, you are a brother, and you are a reporter. I suspect that at one point you were a student. And at one point, you may have even been a teacher. Which one of these things are you?"

Erich's eyes pinched together. "Well, I'm clearly all of them."

The old man nodded. "Precisely. You may call me a murderer. You may call me a monster. But I am also a son. I am a brother. I am a cousin. I am a marine. I am a journalist. I am a husband, a father, a grandfather, and maybe even an asshole. To truly understand someone, you need to see all of their relationships. Take a man for one moment and you may only see one side of him. There are many sides to men. Right now, I'm seeing a reporter. But I can tell by your eyes that you are much more than a reporter. Am I not right?"

Erich nodded, and he pinched his eyes shut. "Yeah, you're right."

"So you understand, then, that I must show you how I found this angel in order for you to grasp how you can find them too."

Erich blinked his eyes open and pointed to himself. "Me? What makes you sure I want to find an angel?"

The old man looked at the drawings on the walls and smiled. He then looked back at the reporter. "I see in your eyes that you are searching for something. You are searching for meaning. You wrote a book—a great accomplishment, certainly—but I can see that you want more. Not just wealth, not recognition or even fame. What you want to know is the meaning of it all and to create meaning in your life. I can see that in you. I can see the hope in your eyes whenever you mention something magical or mystical. You long for this. I am showing you how to get there. But think of this thought and transformation of your mind like a seed. A seed, if planted today, cannot be harvested tomorrow. That seed must first be placed in fertile ground, and then it must be nurtured, fed water and sunlight. If left alone, it could be choked out by weeds, rotted by overwatering, or eaten by some animal or insect. Thoughts and faith are the same as physical seeds. Tend to them, nurture them, and you will get exactly what you want. Abandon them, abuse them, and they will die, rot, or be food for something else."

Erich laughed. "You sound like your pastor."

The old man smiled and poked Erich once with his cane. "Good. That is perhaps the best compliment I have ever received."

Erich shrugged. "You are right about me wanting more. I probably wear those emotions on my sleeve. But I hadn't ever thought about throwing myself into combat just to find angels before. That seems rather foolhardy and a quick and easy way to die."

The old man rocked back and forth. "For most, you would be absolutely correct. But for me, this was not true."

THE FIRST SIGHT
OF AN ANGEL

THERE WERE TWO VERY IMPORTANT clues that told me that the figure before me was not a normal man. I knew what it was when I first saw him. This person was dressed like a man, and he walked like a man, but I didn't believe him to be a man. This is not from a mind of a person who is recalling an event and adding his own twists to it after the fact. This was simply how I felt.

It could have been the way the creature twirled his cane; it could have been the way he wore his black top hat or maybe the way he would sometimes jump up and click the heels of his shiny black shoes. His breath could not be seen in the frigid winter air, and neither the snow nor the chill of the wind seemed to bother him. He simply smiled merrily like he was on vacation and like he didn't have a care in the world. He would sing, he would dance, and all around him, there was the carnage of war.

The creature didn't create the carnage, this was certain. It was clear that the machine guns and the mortar shells were responsible for that. But the macabre site of seeing something play in pools of blood, dancing over bodies and smiling, was very disconcerting.

The second clue was that no one else seemed to be able to see this creature. He danced among soldiers, twirling his cane, singing his song. Mortar shells exploded by his feet, machine gun rounds tore all around him, but there was no effect to him. In fact, there wasn't even a drop of sand, oil, or gore upon his perfect black tuxedo.

I stared at him in wonderment, while trying to keep my head down from incoming fire. I remember my delight, and I remember how my heart leaped into action the moment I saw him. I knew my faith and my mind led me to this junction. I knew that my discipline and my hope manifested something in physical form.

I watched as the creature skipped and danced around us to unheard songs. I knew what I was seeing was not a mirage or other strange thing that men can see when they are in combat. I don't know how I knew this; I just knew it was so. I felt it in my gut.

I was feeling many emotions. I was transfixed upon this creature, and I feared to blink lest he be gone forever. I felt vindicated that my brother, Joe, was not insane. I felt the joy that my quest had not been in vain. I felt relieved that I too was not going crazy. But I also felt very frustrated, because the creature paid no attention to me.

I tracked this creature with my eyes, and at first, I was too afraid to leave my position of cover. The Chinese were all around us, and popping up your head could get you killed rather easily. I tried to get his attention by waving and then by shouting at him. Andy was by my side, as was another marine. George was back some thirty yards, grabbing more ammo, but he was late, and we were already starting to worry about him.

"Who the hell are you yelling at?" Andy asked.

"I'm yelling at them," I said, pointing to the Chinese front. I remember he just shook his head and kept on shooting. "Over here, you dancing fucker!" I shouted. "I'm over here! Why don't you finish the job?"

Andy tugged at my arm. "You need to relax, man. Keep your head down."

I kept yelling, and I even took a few shots at the creature, but the bullets had no effect, and he didn't pay me any attention. I started to get mad because the creature was starting to get farther and farther away.

I wanted to have some answers, and here this creature was dancing away from me like an idiot and paying me no mind. So I did something stupid—I went after him.

I got out from my cover, I stood up among the hellfire, and I ran after this apparition. I shouted, I waved my hands and made a fool of myself.

Andy yelled to me, "Where you going? Get back here, man!"

The noise of gunfire and the confusion of movement that was everywhere drowned out his shouts.

I zigzagged to dodge other marines, body parts, and the other debris of war. I took cover in several craters, but all the while, I followed in the creature's footsteps. With each run, I came closer to him. With each burst of energy, I was able to ignore the sounds around me. The guns, the screams, the explosions dissolved, and all I could hear was my breath. I held on to my rifle, and I ran like a fool toward this thing. He came upon an embankment in a hillside where he stood in front of a line of barbed wire.

I saw a line of bullets that would have torn a normal man to pieces come through the dirt, kicking up six feet high or more. They stopped at this man the way a bucket of small balls would bounce off a brick school. The creature took no notice, no alarm upon his face, and he made no attempt to evade in any manner.

He turned then to look at me, and I stood there foolishly upon the hillside; I was in the direct line of fire of the enemy, but I couldn't take my eyes off of this thing.

"You might want to take a knee, friend. Hell of a day, isn't it?" the creature said to me.

I smiled like an idiot, because the creature spoke. Following his advice, I dropped to the ground. Lead whizzed by me, how close I could never tell. It could have been ten feet above me or three inches above my head. Any man in combat could tell you that when you are faced with a barrage of gunfire, you can never get low enough to the ground. Even with my rifle above my head and my chin pressing into the sand, I couldn't help but feel as though my equipment and even the buttons on my shirt were in the way of me getting closer to the earth. I felt exposed, naked even. I thought that at any moment I would be shot and that would be it. I thought that I was going to die there on some nameless hillside.

I looked up at the creature. He looked as though he wore a halo, but this turned out to be a fire nearby on the horizon. His face was in silhouette, so I could only see a slight twinkle in one eye and the corner of his mouth that looked like a smile.

"Such a beautiful day, don't you think?" he asked as he leaned in to see me more closely. "The air is so crisp and clean here, and those hilltops go on forever. Too bad the war is getting in the way."

"I have to say, it's hard to ignore," I said as there was a flurry of gunfire.

The creature stood up and shook his head. "Not so. All you have to do is listen for the music, and once you hear it, all you need to do is feel the moment, and everything is okay."

The man paused, kicked up his heels, did a small little dance with his cane, and added a flourish and ended with a bow.

"You're insane," I said.

"Oh? Is it me who is seeing a man in a black tuxedo dance upon a hill covered with snow in the middle of a war?"

I thought about that for a moment. Something out of the corner of my eye caught my attention, and where a man had once been, a shell hit. The explosion was close. Too close for me to have survived. And yet, here I am to tell you about it. I didn't even have dirt kicked in my face, and I didn't have the air sucked out of my lungs the way an explosion can do for you.

I turned back to the creature. Unsure of what I should do or say, I simply said, "I suppose you are right, then."

The creature smiled. "I'm just teasing you. You are perfectly normal, perfectly sane." Another few rounds kicked around him in the ground. He ignored them. The ground exploded in flame, dirt, debris, and dust.

"How are you not dead?" I asked, shielding myself from the fallout.

The man shrugged and let out another smile. "What makes you think that I'm not already?"

A terrible sensation crept into my center. My heart sank in my chest. It was the same feeling I felt as a boy when I threw a rock in the backyard and I hit the barn window and broke it. I knew I was in trouble, and I knew that when my father came home I would get a beating. This was the same feeling I was experiencing, but this time, I didn't think I did anything wrong. I wasn't in trouble. I knew what this man was. I wondered if I survived leaving my foxhole, and I wondered if Death was here for my soul. The fear was now mixed with an odd sense of relief that I would no longer have to endure the hell in that cold.

I half crouched in the snow. I felt like I was standing tall, but in Korea, this might have been simply a slouch. "Well, I know why you have come. We should get on with it then, no?"

The man smiled. "Oh, good. I was thinking I may need to explain things a little more. That's always a bore, you know. People tend to have a million questions. So many questions. So unwilling to just let it be. Well, shall we?" The man stretched his arms up high, holding his cane in both hands. He gave a big yawn and turned to face another nameless hill where incoming fire was coming from. "I'll just have to clear the way a bit."

The man pointed his cane at the closest enemy position, and he made a fake machine gun sounds like I would have done as a kid with sticks on my farm. Immediately, the guns stopped. He then waved his cane at the rows of barbed wire, and they parted and recoiled like an elastic that was let go at one end. The creature then moved over the embankment, and I simply followed. The creature turned and said, "Oh, you may need your rifle for a bit of a spell. You should go get it."

"Why would I need my rifle?" I asked.

The creature shrugged and leaned on his cane. "To shoot things with, of course. I'm sure they taught you all about that in your training, am I right?"

I nodded and looked at my empty hands for a moment and then went back to where I had been lying. I grabbed my rifle and moved swiftly back over to him. "Sorry about that," I said.

Death smiled at me, the way a good friend would smile when he saw you come up the driveway or the way an uncle may light up when his nephews have come into the room. He led me to the base of another hillside and moved me by the shoulders so that my back was up against the vertical surface of rock. I could hear Chinese soldiers on the other side of the hill, talking, and they were moving around some equipment. I couldn't see them from where I was, but I knew they were close.

"All right then," the man said. "You should be okay from here on out. I must be leaving. Busy day, you know." The creature tipped his hat and began dancing away.

I was thoroughly confused. I thought he was leading me to the afterlife. I thought I was going to meet the Creator. "How am I to find the way without you?" I asked.

The creature turned to look back at me. "Oh, it's really quite that simple. Just move up the hill, and you will be followed by your friends who remain. You will find a nice little crater with plenty of bodies in it. There you will find an excellent hiding spot for when your enemy overruns your position and kills everyone. After that, you can move back south and rejoin with the rest of your regiment. You will know what to do after that. You don't need me. You just needed a slight push to get you out of that tight spot you were in." The creature pointed at the spot that I had just occupied with Andy. In fact, I could still see Andy pop up from time to time and take a shot.

There was suddenly a huge explosion in that very foxhole, and the machine gun emplacement was in shambles. The cold earth was removed in huge chunks, and the men there were turned to a red paste that smeared the land and covered the bodies of both sides. I gasped, "Andy." I started to shout, but it came out as a whisper. The man next to him I did not know, as he was from another regiment, and now I felt shame for never asking his name.

I saw many men—and many members from our regiment—die in war, but with Andy dead, I felt sick to my stomach. The loss pulled at me from my gut like there was a giant corkscrew in my abdomen that turned in horror as I realized that, had I not gone venturing out, I too would have been a red smear in the snow, just like the others.

The creature poked me with his cane. "Let not your heart linger on the lost. Instead, let it linger on the found. I can't stop this war for you. You are going to have to do that yourself." The creature moved to leave.

"You are leaving me here? I don't understand."

The man's eyebrows shot up, and he straightened his top hat that was tilted off to one side. "So here come the questions." The man let out a long sigh. "I was hoping I could just get on my way. You are far from dead, my friend. That's why you must be cautious from here on out. It's a devil of a day out here, you know." The man smiled and tipped his hat with his cane. He then twirled in one spot. He grimaced a bit and then said, "I still have to work on that turn. It isn't quite right."

"So what do I do?" I asked.

The man shrugged. "I told you. Wait out the battle in the hole over there, and make your march toward the south once it is safe to leave. It will take some time, I'm sure. There will be some hardships, but the worst is over. But this doesn't give you the right to be stupid, you know. Keep your head about you, and you will be fine. Now, if you will excuse me, I have somewhere I need to go." The creature tipped his hat again and danced his way away from there. Bullets screamed past him so much so that my face was in the dirt before I had even a chance to think about doing it.

"Where can I find you?" I yelled.

The man half turned. "At the bridge of tomorrow, over the river of yesterday."

Death left me there; he simply vanished while I was looking at him. There one moment, and gone the next. I looked around for some time, but I never saw him on that hillside again. I'm not sure how long I stood there before someone found me, but the next thing I knew, there was a sergeant nearby yelling something. I looked over at him and shook my head. It took me a moment to figure out what was said, though my body knew the question before I did. He must have asked if I had been hit.

More men came, and indeed, we made our way up that hill and into a pocket of a shell hole that was filled with gore of war.

I never told anyone of this tale; not during the war and not after it. I feared someone would deem me insane and that my life would be ruined. I feared that I would lose Lorraine, my family, and my home. So I kept this story to myself, just like I kept Joe's secret to myself. I told none of my fellow marines, and not even the priest in our regiment knew.

However, I did write about these experiences in a journal. When I read what I wrote, it sounded like pure insanity. I feared that someone would find that journal and that my horrible admission would be known to the world. So I crumpled up that page and tossed it in a campfire and watched it burn.

And so it was that my secret was guarded and was safe deep in my own mind. Or at least that's what I thought.

THE AWAKENING

ERICH TOOK A DEEP BREATH and looked at his watch, but there wasn't one there, only the rash on his wrist. His face was strained like he was experiencing mild pain or discomfort. "I'm still surprised that the Angel of Death would appear like this. That's not how I imagined him."

The old man smiled but did not look at the reporter. He stared off into the prison cell while taking slow, calm breaths. "Nor did I until Joe's account."

Erich drew something in his book. "I always thought it would have a scythe, at least, a black cloak, or maybe even black wings."

The old man looked at the ceiling. "Well, that's what artists have been showing us for years. My guess is that they've never really seen an angel before, but they had to draw something. So they made Death frightening."

Erich threw up his hands. "Well, to be fair, most people are afraid of Death."

The old man nodded. "I suppose that is true. Though they needn't be. Everyone has to die sometime. None of us are getting out of this alive. The more we are able to accept that, the more we can truly live and do the things we would rather be doing."

Erich's eyes widened, and a smirk rested on his face. "Like going to war to chase Death?"

The old man laughed. "That does sound pretty crazy, doesn't it?"

Continuing to draw in his notebook, Erich said, "I'm assuming you met this angel again. Was he the one who showed you the magical sword?"

The old man looked Erich in the eyes. "I can see in your face that you don't believe in any of this, do you?"

Erich shrugged. "I believe that you believe it."

The old man looked down at his hands. "Well, that really doesn't inspire much faith, does it?"

Erich ran a hand through his hair. "You have to admit, this all seems pretty far-fetched. If you were indeed from the future, wouldn't you have something with you to prove it? Some books, a better watch, or fancier glasses?"

The old man shrugged. "There was not much time to gather things when I went back through time. The angel didn't seem to think I needed anything."

"So you met with this angel again?" Erich asked, straightening himself in his chair.

The old man nodded and twirled his cane once. "Yes, but it was much later."

Erich stopped. His pencil snapped upon his page, and he stared at the cane in the old man's hand. It was not a cane this time but a sword. It wasn't a long bladed weapon but short like something an ancient Roman or Greek might use.

The old man reached over and touched Erich on the knee with his free hand. "Are you okay? You look rather pale. Perhaps some water would be good for you."

Erich jumped a bit from the touch, and his eyes locked upon the cane that the old man had now laid upon the bed. It was a black cane with white tips and was no longer a short sword.

The electric lights in the room blinked out, and a shout from a guard echoed in the hallway. There were still lamps along the wall in the hallway, but the cell had become dark. However, there was a glow about the room that was brighter than ten candles burning, and it was coming from the old man's cane.

Erich stood up so quickly that he almost fell over. He backed away from the old man and pointed at him. "Who are you?"

The old man leaned over and picked up the book that Erich had dropped and opened it to a page with a drawing of an angel on it. He faced the book toward Erich and then pointed at the pictures of angels that were drawn upon the walls. "I see we have come to that point, but that's a question you should ask of yourself."

Erich's face was turning red. "What the hell are you talking about?" Erich asked as spit came out of his lips.

The old man's eyebrows rose. "This isn't my prison cell, Erich. It's yours."

Erich looked around the room, and his eyes fell upon drawings of angels on the walls and a set of clothing near the bed, and when he looked at the cloth on his arm, it had the exact same appearance. He looked for his hat, but he couldn't find it. He shook his head, and he paced about the room, making sure to stay away from the old man. "You're a liar."

The old man held up both hands and then pointed to the wall. "Why don't you take a look at the name of the drawings on the wall there?"

Erich glanced at one of the drawings, which had Erich's signature at the bottom right corner. He then tore it down and crumpled it up. "That proves nothing. You could have easily written that there."

The old man showed Erich his book again. "Isn't it time that you face what is happening to you here, Erich? Don't you think you owe yourself that much? You are the one, after all, who wants to get on with the story. But the story isn't about me, is it? It is about you. It has always been about you. This is your story and not my own. We are writing the final chapter of your book as we speak."

Erich moved swiftly to the bars of the cell and yelled as spit flew from his lips, "Guards!"

The old man rubbed his knee and looked at his feet.

Erich pulled furiously upon the prison bars, but they did not budge. "Guards! Get me out of here now!" His shouts echoed down the halls, and other inmates could be heard shouting back obscenities at him.

Passing the cane from one hand to the other, the old man said, "You don't have to torture yourself like this, Erich. I'm here to help you. You just need to take the reins and slow this horse down."

Erich spun around and pointed a finger at the old man. "I don't need anything from you, you monster. You got into my head is all. That's probably how you killed those people. That's probably how they let you into their house in the first place. They had their guard down, and you chopped them up into bits. You freak!"

A guard came by the door. "What's all the racket?"

Erich reached out of the cell with both of his hands. "Please. You have to let me out of here. I've had enough. This interview is over. I can't be in here anymore."

The guard smacked at Erich's hands. "Shut up and get back in there, or I'll beat you down again."

Erich tried to reach out to the guard again, and the guard smacked his hand a second time. He pulled out a truncheon from his belt and hit the iron bars before pointing it at Erich. "Don't make me come in there. Shut up, and get on your bed now. It's late. You should be in bed sleeping. If I have to order these lights on, I'm going to have every guard in here take turns beating you down. Am I clear?"

Erich retracted his arms. "Don't you see the old man sitting on my bed?"

The guard's face twisted, and he said through clenched teeth, "That was your last warning. One more word, and I will beat you senseless."

Erich moved away from the door and massaged his wrists.

The guard lingered there for a moment, spit into the cell, and then left.

"Your wrists are red because they have been chafed by irons. You know that to be true. Now, come and sit with me," the old man said.

Erich held his head with both hands, pulling back the skin on his face. "This is insane. I can't believe this." Erich turned around looked at the old man, and then his eyes drifted down toward the cane that was next to him.

Erich lunged for the cane, and the old man made no attempt to stop him. Erich found himself unable to grab it. He tried again and failed; it was like it was made out of smoke or mist. "What the hell is going on here? What the hell is that thing? Who the hell are you? What do you want from me?"

The old man smiled. "Why don't you sit down? I will finish my story, and it will all become clear to you then."

"I don't want to hear another word of your story," Erich said.

Cocking an eyebrow, the old man said, "I don't believe that to be true. In fact, I think this conversation is the exact thing you have been waiting for. It is you that called me here. Now sit."

Erich paused and swallowed. He then sat down in the wooden chair and folded his arms across his chest. He was looking away from the old man as he gently rocked himself back and forth.

Erich bit at a thumbnail. "What does this all mean? Who sent you?"

The old man smiled. "You sent me, Erich. You are one of the few who can see me."

"Are you saying that you are an angel?"

The old man took a deep breath. "You need to think about what is happening to you right now. You need to focus. Do you know where you are?"

Erich grunted. "I'm in prison, locked in a cell with a freak."

"What crime were you sent in here for?"

Erich looked down at the floor and then put his face in his hands. His body shook as he tried to hold in sobs. "I didn't do anything. I'm a reporter."

Waving the cane in the air above Erich's head twice, the old man said, "You know that isn't true."

Erich gritted his teeth and continued burying his face in his hands as he massaged his cheeks and temples. "I'm a reporter. I'm here to interview the killer."

The old man sighed. "Part of that statement is true. Look deeper into your heart, and you will see the truth."

Looking away and still rubbing his head furiously, Erich said, "It's me, isn't it?"

"What does your heart say?"

Erich's body began to lurch as he held back sobs. "I am the killer. I killed them."

The old man put a hand upon Erich's back and rubbed it lightly.

Erich continued, "I didn't mean to do it. I was so angry. I had been drinking. They stole another one of my chickens. They didn't seem to care that the chickens were mine, and they didn't seem to care that they had taken them. I didn't go over there to kill them, you know. You have to believe me."

"It doesn't matter what I believe. It matters what you believe."

Erich looked up, and his face was wet with tears. "What are you saying?"

"Even the ugliest of men can return from misery and turn toward hope. Every moment is a new moment. Every moment we have the choice, and we can choose our fate."

Erich threw up his hands. "What fate can be found in a place like this? This is the end of the line. There is nothing after this but death."

"Faith only needs a heart to live in. You think these walls mean anything? You put yourself here, and you can get yourself out of here."

"Are you going to break me out of here?" Erich said through a laugh.

The old man shook his head. "I'm going to do much more than that if you allow me. Listen to my tale, and another option will be open for you, should you choose to take it. Trust me."

Erich closed his eyes and rubbed his temples. "Will listening to your tale set me free?"

The old man shrugged. "It might. What other choices do you have right now?"

Erich wiped some snot from his nose. "What happened to George?"

The old man sat up straight and looked at Erich for a moment before letting out a long sigh. "George had been wounded. Not badly. There was some shrapnel in his leg, and he couldn't run, so he crawled out of that battlefield. He must have crawled five hundred yards or more before he found a medic. I felt guilty for not being there for him, either. I left Andy, and he got killed. I let George fetch more ammo, and he got hit. But you can't overthink these things. It can drive a man crazy. I'm sure this is also what factored into Joe's ordeal."

AFTERMATH OF SEEING AN ANGEL

L osing Andy and finally seeing the angel changed me very quickly. I understood deeply how these experiences could affect the human mind and how this moment could have broken me or could have sculpted me.

The first change that I noticed in myself was renewed faith. I felt like I was pulled from that foxhole for a reason, and I wasn't going to squander it like my brother had. I was going to find out what this purpose was, because I owed that to Andy, to myself, and to Joseph. This is a key ingredient to the story, and I don't want to leave that out. By seeing the Angel of Death, I knew that we were not alone on the battlefield and that I was one of the lucky few who actually knew this to be true. Before that time, I never knew loneliness until I was on a battlefield, hugging the ground like she was my mother.

My resolve to figure this mystery out strengthened, but most importantly, I felt free from the fear of dying. I didn't feel completely free, but I felt removed from it like it was a thought that was far away in another world. I knew it could happen to me at any moment, but I never dwelled upon it after seeing the angel.

Over the coming weeks while George was recovering from his injury, I took more tactically stupid risks to attract Death to me so that I could have another conversation with him. Now that I knew that angels were out there, I wanted to learn more by directly interacting with them.

Our line near the Chinese border was stretched thin. We suffered horrendous losses, but nowhere near the losses of the Chinese. We originally thought with such devastating casualties that our enemy would have stopped or had been rerouted. But we were to learn that we were tremendously outnumbered, and it would ultimately be us who were rerouted.

The position I was in was frightfully low on ammunition and on people. Our line of defense was thin and stretched too far. I wanted to join up with another unit and do a tactical retreat. We lost our commanding officer, a sergeant, and a lot of men. There was no time to bury anyone or dispose of the bodies properly, so we just left them there in rows, with a thin film of snow on them. It was so cold that their bodies froze up, and they just became part of the landscape. They no longer had names, wants, or desires; they were simply pieces of meat that hung frozen to the landscape like beef in a butcher shop.

There were two sergeants on that hill, and I was one of them. The other sergeant wanted to stay put, and I wanted to move. I felt this impending dread, like getting into your car with a drunk friend behind the wheel. I knew something bad was going to happen, but I felt helpless and unable to steer the car.

There were twelve of us in total, holding this ridgeline. It was an impossible task with so few people and so few supplies. I argued that we needed to either leave or get resupplied somehow, but no one wanted to budge. I think the cold had a lot to do with it, because it was so cold that I could barely think. A lot of the guys had frostbite, and we were all just one step away from death. We couldn't even light big fires to stay warm out of fear of being seen by the enemy. There were tricks, of course, but a huge bonfire would have melted all of us into reason, and we would have escaped that insanity. However, we just couldn't risk it. I was glad that George wasn't there. I didn't want to lose him too.

Since I wasn't an officer and these men were not from my unit, people weren't listening to me or my ideas. They were scared—and rightfully so—because everyone else was dead. Our position was almost overrun; we were tired and cold, and our time was limited. Because I didn't see the Angel of Death, I knew that my time was not over, and so I decided to take a chance.

I did something dumb; I went out on my own at night. I left my rifle behind, because I didn't want to be bogged down by the weight; I only had my .45 and my bayonet for protection.

I made my way off that ridgeline, and I went to one of our previous positions that had been destroyed. I could hear enemy soldiers nearby, and I hid. There was no way I was in any shape for fighting, and there was no way I could take all of them on. I sat there, hiding my breath in case they could see that in the dim light.

I couldn't see the Angel of Death anywhere, and this was very telling: if I couldn't see Death, then I wasn't going to die. I found some dead marines, and I took their ammo. I found some of our supplies, and I took as much ammo as I could carry. I wrapped belts for our machine gun around my neck and filled sacks full of rounds. I even took a spare barrel for our machine gun.

It was incredibly heavy, and even just standing in place was a chore. On the way back, I didn't bother taking cover, and I didn't take the usual precautions. I simply plodded along in the snow like I was carrying bags of potatoes back on the farm. With my head down and having faith that I would somehow make it back to my unit, I just put one foot in front of the other. As I stared at the ground in front of me, the snow reminded me of Christmas back home, and I suddenly felt like I chopped down a Christmas tree and was simply on the trip home with it. Or maybe I was Santa Claus delivering presents to some friends and children. I amused myself with this imagery, and I imagined that instead of combat fatigues, I was wearing a red suit and a red hat with a long white beard that would tickle anyone who came near. The ammo I carried, of course, was the bag of gifts.

This act would have probably gotten a normal man killed, but I was used to doing these things now. I could have been lost, I could have been shot, or I could have even broken a leg and lay in the snow to die. Again, because I didn't see the Angel of Death, I felt free from worry, doubt, or fear. I marched back to our line.

I got back to my unit just after dawn. I scared a few of the guys when I came up.

"Jesus, man, I almost shot you," one private said, lowering the Garand that he had been pointing at my face.

The other sergeant came up to me, his face twisted in anger. "I was going to write you up for desertion. What fool thing have you done?" He grabbed a belt from my neck and threw it over one of his shoulders.

"You're welcome," I said.

I put my ammo and packs down, and I lay down. I was tired and worn out. The other guys grabbed the ammo and gear and went to work. We checked our weapons again. The cold made the oil in the guns really gummy, and sometimes they would fail to fire, especially when they were really cold. The M1 carbines were even more susceptible to the adverse conditions, but by this time, we were all using Garands and one .30-caliber machine gun.

I lay down for probably only a half hour. I was still tired and cold, but the enemy didn't seem to care about that at all; they had started another wave of assaults.

I found my rifle and took a prone position. I'm not sure how many men we killed that day, but it was certainly many. It probably would have been more if we weren't so cold, delusional, or half-dead with fatigue. The Chinese kept coming over that hill, wave after wave. When it was time to change barrels on our machine gun, that's when things got really terrible. That's when the Chinese actually made it to our ridgeline. We fought man to man, and on several occasions, I used my bayonet and my pistol. We lost three guys during that assault, which left us with only nine men.

It was clear that our machine gunner would have run out of ammo had it not been for my little nighttime excursion. For this, I—and I think everyone else—was certainly very thankful.

#

Erich cleared his throat, and his eyes were swollen. "Did you see the angel on that hill?" he asked.

The old man was staring at the wall. "What? Oh, sorry. I forgot how terrible those few days out on that ridge were. It was relentless. I don't often revisit those nightmarish times. I really don't think of myself as a soldier anymore. I'm Grandpa, not GI Joe."

"GI Joe? I'm not familiar with the term. I've never heard of the weapons you mention either," Erich said through a few sniffles.

The old man waved away the questions.

Erich fiddled with his hands and then asked, "Did you get a medal? Were you decorated for your actions? Sounds like that is something one would get a medal for."

The old man pointed at his feet. "You know, you take for granted how important a good pair of shoes can be—and even socks, for that matter—until you are knee-deep in snow, ice, or mud and don't have these basic things. A lot of guys lost toes and feet because of that cold. I'm sure it was happening to the Chinese too. My father once said that only the colder-climate countries start wars. You never hear about wars that are started in the tropics. It's too pleasant and nice, you see. There's nothing really to be all that angry about. Countries like France, Germany, and Russia have severe cold. I suppose that's why everyone is so angry in those parts."

Erich half smiled. "Well, if that were true, places like Antarctica would rule the world."

The old man winked. "Maybe penguins are onto something? You know, they called the Korean War the 'forgotten war.' It was not as dramatic as World War I or II. And it didn't have as much hate as the

Vietnam War that came afterward. It's like all that fighting we did out there was just a bunch of nothing."

Erich shrugged and rubbed his eyes, which just made them redder. "One could say that about just about every war—even skirmishes where only a few handfuls of people die. We may look at that and say, 'Oh, only twenty-two people died.' But if one of those people happens to be your father, your brother, or you, that number is very significant. It's perspective, really."

The old man grunted. "Perspective. That's the word. That's what we are looking at right now."

Erich rubbed his face, and there was a moment of silence.

"Should I leave you to sleep? You look exhausted. And so you should choose to hear the ramblings of an old man or sleep," the old man said.

Erich shook his head. "I don't want to sleep." After taking a deep breath, he said, "You never said if you got a medal for your bravery. Certainly you saved those men's lives on that ridge."

The old man closed his eyes and rubbed his face with both hands. A single tear was wiped away quickly. "Well, that's the thing. None of those fellas made it out of there alive. To get a medal, you have to have survivors to tell the story, but they didn't make it. That position was overrun, and they were all killed. I barely got out myself."

"I'm sorry. I didn't know," Erich said, bowing his head and looking at the floor.

The old man sighed. "It was a long time ago. I don't think about those parts too much. I like to think about the parts about angels, as they seem to brighten my spirit a whole lot more than talk of the bad parts of the war."

Erich nodded. "I can relate to that. I had manufactured my own reality here. It's funny. I can't believe all of this is happening to me, and yet at the same time, I'm more comfortable with it than I have ever been."

The old man touched Erich on the shoulder, and there was a long moment where no one said anything.

Erich cleared his throat. "Did you see the angel there again?"

The old man rubbed Erich's shoulder like he was patting one of his daughters on the back. "Are you sure you want to continue with this tale?"

Erich shrugged. "There's not much else to do, I'm afraid."

Nodding his head, the old man said, "I never saw the angel again in Korea, but the memory of seeing him kept me sane. I wasn't broken the way the other men were. Two of them became near-hysterical, but that ended after another wave, when the Chinese got on top of us. The ones who lost their cool usually were the first ones to die. That sounds callous. I didn't mean for it to sound that way. I was scared too. I just felt like I had an inside man. I knew I was going to be okay, so I wasn't as scared."

"How did you get out?" Erich asked.

"I did what the angel told me to do. Once everyone was dead, I hid myself among the bodies. I was overlooked, and when the Chinese left, I crawled out and headed south. Eventually, I met up with other American troops, and I was rolled into another unit."

THE FROZEN CHOSIN:
THE CHOSIN FEW

T HE WAR DIDN'T END BY Christmas. Our whole line was abandoned, and we were now doing a tactical retreat all the way back into South Korea. When looking on a map, that distance doesn't seem so bad, but it wasn't like the fighting stopped and they allowed us to pick up our things and go. They threw everything they had at us.

We left behind the dead and a lot of our equipment as we made our escape southward. There were also a number of units who were captured, and we abandoned them as well. Our units were scattered and displaced. It was luck that we got our asses back as well as we did. There were simply too many of them and too few of us.

By this time, I learned that George was being sent home. He sent me a telegram that explained that he lost three toes—two from his left foot and one from his right. A man can't run or fight well with only seven toes, or at least that's what the Marine Corps decided, and they sent him home. I was very relieved to hear this, not only because he was alive but also because my responsibility to ensure his safety was no longer present.

Of course, I was sad that I was alone, and I never did make the same sort of friendships with others like what I'd had with George and Andy.

I found that I began to isolate myself from others. I found that I didn't want to get close to people, because people all around me were dying left and right. I hardened myself to this reality, and I understood how this changed Joseph. It wasn't just the fighting, and it wasn't the cold, the lack of sleep, and the fear. It was the constant loss. Each day, someone we knew died, sometimes quickly and other times not. It got to the point where if I heard a man screaming during the night, I would pray that he would just die quickly so we could all get some sleep.

This was not what I signed up for. This is not the lesson I thought I would be learning, and it wasn't something I could quit or run away from. I was forced to face it.

Chesty Puller, who would later be promoted to brigadier general after the Battle of the Chosin Reservoir, called our mission a tactical retreat, which was meant to sound positive to the troops. One general even said we were simply attacking in the other direction. To the men on the ground, there was nothing glorious about what we were doing. We were like a wounded rabbit trying to run away from the fox. We knew we couldn't run forever, and we knew that at some point we would have to face the fox.

We fell back to the line where the war pretty much started. Korea was still divided in two. Our job was for it not to get too bad, and we basically held the line for the remainder of the war. This is a simplification, of course, but the end result was that Korea was divided into a north and south. Peace was reached, and after the war, an exchange of prisoners and bodies was negotiated, but it wasn't a real victory the way World War II was a victory.

I don't think anyone won that war. *Everyone* lost. I'm glad that George got out while he could. We would have been better off putting twenty guys from each side into a room and letting them kill each other. It would have been less barbaric.

After the war, they called my regiment "the Chosin Few," after the battle we fought by the Chosin Reservoir. But I preferred the term "the frozen Chosin."

The war dragged on for several more years, but it was that first Christmas by the Chosin Reservoir that was the most dramatic. After that, everything felt easy. There were plenty of other battles and plenty of casualties. But the lines didn't change much after that, and we simply duked it out across a single line for almost the entire rest of the war. They would hurl shells at us and we at them. This was even happening during the peace negotiations. It was like we didn't want the party to be over, so we made sure to drink all the booze. In war, this meant that what we were doing was expending as much ammunition as possible, mostly in the form of shelling. We wanted to make sure we killed as many of them as possible before the war could end, and they were doing the same thing to us.

Like all good and bad things, the war ended. I was happy to return home and happy that my mission was successful, even if I struggled through a few more years in action. I truly believe that both my purpose and my faith kept me alive through the entirety of that place. Coming back home was one of the best experiences in my entire life. A man will never know joy until he visits with misery and sits at the table of despair for an extended duration. I never knew happiness until I stared at ugliness in the face for much longer than I ever wanted to.

I don't know who hugged me the longest when I came home. I don't know if it was my wife or my mother. Even my father hugged me briefly too, and when we all started crying, he left the room to get us all something to drink in the kitchen. He took a long time, and I could only imagine he was overwhelmed with emotion like we were. Dad believed he should always be strong for everyone, and I admired that he possessed such strong convictions about this. Also, I didn't like crying in front of my father, because I felt like less of a man for doing so, even though I had gone to war and he had not. Of course, my shame didn't stop the tears from flowing. There's something about seeing my own mother cry and indeed my own wife cry that sunk right to the bone.

My daughter, Angela, was just a small baby when I left for Korea, and I missed almost three years of her growing up. I held my daughter close to me; she smelled like hope and sunshine. Angela recognized me, probably from pictures; she smiled, pointed at me, and said, "Daddy!"

I held on to Angela for at least an hour as my mother prepared dinner. I just didn't want to let her go, even though she was squirming this way and that; it was like holding on to a snake. Angela was so big, and I felt like there was a lot of catching up to do.

That first meal back home on the farm was amazing. Each potato tasted like it was prepared for a king. Each bite of turkey soaked in gravy brought tears to my eyes. I held my wife's hand for the entire meal, and my eyes were glued on my daughter. And every time my mother got up from the table to get something, she would kiss me on the head and rub my back like she did when Joseph first came home from the war. It was good to be back.

Each meal at home was the best meal I ever tasted. Holding my wife in my arms was like holding the most precious jewel in the world. I found that I cried a lot during that time, just like my brother, Joe, and now I know why he was so morose. The emotions of joy and happiness were almost painful. When a man gets used to misery, pain, and death, it becomes part of who he is as a person. When life is basically just putting one foot in front of the other and making sure to dodge incoming fire, the world shrinks. When I came home, I saw just how big the world was, and it was overwhelming and frightening. It was like I didn't know who I was anymore or what my purpose was. I was a stranger looking in, and the memories of my life were reduced to an echo in time.

I remember that first day back on the farm like it was yesterday. I looked across the field to the tree line, and I remember thinking that I didn't have to look for cover or listen for the sounds of incoming shells. I didn't have to worry about dirt in my rifle or worry that the Chinese were on the other side of the hill, coming for us. It was a strange experience to come to a place so peaceful that I had a difficult time believing it. Each morning when I woke, I looked around for my rifle, and I would have this anxiety that I'd lost it somehow. This feeling was brief, of course, but it was still a very heavy feeling. It was for this reason I kept a 1911 pistol in my nightstand. Not because I needed it but because I felt much safer with it there, and there were times I even slept with it under my pillow. I always kept my rifles downstairs locked up, because Lorraine didn't like them lying around.

I wrote to George a lot when I first returned from Korea, but because he lived in New Jersey, I never saw him again after the war. I think he felt guilty for abandoning us at the line, and he never quite got over that. I, of course, never blamed him for getting hit with shrapnel or losing his toes. That would be ridiculous, but emotions are rarely logical. I still held George in high regard, but our friendship faded over the years following the war.

As I look back at my experiences of the Korean War, I can see why Joe killed himself. Not because of guilt but because he'd lost his way. I saw firsthand what it was like to lose a friend and the guilt that followed my decision to leave that foxhole. The war was Joseph's life, and when the war was over, he had no more life to live. I witnessed this feeling in Korea, but for me, my mission was not over. I still had a mission. Now that I had seen the Angel of Death with my own eyes, now that my faith was rekindled, I knew that I would have to find this angel again, because I still had a lot of questions.

#

My second daughter, Faith, was born in 1954. Her delivery was a difficult one, and there were complications. As a result, Lorraine's uterus was removed to avoid her bleeding to death.

When Lorraine's surgery was over and I was allowed to visit, I came into the room with Faith in my hands. I held my daughter in my arms, and her cries subsided. Her chubby cheeks reminded me of a cherub, and in my head, she had wings upon her back. Lorraine was still in her hospital bed, and I was next to her so that some part of me was still touching her. I kissed Faith on the forehead, and I realized that she was wet from my tears.

Of course, this made Lorraine cry, and at first I thought she was simply as happy as I was. However, it quickly became apparent that this was not the case. "I'm sorry I didn't give you a son."

I was stunned by what Lorraine was saying, and I said nothing.

"I know you wanted a son to carry on your family name," Lorraine said, still sobbing uncontrollably.

I kissed Lorraine while I was still holding Faith. "I don't want a son. I don't want him to have to go to war like I did or feel obligated to go because of me. I want only daughters. I want a thousand daughters and not a single son," I said to her.

Lorraine was still crying, and she made no attempt to wipe her tears. "But who will carry on your name? Your parents are going to be so upset. They are going to hate me. I failed you."

I was still holding Faith and rocking her gently. "You didn't fail me or anyone. It is not like I am a king and need a prince to carry on my legacy. Besides, my mother is going to spoil these kids rotten, and so will my father. Just wait and see. They will love them like crazy, as will I."

Lorraine grabbed at her hair with both hands. "But your parents lost Joseph, and now you are the only man left in the family. Your cousins were killed too. You are the last man in your family lineage."

I put a finger to Lorraine's lips. "Hear me now. I only want daughters. I only want angels. I want your stunning good looks to carry on; that's what's most important to me. Besides, boys are smelly and will want to use our car the very moment they will be able to drive. Who wants that? I can protect our daughters from harm, but I cannot protect a son from himself."

Lorraine laughed at this, but I knew she still felt a tremendous amount of guilt.

With Faith still in my arms, I hugged Lorraine the best that I could.

GERMAN OFFICER
ACCOUNT

MY INVESTIGATION ON THE ANGEL of Death continued long after my service in the marines. During one of my many trips to the library, I ran into an intriguing statement written by a German tank officer who had survived the Second World War. At the time, my German wasn't very good, and so it was difficult interpreting what was said. I went to a local university, and I spoke with a professor there who helped me with the translation.

The article read thus:

> It was the Battle of the Ardennes. A part of the war that had mostly succeeded. It was a cold morning, and I was looking out of the top of my tank with a pair of binoculars when something got in the way of my field of view. A man had crawled up on my tank and was dancing upon it. The man was unarmed, and so I didn't shoot him. I wondered how a rich civilian had gotten to such a remote place without so much as a smear of dirt or spot of water on his shoes. I went to shoo away the man and jumped off to pursue him when my

tank was hit and destroyed. All of my men were killed. They were good men, loyal to the last.

I believed that this account was actually an account of the Angel of Death. And so I began to track this man down, because I wanted to talk to him. It took me several months to find this man, but I found him living in Switzerland under the same name. He refused to talk to me at first, and letters I sent him asking for an interview went unanswered. So I took a trip to this small town with Lorraine when we were on vacation in Europe. After dinner one night, I told Lorraine that I needed to go for a walk, and I went alone to this tank officer's place of residence and knocked on his door.

When the door opened, I smiled and held out my hand. "Hello. I am a journalist, and I am writing a story on the war."

This was as far as I got. The door shut, and I pulled my hand away so that it wouldn't get crushed. I thought I should have put my foot in the door, but he was a strong-looking man even for his age, and I thought he might have crippled it.

I then shouted through the door, "I'm only here to talk! We have similar experiences, and I sought you out!"

"Go away," I heard through the door in a thick German accent. "I left the war with the rest of the dead. I'm not interested in what you have to say."

I pressed my face up close to the door, hoping my words would reach him better. "I think you are wrong. You would be very interested. I know what it is you saw when your first tank was destroyed. I saw it too. The dancing man in a tuxedo. I know who he is."

There was a long pause, and as soon as I said these words, I felt stupid. I looked around me to see if anyone else heard me, but there was no one there in the street.

The door opened back up. The old man grabbed me by the shirt and dragged me inside. For a moment, I thought he was going to hit me. "You have no business shouting like that in my town. Who are you?"

I explained again who I was, but I got the sense that he wasn't really interested in that. "Please, I am here to discuss what it is you saw when your tank was struck by enemy fire. I too have seen this angel."

The man's face contorted, and he stood up taller. "Angel? What are you talking about?"

"I saw this angel in Korea, but this is a long story. Would you care to hear it?" I asked, studying the man's face. I could see how this man had been an officer. There was a commanding presence to him, and I felt out of place asking him questions. I felt as though he should be asking me questions, and I should be following whatever he asked of me. But that was the soldier in me.

The former German officer squinted and took in a deep breath, knowing full well that talking about war experiences was like opening up old wounds. I could see the man calculate all of this in just a few moments. Reliving war experiences was painful and exhausting, and so most of us veterans chose to forget them.

"A drink?" he asked.

I nodded, and the man left the room briefly only to come back with two glasses of booze which I thought had mix in them. To my surprise, it was straight liquor, and I coughed a bit from my first sip. The man only smiled and sat down on an old reclining chair with the armrests so worn out that the fabric was all but shreds. He motioned for me to also have a seat, and I sat perched on the edge of the sofa like a cat waiting for a ball of string.

He took a long drink before he said anything. "An angel, eh?"

I pretended to take a sip of my drink. "Yes. I know that might be difficult to believe. But what is stranger—being saved by a lunatic in a tuxedo or being saved by an angel?"

The man grimaced a little. "I had wanted to forget what I saw that day. I've told people about it. That was a mistake. I can see that now. That cost me dearly."

I nodded. "I have never spoken about this aloud. You are the first person whom I have ever told. I have gone in search of people who have had similar experiences. I wanted to know if I was going insane or not."

The man took another drink after swirling it around in his glass. "Then you are wiser than I. I had later told everyone that I had been thrown from my tank during that explosion. That seemed to be a better explanation than a dancing man in a top hat."

"Did he say anything to you?" I asked.

The German officer took a deep breath, took another sip of his drink, and mulled over the question. His eyes stared past me for a second, and I felt as though he were watching the scene again from the Ardennes as if it were on a movie screen behind me. "Not really."

"But he did say something, then?"

The man nodded. "Certainly. I lay there in the snow, looking at the burning wreckage of my tank. The man in the hat said to me, 'Best you move. More ordinance is on its way. Take care now.' He then tipped his hat and went on his way. I got up to follow him for a bit. I guess I felt compelled to. Sure enough, more rounds came in, and I surely would have been killed in that moment."

I leaned so far forward I almost slipped off of the couch. "Did he say anything else? Did he mention anything else?"

The man shook his head but didn't say anything right away. "I don't remember. Why?"

I sensed that there was more to the story, but he was too shy or embarrassed to tell it. I decided to tell my part of the story. "My brother saw this angel on Omaha Beach during the D-Day invasion of Normandy. When he returned from the war, he told me about the experience. I believed him, but I thought he might have been just seeing things. But I saw him too in time. I came to see him during the Korean War. My position was about to be overrun. That creature came to me then. He had a black tuxedo, a black top hat, and a cane. He danced over the piles of bodies in front of our machine gun nest. I saw him, but no other person saw him. I felt compelled to follow him, as bullets and bombs had no effect on him. I wanted to know what it was. At the time, I thought I was dead."

The German man nodded. "Sounds familiar."

I cleared my throat and continued, "I was surprised when he told me to pick up my gun. I thought he was leading me to the afterlife. The machine gun nest I was in was completely blown up. I would have been killed if it weren't for him."

I paused to take a small sip of my drink. For a moment, I felt like I was with my brother behind the barn, having rum for the first time.

The German man looked down into his drink. "I remember feeling sad that I hadn't been killed. Is that odd? I was sad that I had to continue on. I had to linger while the dead got their rest. I had to wade through the rest of the war when my men in that tank got to sleep. This was a cruelty that I never understood. I never died a hero. So many others did."

I tried to appeal to him, to see if I could get any more information out. I was excited to talk to someone else who had seen the angel, but I didn't want to scare him away. I didn't want him to push me out of that house, and I wanted more information. "I felt shame for surviving while my brothers were dying."

The man pinched his eyes shut for a moment, perhaps to squeeze a painful memory away, which made the lines on his face stretch like folds in cloth. I continued to talk, in an effort to have him open up a bit. "I tried to talk to the angel, but he became agitated when I asked him questions. I saw bullets pass through and around him. He wasn't natural, whatever he was. He led me away from my death, and I thought he was leading me to my maker. Imagine my surprise when that wasn't the case at all."

The man nodded. "A tall tale. Men see many things in battle. At least that's what people insisted on telling me." The man let out a laugh.

I wiped the sweat from my hands onto my pants. "Sure, but never a man dancing in a tuxedo. I believe this to be some sort of angel. I think it's the Angel of Death."

The man's eyebrows rose as he brought his glass to his lips. "How do you know that? It could have easily been a demon if you believe in such things."

I shook my head. "Would a demon save our lives? Would a demon not try to manipulate things further?"

The man shrugged. "What use is there in saving us? Did you invent a faster car or something?"

I chuckled. "No. I haven't invented anything. I'm just a family man. And that's why I'm still perplexed, and that's why I'm here. I'm trying to figure this all out. I think there was a reason we were all spared."

The old man waved a hand in the air to dismiss my statement. "There is nothing to figure out. War destroys everything. People, places.

Some live that shouldn't, while others die who should have lived. The whole thing doesn't make any sense."

I took another sip of my drink. "Maybe I'm running a fool's errand, but I still would like to know what happened. I may never find out, but I feel like I have to try."

The German man took another sip from his glass and set it on a wooden end table. Nothing was said for a time, and the only noise in the room was the ticking of the grandfather clock by the fireplace across the room. "You said your brother also saw this thing. When would that have been?"

I wiped the condensation from my glass onto my pants. "That would have been June 6, the day of the American invasion."

The man considered this for a moment then said, "Five months before me. How many others have seen this ... thing?"

I shrugged. "I don't know. I don't think people talk about this sort of thing. I met a Chinese man in Korea who claimed to have seen it. So that is at least four of us. You, however, are the first definitive story that I've heard. I'm looking for more stories."

The man grumbled and shifted in his chair. "I don't know how much I can add. It was a long time ago."

I nodded. "I'm sorry to bring this to you. It has just been haunting me for a long time. I wanted to bring closure to my brother's death."

The German man squinted and looked up at me. "I thought you said that this angel saved your brother."

I nodded. "Yes, he did. But the war broke my brother, and he later killed himself."

The German man took a sip of his drink. "I'm sorry to hear that. War can break even the strongest of men." The man's words were both sincere and insincere at the same time. It was a well-rehearsed thing to say to another veteran. It avoided the hard truths and at the same time could protect one from deeper wounds. Even still, I felt comforted by this. It was familiar.

I thought I might have been close to cracking this man's story, but at the same time, I didn't want to stay too long and watch this man get drunk. So I stood up. "Sorry to have taken your time. It was nice to meet you. I'm glad we are both not crazy."

The German man's eyebrows darted upward in surprise. It took him a few tries to get out of his chair, but after he did, he escorted me to the door with one hand gently on my shoulder as if I were one of his children.

"Thank you for the drink and your kind words," I said.

Just before I passed the threshold to exit his house, the man said, "Hey. There was one other thing."

I turned around with my eyebrows raised, trying not to show my excitement.

"I had asked the angel where he was going. He said, 'To the bridge of tomorrow, over the river of yesterday.' What do you suppose that means? I had that in my head for many years, but finally, I just tried to forget the whole thing. I felt like I was starting to go crazy."

"You are not crazy. I have heard these words before. The angel said them to me, and he said them to my brother."

"What do you suppose it means?" the man asked.

I scratched my chin. "I don't know. A clue, maybe. A place where we might find him."

The German man took a deep breath. "I'm sure I will find out one day soon enough."

I hoped to hear more, but that was all there was. I didn't know what it meant, but it was something to go on, at least. Perhaps it would be a clue that I could use to find out more information. I thanked the man again and gave him a solid German handshake. He smiled genuinely for the first time.

"Good luck," he said.

VIETNAM

TIME PASSED BY QUICKLY BECAUSE I was happy. Ten years vanished in a blink of an eye since Faith was born, and I saw no angels in that interim. I was content, I was watching my kids grow up, and my career as a journalist was really beginning to take shape, but I never forgot my mission for one moment.

I went to church every week and had lunch with Pastor Jacob from time to time. Pastor Jacob now was getting very old, and he probably shouldn't have been running the church at all, but his passion for it was too great for him to let go. I never told Pastor Jacob about what I saw in Korea, but sometimes I wondered if he knew, because he would give me these odd looks as though he knew something I didn't. Occasionally, he would come up beside me, put an arm around me like a bear, and nod like he agreed with something I said.

I volunteered at the church for events, and at night, I continued to read books about angels. Some of them I read many times before, but this didn't bother me. It kept me in constant attunement to the world just outside of our own.

When the United States became heavily involved with the Vietnam War in the late 1960s, a lot of my peers were going over there to photograph, film, and document what was happening. Throughout the

Korean War, I took many pictures. Most of these I did not send home right away but instead waited until I returned. My pictures were later published in magazines and newspapers, detailing the trials and horrors we saw there. This pushed me further into a career of journalism, and for a time, I enjoyed this fast-paced world where I was recognized for my talents as a photographer and as a writer.

I resisted the first few offers I received to go to Vietnam, but at the height of that war, I could no longer ignore the call. I saw what was unfolding, and I felt as though it was a historical event that I was missing out on. It was truly a turning point. I knew that my place was there, and I had a burning suspicion that I would find the Angel of Death again, just as I had in the Korean War.

I volunteered to go to the Vietnam War, not as a soldier this time but as a photographer and journalist. My overt mission was to document a very unpopular war and to bring the truth to the people of the world. My personal mission, of course, was to put myself in harm's way so that I might once again see the Angel of Death so that he could answer a few of my questions.

When I told Lorraine I was going to Vietnam for work, her face drained of color. She gritted her teeth and clenched her fists. She said nothing and walked away from me.

I followed her into the kitchen and asked, "Are you okay?"

She turned her back to me, opened up the cupboard, and grabbed the first bottle she could find. It was a bottle of single-malt scotch, something I saved for when my father came over, and she opened it up and took a swig straight out of the bottle. This shocked me, because Lorraine did not drink very much, and she certainly would never drink anything from the bottle.

"What are you doing?" I asked.

Lorraine gasped and spit up some of the scotch. "Well, if you are off to go do something stupid, I should join you."

She took another swig, but this time, her body pushed it out, and she had to catch it with her hands to keep it from splashing everywhere. "This is disgusting. It tastes like burned Band-Aids." She then grabbed a bottle of rum and took a drink of that. The look on her face told me she liked that a whole lot better.

I leaned on the counter. "Lorraine, can we talk about this? Put the bottle down."

Some rum dribbled down her chin. "Talk? What am I going to say, huh? You've already made up your mind. So I might as well get drunk, because you aren't going to listen to a damn thing I have to say."

I sighed. "You aren't making any sense."

Lorraine's eyes were like daggers. "And you are? You are deliberately going back to some backwoods country so you can get shot?"

I took a deep breath. "I'm not going to get shot. I'm going to be with a crew of journalists. We are going to take some pictures of some soldiers and some rice fields. We aren't going into the thick of things. I won't be in battle or anything."

Lorraine harrumphed and took another drink. She wiped her mouth on her dress sleeve, pointed a finger at me, and said, "Right. Don't lie to me. I know you very well. You can't sit around while everyone is in danger. You have to be right up in there!" She made a rude gesture with her free hand.

I sighed. "It won't be for that long."

Lorraine's eyes went wild, and she slammed the bottle on the counter. "Long enough to get shot, I bet."

"I'm not going to get shot," I said as I folded my arms.

"You think your angels will protect you?" she asked.

I wore a startled look on my face, and Lorraine's eyes widened as she went in for the kill. "I've read Joseph's poem. And you read a book about angels every night. Maybe Joseph saw something in Normandy. Maybe he didn't. Going to Vietnam will never bring him back. Just like going to Korea never brought him back. If you care for this family, you will stay here."

Unannounced, Faith walked into the room; she was fifteen at that time. Her sister, Angela, was twenty and was off in college in Seattle. "What's going on? Why is Mom crying? What did you do to her?"

I raised my hands in protest. "I didn't do anything, dear. We were just having a discussion."

Faith crossed her arms tightly about her chest and tossed her head in such a way that her long hair flung over onto her back. Her eyes narrowed.

At that moment, I just noticed how short Faith's skirt was. It looked as though she were wearing a belt. "What the hell is that?" I said, pointing to her outfit.

"It's called a miniskirt, Dad. Don't change the subject. Why are you making Mom cry … and drink?"

"Faith, it's nothing. Can you give us some space so that we can talk?" I asked.

Faith stomped her feet. "No. I live here too. Why are you driving Mom to drink? She's going to become an alcoholic."

I took a deep breath and tried to have a calming tone. "Your mother is not an alcoholic. Can you please leave us for a bit while we sort a few things out?"

Faith rolled her eyes and sighed. "Whatever. I'm going out."

I took a few steps toward Faith. "No, you are not. Go put something decent on."

Lorraine slammed down the bottle of rum, and all eyes darted to her. "She can wear what she wants. All the kids are wearing them." Lorraine then looked at Faith. "Your father is going to go to Vietnam to take some pictures of all the evil and all the dead people. That's what's going on."

Faith's face went white, and her arms unfolded. I knew this was her upset face, but she didn't give me any time to explain. "You are going to film all those baby killers?"

I blinked. "Who said anything about baby killers? I'm going to take some photos, and I'm going to come back home. That's it."

Faith stomped one foot. "Haven't you been watching the news? People don't come back from Vietnam the same. They spray chemicals out there and put things in the food that make everyone crazy. So many people die out there, and for what? Are we being saved from communism?" Faith asked, but she didn't give me time to respond. She turned quickly and ran upstairs.

That was pretty much the end of the conversation. Lorraine kept on drinking, and she retired to the living room and gave me the silent treatment for the rest of the night.

The next while before I left for Vietnam was very difficult for my family. Things were very strained between Lorraine and me, and we barely spoke to each other. Not that I didn't try, of course, but Lorraine was extremely upset with my decision, and so was Faith. Lorraine destroyed my passport in an attempt to stop me from leaving the country, but I simply applied for another and hid it where she couldn't find it. Faith barely talked to me during this time, spending the majority of her time with kids I didn't like.

It was only when it was the day that I left that my wife embraced me like she did when we were first married, and she cried in my arms. "You be careful out there. I love you so much, and I don't know what I would do without you."

I whispered, "I will be fine. I'm an experienced soldier. I know how to handle myself out there. Once a marine, always a marine."

Lorraine made a funny face. "Semper fi."

I smiled. "Don't make fun."

Lorraine took off a white silk scarf from around her neck and gave it to me. "I'm going to buy a miniskirt. I will send pictures of myself until you can't stand being away, and you will want to come back to me."

"Wait. Why wasn't this up for discussion earlier?"

#

It was 1969. I was forty years old, and I was going to a war zone as a man and not as a boy. I knew that Vietnam was going to be a very surreal experience the moment I stepped off the plane. It was something I could feel in the air; it was tangible like the clothes on my body. There was something very odd going on in Vietnam, and I believed that I could sniff this paranormal source out and find it. My mind was hell-bent on discovering the source of this, not only for the newspapers and for the magazines but for myself. If that angel was anywhere, he would be here.

However, my initial assignments were quite dull. I took pictures of the men of combat and the wake of destruction they left behind, and I documented stories of the war, but these were all after the fact. I had seen similar things in Korea, so it wasn't a shock to me like it was to some of the other younger journalists there. I sympathized with the fighting men, of course, but I was not in any danger, and I was far behind the front. I was watching the war from a safe distance, and I knew that I would never see the angel by doing what I was doing.

And so I asked for more dangerous assignments so that I could be closer to the action and hopefully catch a glimpse of the angel. Because of my run-in with Death during the Korean War, combat did not frighten me like it did most people. Don't get me wrong—when bombs went off and when bullets whizzed by, I didn't laugh and dance, and I certainly did not wear a tuxedo. I dropped down to the ground like everyone else, but this isn't what I'm talking about. I'm talking about a deep-seated emotion: I simply wasn't afraid. I felt as though Death knew when my time was, and that I would see him again when my time was up.

I eventually got assigned to an infantry unit that would do reconnaissance missions out in the jungle. The air force would drop a lot of bombs or napalm, and my guys would try to outmaneuver the enemy and flush them out. The vast majority of my time was spent either digging foxholes with the men or going out on marches through the jungle. Since I was older than everyone else, everyone looked like young boys to me. In fact, some of them were younger than my eldest daughter. Some of the guys called me Pops.

Hiking through the jungle was not a pleasant experience. It took all of my power to keep up with the men whom I was documenting. I wasn't armed, but I was holding a lot of camera equipment. It was hot, wet, and miserable. If I leaned upon a tree, there would be ants crawling down my back in a matter of moments. The mosquitoes were terrible; I felt as though I were breathing them.

The initial type of action I saw was very brief. Since the sight distance in the jungle was exceptionally short, many times people would be shooting, and there was really nothing to see. An hour could go by with a lot of ammo thrown out into the beyond, but not a single target was hit on either side. It reminded me of my first combat experiences in Korea, except with even shorter engagement distances. It was clear that this type of environment was making the soldiers paranoid, because they simply had no idea where the enemy was or when they would be ambushed. This sense of doom was like a dark cloud that pressed down on everyone. It was infectious, and I too was beginning to bend lower when I walked.

I prayed every time I went to bed and every time I woke up. I made sure not to interfere at all with the men, and I took a lot of pictures. I tried to capture this sense of doom that I was feeling in my bones. Occasionally, I was successful, but it was like trying to find an endangered species of butterfly. There was just a lot of noise, and most of my pictures were useless.

Because of my sincere desire to see Death again, I took some pretty stupid and careless chances just like I did in Korea. In my head, I could hear Lorraine yelling at me, but I still felt compelled to do the things I was doing. One time, I walked out into a street that was alive with machine gun fire in order to get the picture I wanted. Another time, I ran out from behind cover to grab a soldier who was shot in the leg. I even made the rookie mistake of standing up on a hilltop with my silhouette easily seen, in order to get a better photo.

The guys in my unit started calling me Lucky when a mortar shell exploded near me and somehow missed me completely. I then told them that this was also my nickname in the Korean War, and I had to explain how I escaped death. I left out the critical part of the angel, of course. One day, when we were making our way through the jungle, I was standing next to someone when a land mine went off. I was fine. The other man wasn't so lucky. Another time, I was at the trailing end of a misdropped napalm strike. I was separated from my group but not by much, and as luck would have it, I managed to find a concrete building that took the blast, and there was enough oxygen in there to keep me safe.

In Korea, I didn't mind being called Lucky, because I was in the shit just like everyone else, but in Vietnam, I didn't like the nickname. I was a journalist and not a soldier. I could quit my job at any time, but the rest of the grunts couldn't just quit. They were forced to endure the pain of combat just like I was many years before. Also, the nickname implied that everyone else was unlucky, and I didn't like that so much.

If there was one word I could use to describe the Vietnam War, it would be "chaos." There were no lines, and an attack could come anytime from any direction, even from behind. The unit I was with would zigzag in the jungle or through ruined towns, trying to find something to shoot at. Since I was trying to get a good picture during firefights and because I was often left in the rear, I sometimes became separated from the other men. Through a camera lens I saw even less, and so this made me take risks, and I would wander off. But sometimes I was just tempting fate and hoping that the angel would show himself.

We came upon a town whose name I couldn't pronounce then and I can no longer remember now. There was concrete and debris everywhere, because the whole town was burned to the ground, and there wasn't a tree for miles that was still standing. And yet, the enemy was now hiding in holes in the concrete and the dust. This was more unnerving than fighting in the jungle. In the jungle, the enemy could still be anywhere, but there was something more natural about it. Being surrounded by vegetation and greenery was like being surrounded by life itself.

During this firefight, I heard the sound of a baby crying.

"Do you hear that?" I asked a soldier next to me.

The boy shrugged and said in a Southern accent, "I don't hear shit."

"Dude, what's your problem? You should hunker down, 'cause I don't want to be carrying your ass all the way back to Saigon," another man said.

This elicited some laughs, but it was brief. Lieutenant Anders, the officer in charge, ordered his men to move in the opposite direction of the crying. I, however, made sure that I was last in line, and when I got the chance, I moved over to where I heard the baby.

I knew it was stupid to wander from my unit. After all, I wasn't armed at all, but something drew me to this place, and I couldn't help but follow it. The cries of this child were like a siren calling to me out to sea.

What I came to find was a Vietnamese woman shot to death lying on her side in a pool of congealed blood. There was a crying, naked baby by her feet.

I was standing right beside the baby and looking down at it, wondering what on earth I should do with a baby. It was in this very moment that the Angel of Death appeared right next to me. I stared at him blankly. Although I pursued him every day, I was still not ready to see him there so suddenly and without any warning. I was convinced that I would only see Death if I was close to death. And so, when I saw him again, I couldn't help but think that today was my last day on this earth. I choked down air, and my heart raced like crazy.

I stood there like a moron with my arms dangling uselessly by my sides and my mouth agape. It took a few moments before I managed to snap a few pictures of the angel. Death smiled at me, a smile a man will never forget. It wasn't exactly peace, but it wasn't exactly evil, either. It was neutral—like an inevitable thing that must be done. No one wants to put down a cat or a dog when it is time to go, but we all recognize that point in time when we must say good-bye.

It was that smile that gave me pause. The angel wasn't dancing among the dead this time, and he was not twirling his cane. He was standing next to me, unmoving. His black tuxedo was pristine, as were his cane and top hat. His face was exactly how I remembered it; he wasn't a day older.

While I was standing there like a fool, he scooped up the child and passed it to me like a football. I caught the baby with both hands and rearranged it so I was supporting the head. It was a baby girl, and she was so small that I could hold her with one hand. I grabbed my wife's silk scarf from my pocket, and I wrapped her up with it the best I could.

"Take her," Death said. "You will know what to do with her when the time comes."

Death then walked away.

"Wait!" I cried. "I know you don't like questions, but I have many."

Death turned and looked over his shoulder at me. "Life is questions, my friend. When questions are answered, there is nothing left to pursue. Nothing left to discover. Don't you agree?"

"Yes. But—"

The angel shrugged. "But what? Everyone wants answers. Not everyone deserves answers." With that, Death tipped his hat and danced away.

I ran after him. By this time, I was aware that there were bombs and bullets whizzing by us, but I no longer cared. I ran up behind the angel and tapped him on the shoulder like he was waiter at a restaurant. He turned around and looked at me, his face growing serious, but there was still a smile on his face.

"Best you take some cover. I won't be around forever, you know."

Bullets did nothing to Death; he simply stood there, unaware of what was happening. Bullets and shrapnel detoured around him like scared flies, but none hit him. This wasn't just ten or twenty bullets, either. This was hundreds of bullets all doing nothing. Explosions too baffled the laws of nature, because the concussive force should have shaken the skin off of our bones. We were both unharmed, and the only thing that told me that explosions had indeed occurred was that my ears were ringing.

I cleared my throat. "I'm sorry to bother you, Death, but I've come a long way to meet you again."

"Death?" the angel said, cocking one eyebrow.

My eyebrows rose as if to mimic the angel. "You are the Angel of Death, are you not?"

The creature seemed to contemplate this for a moment with his arms folded and one hand on his chin. The angel's brow furrowed, and his lips turned downward. "I'm not sure why one would call me such a thing."

I shrugged. "Well, maybe it is because you hang around battlefields and dance on bodies. What else would you be?"

The angel looked down. He was standing on a severed leg; he stepped aside. "I prefer the name Kyle."

"Kyle?"

The angel nodded and smiled. "Yes, Kyle. I like the way it sounds. Besides, you probably couldn't pronounce my real name. So call me Kyle."

I cleared my throat. Another shell hit close by, and debris went flying harmlessly about us. "Okay, Kyle. Why are you helping me?"

Kyle laughed. "I'm not helping you, silly. You are helping yourself. If you continue on this line, great things shall happen. It is faith, then, that has helped you, don't you think? Your faith has guided you here, and infinite intelligence has a plan for you that is better than your own. Faith is the only known antidote for fear. And fear of unanswered questions is simply another fear. The point, then, is to have faith."

Kyle then tipped his hat with his cane, and he turned and walked away.

I let him go.

I watched him dance his way out of that battlefield, and when he turned a corner of rubble, I never again saw him in Vietnam.

I came to a harsh realization that I was in a very dangerous position. I was in the middle of a street with absolutely no cover. I was still holding this baby, and people were still shooting at me. I don't know how I wasn't hit. I don't know how I survived without Kyle there.

I moved away as quickly as I could and tried to find someplace to hide. I doubled back to where I believed my unit to be. I ran from cover to cover and sometimes changed my direction just in case someone was following me or anticipating my movements. I kept the baby close and in my shirt. When bombs went off, I did my best to protect her. To my surprise, she didn't cry much, and when she did, I rocked her gently, and she would go back to sleep.

When I finally returned to where my unit was, I found only bodies of soldiers. And because I couldn't find anyone, I assumed that they were all killed. It was getting dark, and I had no idea where I was or where I was going. I kept looking around in the rubble.

There was a horrifying foot-wide blood smear upon the ground, as if someone was dragged. I followed this blood smear and found that it led to a man leaning up against a brick wall in a half-bombed-out building. When I came closer, I could tell the man was American. I raised my hands, showing that I was unarmed as I approached. I could see that the man was holding a pistol, though it was not pointed at me.

As I came closer, I kneeled down when I recognized the man as Lieutenant Anders from my unit. He was a strong-willed man, and I grew to like and admire him in the short duration that I knew him. He was still breathing, albeit shallowly, and he was wounded in the stomach. The bloodstains were almost up to his neck and were all the way by his knees. I'd seen men hit this way in Korea, and none of them lived through it.

"Hey, Lieutenant. It's me, Lucky," I said.

Anders looked up at me. His breathing was erratic and his eyelids heavy. "Are there any others?"

I shook my head. "I don't know. You are the first person I've found."

The lieutenant slumped over, and I thought he'd died, but when I checked for a pulse, it was clear that he'd only passed out. He was too weak to move and too far gone for my aid to do any good, but I had to do something, so I tended to him the best that I could—which is to say not very well. With the Vietnamese baby still tucked inside of my shirt, it was difficult to dress the man's wounds properly, but I did what I could. My movement comforted the child, even though there were sounds of war all around us.

Tending to a dying man and a newborn baby was not the job I imagined I would be doing. And yet, there I was doing just that. I rocked back and forth to keep the baby quiet, and I held my friend's hand to let him know that I was still there. I tried to whisper some comforting words with the hope that he could hear me. I found some morphine, and I gave him some of that. He didn't moan much or say anything. He choked from time to time and winced with each cough. His eyes danced around a lot like he was looking at other people standing around us, which caused me to look behind me to see if there was anyone there. But there wasn't. It was just the three of us.

I took a few pictures, but I didn't want to be too rude or morbid. I didn't know what else to do, and it felt right to capture this moment.

Just before my friend died, he made eye contact with me. He smiled weakly and said, "You're lucky."

I shook my head. "I'm not lucky to be the only one left."

He shook his head again. "You are lucky to have talked to him. They are coming for me. They are all around me. It's beautiful."

This was all I could understand. He said more, but it was nonsense, and soon he was unconscious. I looked around, but I never saw anything. I knew his end was coming, so I stayed with him, tending to him and to the baby. I wondered what eyes might be on us.

He died in the night, while I dozed off to sleep with the baby tightly in my shirt. When I woke and noticed he was no longer there, I said a short prayer for him, and my eyes were blurry with tears. So much so that I didn't notice what was around me.

Soldiers found me—and not soldiers from our side. There were five men and one woman in the group as they approached me with their AK-47 rifles trained on me. Their weapons looked much larger in their hands than one would expect. They were short, tired looking, and smeared with blood, dirt, grease, and the stench of days in the field. They looked like a ragtag band of misfit children more than soldiers.

The woman in the group also carried a rifle and other equipment soldiers carry. Her hair was long, black, and tied back in a ponytail. She was a pretty woman, but she wore a hard look about her the way only soldiers can get; she clearly had seen too much. She held her rifle tight to her body and pointed it at me. She said something to me that sounded like a swear word.

It was far too late for me to do anything, I had no weapons, and I didn't think to take my lieutenant's pistol in time, but in hindsight, that is the only thing that saved my life. I raised my hands in the air and didn't move.

I don't know what was said, but there came an argument. When I opened my jacket to reveal the child, the arguments stopped. I handed the baby to the woman soldier. She pointed her rifle at me and could have done away with me right there and then.

But she didn't. She cried and nodded to me.

There were more words spoken, but I didn't know what to make of any of it. I sat there waiting for my end next to my dead lieutenant friend, but that didn't happen. The soldiers simply cleared out and left me there.

#

After the Viet Cong moved out, I spent the rest of the night by the side of my dead friend, Lieutenant Anders. I wanted to take a picture of him after he passed, not because I had a morbid fascination or anything of the sort but because I wanted to capture just how peaceful he looked. I refrained, however, when I thought of how his wife or how his family would react to such a thing.

It took me another day to find the unit I was with. Some soldiers had survived the firefight and retreated to find another unit of Americans. I heard the soldiers long before I saw them, and I called out to them. "Don't shoot!" I yelled. "I'm a journalist, and I'm lost."

"What the fuck are you doing out there?" someone cried out.

I was hiding behind a concrete barrier. If there was one thing I learned about Vietnam, it was always be overly cautious. People were very twitchy.

"When was the last time the Red Sox won the pennant?" another voice called out.

I was confused. I wasn't much of a baseball fan. "Who cares?"

This produced some laughter.

"Lucky, is that you?" a soldier called out.

"Yeah." I stood up slowly with my hands up. There were several rifles pointed at me, including an M60 machine gun.

When rifles were lowered, I made my way over to the Americans and fell over exhausted. I didn't eat or drink anything all day, I was covered in filth and blood, and my skin felt like a giant raisin.

One of the soldiers gave me some water, which I gulped down, and it splashed all over my face. I was so glad to be found and so happy that I was both crying and laughing at the same time.

"Easy now. You don't want to get drunk," one of the soldiers said, laughing. "How did you survive out there?"

I shrugged. "I guess someone is in my corner. I found a baby, and I put the baby in my shirt. I found Lieutenant Anders too. He was hit in the stomach. I tried to help him best I could. But he didn't make it."

I saw one of the boys lower his helmet so it obscured his face. Lieutenant Anders was popular with the guys.

"How did you get through the line? This place is crawling with VC."

I choked a bit and wiped my face the best I could with my sleeve, but this just put more dirt everywhere. "They let me go. One of the Viet Cong was a woman, and I gave her the baby. She let me go."

"Wait, they came up to you?"

I nodded. "Yeah, I was sleeping next to the lieutenant. They got to me right after he died."

"You's a lucky fucker," someone else said.

It was then that I knew I was done in Vietnam.

The next few days were a blur. I was extracted from the front line by helicopter and taken to Saigon. It's not really important to know what a helicopter is, it's just a flying machine that can take off and land vertically.

At any rate, once there, I requested the next flight out, which was in two days. I didn't leave my room much, and I slept most of that time. In another blur, I was in Tokyo, Japan, and in another blur, I was in Seattle. It would take me a long time to get back to my hometown, but it didn't matter. I was home. I was safe, and my mission was completed.

I took a train back to Spokane, and Lorraine met me at the station.

I saw Lorraine standing there in a blue miniskirt, and my eyes popped open. I walked up to her, placed my bags down, and opened my arms wide to receive a hug. I got a slap in the face instead.

"You son of a bitch," she said right before she kissed me so hard that I thought she was going to bite through my lips and into my gums.

I hugged her tightly, and we didn't say much for a long while. In fact, I didn't even see Faith until I heard her sigh and mutter something under her breath.

"Come here," I said to her. And Faith joined our embrace.

#

Erich stretched and cracked his back by twisting left and right in his chair. "Well, how did the pictures turn out?" The old man cocked an eyebrow, and Erich continued, "You said you took pictures of the angel, or Kyle, or whatever his name was."

"Oh!" the old man said, raising a finger into the air. "Those pictures, I'm afraid, never turned out. They were overexposed as though I had taken them while aiming my camera into direct sunlight. I never did get a photo of him."

Erich grunted. "So you never had proof that he even existed. That must have been frustrating."

The old man shook his head. "Not really. I left Vietnam knowing a great deal more than when I went, and so that was enough for me."

"You were how old then?" Erich asked.

"I returned home in 1970. I was still forty years old."

Erich grimaced. "You look like you are a hundred years old. I don't have much time left. I hope the rest of your story doesn't take as long. I may never hear it."

The old man examined the other. "I'm not a hundred years old!" The old man paused and then nodded. "But you are right. There are many details that are not relevant to the story. I shall omit those."

Erich pointed to the cane by the old man's side. "You still haven't told me what that is. Where it came from or why you have it."

The old man took a deep breath. "I will get to that. Vietnam was the last battlefield I would witness, and since I didn't know the true nature of the angel named Kyle, I didn't know if I was ever going to see him again. And so, for a time, I was at peace with having my questions unanswered. I slowed down my pursuit, and I began to live my life.

"I know you might not care to hear about how good my life was, but it was simply just that. It was filled with joy, love, and dedication. I watched my daughters grow up, get married, and have children of their own. I watched my parents grow old, and eventually, they passed away. My father died in 1984; I was fifty-five and my father was eighty. My mother died just two short years later in 1986 at the age of seventy-eight. I really thought my mother died of sorrow, because she was in excellent health her entire life. There was always so much love in her heart for my father, and when he left this world, her world crumbled around her. Her soul was linked so strongly with my father's that she just couldn't stand living without him. At least that's how I saw it."

Erich took in a deep breath. "Both of my parents are still alive. I haven't seen them in a long time. They've disowned me. I suppose I can't blame them. It must be hard on them too. Being the parents of … you know. And now they will have to live on after I'm gone. Not really fair for them."

"There are consequences for every choice we make in life. The bad news is that you are responsible for all of them. The good news is that you were responsible for all of them. This means we are in complete control of our lives."

Erich pondered this for a moment and then said, "Sorry. Please continue."

The old man looked at the far wall. "For me, my life really ended on July 17, 2011, the day that Lorraine passed away from cancer. She was eighty-one years old."

THE GREAT LOSS

T HE SUN WAS OUT, HEAT waves were coming off of the concrete, and Lorraine and I were in the hospital, waiting for the doctor to come tell us her results from the battery of tests they did on her. Lorraine and I were sitting next to each other, holding hands like we usually did, but we didn't have much to say, so we sat there in silence. She coughed several times, but it wasn't anything serious. We were wondering why it was taking so long for the tests to come back.

We waited what felt like days, and those chairs in the hospital were not very comfortable, and my knees started to ache. About the time when I got up for a walk, the doctor came out, followed by two other doctors. We were escorted into another room, and they closed the door.

"What's the scoop?" I asked. "We've been waiting for a long time. We have some errands to run today."

One of the doctors, who looked young enough to be my grandson, pushed up his glasses on his nose and said, "I'm very sorry to keep you and your wife waiting. I wanted to be sure of the results, and I wanted a second opinion."

"This sounds serious," Lorraine said.

The young doctor swallowed and said, "I'm afraid it is quite serious."

While he was talking, another one of the doctors put up an x-ray of Lorraine's chest, and even though I was no doctor, I could tell that it didn't look normal.

The young doctor continued, "I'm afraid Lorraine has stage-four pancreatic cancer."

The doctor paused, and there was a moment where no one said anything.

"There must be some sort of mistake," I said. "We came here to get some antibiotics for Lorraine's cough."

One of the other doctors pointed to a blob on the x-ray. "Your wife is experiencing flu-like symptoms because the disease has affected her lungs."

"What the hell does this mean?" I asked, my voice angrier than I intended.

The young doctor cleared his throat, looked at me once, and then looked at Lorraine. "It means that your cancer started in your pancreas and has already spread to other organs in the body, particularly the lungs, as you can see in the x-ray over here." The doctor paused to point to a baseball-sized lump.

"Can't you cut it out? Shoot it with lasers? Or radiation?" I asked.

The doctor kept his eyes on my wife. "You are not a good candidate for surgery; we believe that you would not recover from it. Radiation therapy is possible, but at this stage, it is unlikely that we would see any significant change."

I cleared my throat. "Okay. What about chemotherapy?"

When Lorraine failed to say anything the doctor finally looked at me, and I knew the answer before he spoke. "That is certainly an option, but this will make Lorraine very ill, and so the concern then is quality of life."

I bit down hard on my tongue. I did not want to be weak in front of these people.

"How much time do I have?" Lorraine asked. She was playing with a balled-up napkin.

The young doctor looked at the ground and then put his hands together while still holding a clipboard. "Not very long. A few weeks at most."

I gulped. That was not the answer I wanted. "Weeks?"

The doctor nodded. "Perhaps less than that. I'm sorry."

I wiped my nose. "So there's nothing you can do?"

The doctor nodded again. "We can try chemotherapy if you want. That decision rests with you."

Lorraine took a deep breath and then coughed a few times. "I don't want chemo. I don't want my last hours choking on my own vomit. What are my other options?"

The doctor bit his lip and did not look directly at us. "Well, there is hospice. You might even be able to do this in the comfort of your own home."

"Hospice?" I asked, but it was more to myself. Hospice was something I only knew as the last exit before toll. There is only one way out of hospice. I shaded my eyes with one hand, and I squeezed Lorraine's hand with the other. "Can we have a moment?"

"Sure," the young doctor said. "I will be here if you need me. A nurse will come by to explain all the details of hospice to you if this is the decision you come to. I'm sorry this couldn't be better news."

I waved the doctors away, and they disappeared from the room.

I immediately embraced Lorraine. I pressed her face against my chest as she sobbed. I rocked her back and forth, and we said nothing for a long time.

After about twenty minutes, a nurse came in with an armload of brochures and pamphlets that neither Lorraine nor I felt like reading. The nurse talked at great length about the process of hospice, where we would go, and what would happen. I didn't hear much of what was said, and I doubt Lorraine heard much, either. The nurse was young and pleasant, but we were just not ready to hear much of anything. The only thing I remembered from that conversation was that I would be able to stay in a bed next to Lorraine during her stay.

Once the nurse had left, Lorraine began crying again. "I'm not going to make it for Thanksgiving, am I? Or Christmas?"

I was so overcome with grief that I couldn't answer her.

"You will take care of the girls, won't you?" she asked. "And the cats, of course. You know Skipper loves tuna in the morning, and Felix will need his milk before noon, or he will go all crazy. He will claw up the couch."

She then proceeded to tell me all the things I would need to know once she passed. I was quiet, but I was not listening. All I could think of was how much I would miss her and how lost and alone I would feel. I didn't care about how the laundry was to be folded, and I didn't care about how to clean the inside of the oven. I figured if those things got bad enough, I could always call on Faith and Angela to help me.

This conversation went on a long time, maybe even hours, but at some point, Lorraine ran out of things to say. She looked at me. We embraced and cried together.

We left the hospital and went to the hospice center immediately. By this time, it was evening, and both Angela and Faith met us at the facility. Angela at this time was sixty-one, and Faith was fifty-seven. Even still, whenever I saw them, they both appeared as small children to my eyes.

The girls were wonderful. They took care of all the paperwork that needed to be done and made sure that Lorraine and I would not have to do much except sign a few forms.

By the time we got Lorraine's room figured out, she was very tired and lay down immediately. I got her a cup of water with one of those bendable straws she liked, and I set that by the bed.

With Lorraine sleeping and Faith and Angela working out all of the details, my head was exploding, and I needed to not be there. I needed to get out and have a walk.

"Dad, we need to talk about your insurance," Faith said.

I groaned. "I gave you my card."

Faith shook her head. "That one has expired. Does Mom have a newer card?"

I shrugged. "Check her purse."

At this point, I got up to leave.

"Where are you going?" Angela asked.

I avoided eye contact. "I'll be back."

Angela gave me another hug, and for a moment, I thought it was the fifties again. I patted her on the back and went about my way.

I'm not sure why I didn't see angels when I was feeling this sorrow. I studied angels all my life and witnessed angels under duress. But I thought an angel would have visited me in those last few days in Lorraine's life. Maybe that's why I went for a walk. Maybe I was hoping for some divine intervention, but the dancing, tuxedo-wearing angel named Kyle didn't come to me then. With all the sorrow and all the praying I was doing, I felt alone and abandoned.

Perhaps this may have been a negative feeling, and maybe that's why Kyle didn't come. I'll never know. After my walk, I returned to Lorraine's room.

Lorraine looked different now. It was as though she, in that short time, had given in to the diagnosis that was given to her. She was tired-looking and withdrawn, and she didn't connect much with us.

The girls and I chatted, of course, and the conversation went around in circles the way that only women can make happen. But I knew that they were there for me, and that was the important thing. They both stayed until it was after 10:00 p.m., Lorraine was asleep, and I was already dozing. I hugged our children good-bye, saw them to the door as if we were home, and got ready for bed.

Sometime in the night, Lorraine woke in my arms and tried to get up. "Can I get anyone anything? Some tea, maybe?"

I gently directed my wife back to her bed. "We can send for some tea. You don't have to worry about that. Angela and Faith have gone home to their families."

Lorraine smiled. "Do you think they will have some milk? I do like milk in my tea."

I couldn't stop the tears from my eyes, and Lorraine wiped them away. "I'm sure they have some milk," I said.

Lorraine's condition deteriorated rapidly. I sat there with her for the next few days. My girls and their families were in and out of that hospital too; I wasn't the only support for Lorraine. Some longtime friends visited, and some family came in on her side too. But this was all a blur to me, and I didn't really pay much attention to it. I was so focused on my own suffering that I didn't have the energy or the power to care for anyone else. I was exhausted, and any energy I had went straight to my wife and no one else. I wanted as much time with her as I could possibly have.

Lorraine came in and out of consciousness, and they made sure to give her drugs to soothe the pain. But this made it so that she was more unconscious than conscious.

One time, I was watching TV and reading a book, but I wasn't really doing either. Angela and Faith were there, and when Lorraine began to stir, we all moved in closer. I held Lorraine's hand with both of mine.

In almost a squeak of a voice, she asked, "Will you be okay?"

I smiled, and I think she saw that. That was important to me. "Of course I'll be okay. The girls will take care of me now. You taught them well."

Faith and Angela were in tears, and they hugged her tightly. One of our granddaughters was there too, and it was all tears.

Lorraine's eyes were already closed, and she smiled and drifted back off to sleep. But I kept talking while stroking her hair.

"I'll be fine. Felix and Skipper will be fine too."

The girls took turns saying their last words to her. Lorraine didn't say anything, but she nodded from time to time. I think she could hear them. The girls stayed as long as they could, but night soon came, and Lorraine didn't show any more signs of responsiveness. She moved some in her sleep, but there were no more words. And so I said good night to my daughters and my granddaughter, who was almost twenty-nine at that time and had a child at home too.

I don't need to draw out the details, but I stayed with my wife until she died, which was hours later and in the middle of the night. Everyone else had to go home to be with their families. This was understandable, of course; I wanted a nice bed to lie in too. The hospital was kind enough to give me a bed so that I could lie down and hold Lorraine's hand.

When I could tell that her time was coming to an end, I sat up in my small bed, and I held her hand, stroked her hair, and talked to her, even though she was unconscious and not responsive.

I felt as though that on some level she could hear me. I felt that even though we were connecting, I needed her to know that I was okay so that she could let go. I know she worried about me. Worried about whether I was warm, worried if I had enough to eat, and worried whether I was comfortable or not. I didn't want her to worry anymore. I wanted her to be at peace, and I wanted her to be safe when she crossed over.

And then it happened. Her last gasp of breath and a long exhale—I knew it was done.

I didn't call the nurses right away once she passed, though I think they already knew. One nurse poked her head into the room, and I'm sure my face said it all. She disappeared, and about forty minutes later, my girls were there. It must have been six in the morning when they arrived.

They came in, hugged me quickly, and said good-bye, and that's the important thing. The rest of what happened was another blur. Faith was great in taking control over the details. She just scooped up the paperwork and handled it. She talked with the nurses and got all the details we would need for the next steps. Angela stayed right by Lorraine, hugging her close.

More time had passed, and Faith's husband and Angela's husband and their children joined us later that day for dinner. I really didn't eat much. I ordered a BLT and some fries, but I could barely manage more than a few bites; that's all I could stomach.

The girls took me home, stayed with me awhile, and then left to take care of their own affairs. This is when the sorrow really hit me.

I was there, alone in my house, our house. I was dizzy, and I lay down to rest for a while. When I woke up, I swore I could hear Lorraine in the kitchen, and for a brief moment, I thought she was actually there. But after brief exploration, I found that she was nowhere. I was alone now. And the house was very quiet. I sat down on a chair in the living room and stared into the kitchen, hoping that she would be just around the corner. Even the cats did not howl the way they normally would when they didn't get food. Felix was on one of my thighs, and Skipper was on the other. I gave them both a quick pat and kiss, the way Lorraine would, and I got up and went about my day.

DISCUSSION ABOUT LORRAINE

T HE OLD MAN WIPED SOME tears from his eyes and wiped his nose on his sleeve. "I'm sorry. For me, the memory is still very new."

Erich shook his head and handed the old man a handkerchief from his pocket. "You don't have to apologize. I'm a mess right now too. I feel like I just woke up from a drunken three-day binge."

The old man took the handkerchief and studied it for a moment before wiping his eyes. "Well, I know you don't want to hear about any of my family crap. You certainly don't want to hear about how I have a heart and how I have loved."

Erich took a deep breath. "Actually, I am beginning to see that this is an important aspect for your tale." Erich looked down. "I think you were right."

The old man smiled weakly and took a deep breath and leaned back on the brick wall behind him. "Since I was very young, I understood that we all grew old and we all died. I saw my father grow old and die, and my mother. And all of our childhood friends. But when it is happening to you, it seems like we resist it. Maybe it is denial, maybe it is that we just don't want to face it, or maybe we just don't know what else to do. But time keeps ticking away. You are playing a game of chess with Father Time, but it is folly. You can never really win. You may win a round or two, but eventually Father Time takes the board."

"That's probably the most fatalistic thing I've heard you say." Erich looked up and stretched; his eyes were wide like a cat that was caught doing something it shouldn't be doing.

The old man nodded. "That's how I felt after I had lost Lorraine. What's the point of coming home when there is nothing to come home to? What's the point of getting out of bed if you have no one to share breakfast with?"

Erich shrugged and shifted in his chair. "That argument could be made for anyone. What's the point of anything, really? We are all just living off of borrowed time, and eventually we all die. That's why we have to do the things we love. I wish I had never gone over to my neighbor's house that day. So he stole my chickens. So what? I should never have been drinking, either. It's all such a waste."

The old man picked up Erich's notebook from the table and flipped through it. There were a lot of pictures, mostly of angels, though there were some portraits. There was even a self-portrait of Erich with his eyes closed.

"You love to draw, don't you?"

Erich nodded and smiled. "Yes, it has always been a hobby of mine. That and reading. I try to read two books a week, though sometimes I only get around to reading one. If I'm not reading, I'm probably drawing something."

"Good. It is good to have a passion. That's the most important thing in life. Your way of life will sustain you if you allow it. Your way of life will give you power and determination to see it to the next day. It gives you a reason for getting up in the morning and drives all of your actions." The old man paused and looked up at the ceiling.

Erich's eyes followed, but he saw nothing and looked back at the old man.

"What is it?" Erich asked.

"Hrm? Oh. I think my passion for answers is the only thing that kept me alive after Lorraine left."

Erich chuckled.

"What's so funny?" the old man asked.

"Oh, nothing. You just switched to speaking German again. You had been doing very well with speaking English consistently."

"I said that in German?"

Erich nodded. "Yeah, and fluently. Like you grew up here."

"I wonder why that is. I was thinking about something I saw in a movie once that was relevant to my story. But then I wondered if you had movies or not in your time. I think you called them motion pictures."

Erich nodded. "We have motion pictures, yes. I don't think they will really take hold. It is a novelty, really. Though the one I saw had a piano player, I don't much like the sound of pianos. My mother made me play piano as a child, and I hated it. I made sure to play badly so that I wouldn't have to do it anymore."

"How did that work out for you?" the old man asked.

Erich shrugged. "It just earned me more lessons."

The old man rubbed his hands slowly. "Well, in my time, movies were two hours or even three hours long, with sound, in color, and with special effects ... ah, that's not relevant."

"What are special effects?"

The old man waved a hand. "I've said too much. It's not important. It was just a memory is all. In this one movie, a father was explaining to his son the value of the sword. He explained that through life there will be no one you can trust, and then he pointed at the sword and said something like 'This you can trust.'"

Erich put a finger to his lip and looked at the old man's cane. "Are you saying you put your trust in violence?"

The old man shot Erich a quizzical look. "What? No. The man was saying that the only thing you can really have faith in is your life's mission. In this case, my life's mission was finding that angel and getting the answers I desperately wanted from him. There were so many things unanswered. Why did he spare my brother, only to allow him to kill himself a short while later? Why did he save me and then abandon me in the years to follow? Did I just dream up this whole thing? Did I see a vision, or did I imagine everything? I wanted to know if I lost my chance at having a true purpose in life. Did I allow myself to grow old and wither away before my destiny was to unfold? Did I miss my calling? Did I ignore some clue that Kyle gave me as to what I was supposed to be doing?"

Erich rubbed his eyes and yawned. "Sorry. I'm sleepy, but I still don't want to sleep. Is this when you found the magical sword?"

The old man grimaced. "This was a dark time for me. I lost everything that I ever needed to fight for. My children were grown up and didn't need me. My grandchildren were grown and were scattered all over America pursuing their dreams. My friends were either dead or too old to do much. I sat at home alone. I sat there reading my old books on angels. My daughters came home often to look after me and even to cook and clean up the house. I became a slob once Lorraine died. You never know how much your wife looks after you when she's no longer there to do it."

"That must have been difficult for you."

The old man didn't say anything for a time and then nodded and stared off into space. "I was lost. I was filled with sorrow. I thought about suicide a great deal. I kept my gun in a drawer by the bed. Sometimes I would wake up in the night, and I would open that drawer and look at my pistol. You have to understand how lonely I felt. And oddly, I felt like I was abandoned. I know it was impossible for Lorraine to abandon me, but that's what the loss felt like. Abandonment. One night, I took out my pistol, and I put it to my head. I was about to pull the trigger too. I thought maybe this would make the angel appear again. Tell me what to do or something. But no angel came."

"So what stopped you from doing it?" Erich asked.

The old man used the handkerchief and wiped his eyes and nose. "The cats. Skipper had jumped in my lap, looked into my eyes, and started purring. I think he thought it was breakfast time. I couldn't abandon them. Lorraine would have never forgiven me. I put the gun down and went to the kitchen to give the critters some food."

Erich chuckled. "A chicken condemned me to death, and a cat saved your life?"

The old man laughed too. "No. I think it was Lorraine. Or a memory of her, to be more precise. But it was then in the kitchen that I saw a cross we had there, and a thought dawned on me. If I was willing to throw everything away, I should have the guts to do anything I wanted to do. After all, this was the end of my life. Why not do something stupid? Why not go out with a bang?"

TRIP TO ISRAEL

AFTER I DECIDED NOT TO kill myself, I determined that I needed to take action; I decided I needed a vacation. I needed to get out of the house and far away from my daily affairs. I decided that I needed to be in the most holy place in the entire world, so I packed my bags, and I bought a plane ticket to Israel. Israel was a country formed in 1948 out of Palestine. Its politics are exceptionally complex, and I won't bore you with the details. The important thing is that Israel was a very sacred land to me.

Of course, I almost lost my mind when I found out how much this was going to cost and how long it was going to take to get there. But what did any of that matter? I wasn't going to need money anymore, and just a short while earlier, I was willing to put a bullet in my head. I could afford to spend every dime I had, because there was really nothing left to lose for me. So I might as well spend it on things that I wanted and needed to do. My mother used to say, "You can't take money with you when you are dead."

I called Angela and Faith to tell them I was taking a short trip to Montana. This was a lie, of course, but if I actually told them where I was planning to go, I'm sure there would have been an ambulance and a police car at my house before I could put the phone down. I felt bad about this, but I knew they would try to stop me if they knew the truth.

My girls were upset that I was going to drive for so long, but they understood, and more importantly, they agreed to come over and feed the cats while I was away. I took the car to the airport, paid the horrible fee there, and then hopped on my first flight.

I am fortunate that Lorraine always kept my passport up to date. We used to travel more when we were younger, but after seventy, I don't know if we ever took a trip outside the country. Lorraine was always prepared to go on some adventure, and she wouldn't let something like a passport renewal to get in her way. That being said, when we got older, we didn't have the same energy to be on flights for very long.

I took what felt like a dozen flights to get to Israel. This was not a fun adventure. It was an exercise in pain and frustration and consisted of many trips to the bathroom. I was feeling this sense of dread on my second flight that I made a really big mistake by taking a trip across the world. I thought that I should just get out at New York and look at the museums or something and then come home. But something kept me going. Something pulled me along, and I got on my next flight. My back was hurting, my knees were aching, and my ankles felt like they were on fire. In hindsight, I should have bought a first-class ticket. Why not, right? I wasn't going to live much longer, so why wouldn't I spend money to be more comfortable?

When I landed in Israel, I immediately felt stupid. I didn't know anyone there, I didn't speak the language, and I had no idea where I was going. This both scared me and excited me, and when I got off that plane, I was already sweating head to toe. No one knew where I was, and I had no idea what I was going to find or even what I was going to do there. There is power in uncertainty, though, because when things are uncertain and no plans exist, you are naturally open to infinite possibilities.

I mustered my courage by pretending that Lorraine was there with me. Lorraine liked to be on my left side when we would walk; she would wrap her hands around my elbow. So when I was walking around, I tried not to look to my left. I didn't want the illusion to be shattered by seeing that she was not in fact next to me. I felt the weight of her hands on me, and I felt her head nuzzling me on the shoulder. It was very comforting, and it gave me the strength to carry on.

What would Lorraine do? I asked myself. Lorraine was an organizer, and she would have planned this vacation down to the last detail. I thought about how she would go about planning the trip, and so I asked around and managed to get a few leads about a place to stay. I felt like I was channeling her energy and her spirit. This wasn't as lonely as it may sound. In fact, this gave me the optimism that I was yearning for. Humans aren't meant to have sorrow, at least not for long. Humans are meant to create and to explore. To learn and to love.

With Lorraine's magic and her charm, I managed to get the cheapest hotel I could find, and for the next two days, I became a tourist. I didn't sleep much. I was like a child who was awake on Christmas Eve. I went out for long walks, I did some sightseeing, and I stood in some of the grandest synagogues the world ever knew. When no one was watching, I would talk to Lorraine, a habit I developed ever since she died, but I was always careful not to do it when others were looking. Lorraine wouldn't like it if people called me crazy. And I would be no good to anyone in a mental hospital.

I found some people who spoke English, and so I could get around even if I had to backtrack a little bit. I didn't know where I was going at first, so I simply just wandered around looking at things and stopping only to have some food. I don't know how much I spent, but I felt so free of the burden of caring where my hard-earned money was going at this point. I was in my winter of my life, and it was time to not worry about what tomorrow would bring, because there might not be a tomorrow for me.

I woke up from a nap on my third day. I'd had a dream about catching fish, and I remembered something that the angel Kyle had said: "The river of yesterday." I woke with a start when I had an idea. I hastily had a shower, threw on my clothes, and got out of that hotel. I waited for the hotel staff to finalize my bill, and I was getting impatient. But then I felt the familiar tug at my elbow, and I smiled. I finally saw a concrete goal in Israel, and I set out to get a taxi; I was going to the Sea of Galilee.

I was driven by an image of catching fish, and I thought, *What better place to do this than in the Sea of Galilee? This is where it all began, right?* This is where Jesus taught his disciples. I thought that I would be shown a sign here, because it was one of the holiest places on earth. I felt that if I could see angels on battlefields in the worst human misery, I would be able to find an angel in the Holy Land.

I found another hotel in the area, dropped off my bags, and set out on foot. I don't know why I didn't take another taxi, because my knees were already aching. But I wanted to see the sights the way a man would have seen things thousands of years ago. It was important to me to do this journey with my own feet. So I took to the roads.

Israel wasn't at all what I had imagined. Everything was much more modern than it was in my mind. I suppose I should have guessed this, and perhaps I should have done a lot more research. I didn't do much in the way of preparation; I just went out there with the faith that I would find what I was looking for. In my head, Israel was supposed to have people in desert attire, walking camels and herds of goats everywhere. I know that sounds stupid, but I think I'd just read so many old books on angels … and all the artwork I saw depicted this old-time image, as well.

I stayed in Israel for seven days and seven nights, four of which were by the Sea of Galilee, hoping that something would come to me. I actively searched the area there and came up empty-handed each and every day. I think I became more and more desperate with each passing hour. I prayed often, I went to church, I kept asking for guidance, but I found nothing. No angels came to me. No angel showed me the way, and there were no more clues than when I'd left my home.

What followed immediately was complete and utter disappointment. I thought that something would be shown to me, and nothing was. I thought that there would be some fanfare or something, but this was not the case.

Having nothing to show for my time, I packed my bags, went to the airport, and began my journey home.

On the long and lonely flight home, it came to me, as things usually do when I am calm and at peace. I think this is because when we are relaxed, we can hear the whispers of angels who guide us to the truth or along the right path. Opportunity in life is rarely met with trumpets, fireworks, and huge neon signs that point the way to success. Luck is where preparation and opportunity meet—at least that is what Roman philosopher Seneca said.

I came to an epiphany somewhere over the Atlantic Ocean. I was looking out the window at the water below us, and I let my mind wander. It was that moment right before one falls asleep. Where your mind is open to suggestion and relaxed enough to let go of all the things that occupy your mind. It was as though the fog in my mind was lifted. I didn't even know I had a fog in my mind until such a time when the curtains were drawn. The veil was lifted.

The river of yesterday was in my own backyard.

As a boy, Joseph and I had fished in a nearby river. I believed this is what the angel was referring to and that this was where I would receive my next instruction from the angel. All I had to do was go back there to find whatever it was. I made up my mind to head straight to that river with a fishing rod.

A smile came to my face—the type of smile like I remembered a funny anecdote or memory. I was wide awake now, and my mind was spinning into a new frenzy. I didn't care that I'd spent a week in Israel. To me, this was not a waste, because I had to go all the way to Israel to understand the clue. The journey was necessary to open my mind enough to see the answer.

I was delighted. There was a weight off of my shoulders, and I knew I was heading in the right direction. I knew that I would find whatever it was that the angel left for me there. Now all there was to do was wait.

I tried to read to pass the time, but this gave me little comfort. I felt like I was close now, closer than I'd ever been, and I wanted to be done with the chase.

Little did I know, the chase was just beginning.

BRIDGE OF TOMORROW

O F COURSE, BY THE TIME I got home, I was exhausted. So
much so that I just couldn't pick up and leave on a fishing
trip. So I called my daughters to let them know that I was
back home, and I went straight to bed without so much as a piece of
toast to eat.

I got up early the next day, got ready within twenty minutes, and
gathered all of the things I would need. I hadn't been fishing in years,
and it took about an hour to find my tackle box and my fishing rod. I
had to fix a few things, and some of my gear had rust on it, but it was
good enough to catch a fish as long as my old hands could still manage it.

By the time I ate and got all my things in order, it was noon. I packed
up my car and headed down to the old spot where Joseph and I fished
when we were kids. Of course, a lot of that riverside was now developed,
but the spot where Joseph and I fished was still fairly wild.

I didn't have a fishing license, though I was pretty sure no one
would care if they saw an old man fishing in the river. It's not like I was
committing acts of terrorism or anything. I was just out enjoying the sun.
There wasn't anyone out on the river, anyway—I had the river to myself.

I felt like I was a teenager again, coming up to that river. It shimmered
in the golden sun, and the rustling sounds of the water flowing by made

me forget my own thoughts for a time. I got out my gear and prepared my rod and my lures in a meticulous fashion that only a grandfather could stomach. It took me a few hours to set up on a large rock that I used to fish off of so many years ago, though I was not as quick as I had once been. When I was finally done, I sat there on that familiar rock and cast my line into the water.

I caught nothing. I sat there all afternoon and all evening, and I didn't catch a thing.

Even when the sun was setting and the fish were jumping, I caught nothing. I tried the yellow lures, the orange ones, the ones that spin, the ones that float, big ones, little ones, medium-sized ones. But nothing worked; the fish just were either not interested or were avoiding me.

My hope began to fade then, and I lowered my rod and sat down upon the rock and began to sulk. Not because I didn't catch anything, but because I was starting to lose faith. I was starting to doubt everything, and I was starting to feel like an old fool. Negative thoughts flowed through my mind: I was not meant to see the angel again, I was not meant to be on this mission, I was not worthy of such a thing. I was just a man who was lucky to survive Korea and Vietnam and who was lucky not to die somewhere along the way. I wasn't a genius, and I wasn't a wealthy man, either. I was simply an ordinary guy who had dreams that were much bigger than could ever be resolved.

Maybe that was my weakness. Maybe I built a dream so big that I could never possibly create it. Maybe that is how I protected myself all of these years. I was a middle-class man, because I lacked the inspiration and the clarity of mind to make something more of myself. I could have pursued journalism in such a way that could have improved the life of my family, but I didn't do so. I could have pushed myself, climbed the corporate ladder, and gotten an office and a bigger title. But I didn't. My obsession was always about angels. Because of this, perhaps my true potential was never reached.

Since angels became my single fixed power in my mind, a burning desire so fierce, I in fact let everything else slide. Of course, I led a good life, and I shouldn't complain. I had a house, a loving wife, and two beautiful children. What else could a man possibly want in life?

Again, I felt this aching in the pit of my stomach, and I knew I was taking a wrong turn. I felt stupid and alone. I doubted myself, my calling, and the very reason I was out there in the first place. I felt as though something was whispering to me as if the doubt and fear were not my own. I decided then to listen to my other inner voice: the one of peace, kindness, and hope. I took a deep breath and closed my eyes. I allowed the sounds of the running river to fill my mind and wash away all the negativity that I was feeling.

I stood up. My heart was racing. I knew that I must wash away this negativity. But how?

Thinking that I may have to take a leap of faith, I jumped into the water, and I thrashed around for some time. But again nothing happened. I prayed again. Nothing happened. Still in the water, I became angry. I tried to hold it back, and I tried to wash away my negativity in the water, but it just grew more intense. It was dark, and here I was, an old man thrashing around in the Little Spokane River like an idiot child on a dare.

I shouted with every fiber of my being, "Why? Huh? Can you answer that? I've traveled the world looking for you. I know you can see me. I know you know my pain, and yet you do nothing. Nothing! What the hell am I supposed to do? If you truly want me to do something, you need to be a bit more proactive. Don't you think? You need to help me help you. I don't need more riddles. I need a straight answer. Enough already!"

I waited a moment to listen for an answer. I felt like I was yelling at the Lord. When I didn't hear a response, I continued to yell, "Do you want to baptize me? Is that it? Well, fine. I'll baptize my damn self!"

I ducked my head underwater. The light from my flashlight shining from the rock above cut into the water at a strange angle. The water was murky, and the light coming through it was warped and strange-looking. I saw shapes in that water. Not frightening images, just images. To my surprise, I was still shouting.

I thought to myself, *Why not just take in as much water as possible? Take it deep into my lungs and end it all right here and now.* The only epiphany I would ever have is once I crossed over into death. Only then would I truly be free. I wasn't afraid to die, and I didn't feel like I had much to live for. My children no longer needed me, and my wife was already gone, and my children could feed the cats. What was I holding on to, exactly?

As I looked up, I realized that there was more light coming into the water than was possible from my flashlight alone, and I assumed it was someone else's flashlight. After all, I was making a lot of noise.

I pulled myself ashore. But the light that was so bright a moment ago passed. I didn't hear anyone, and I didn't see anyone. I was alone in the dark, dripping wet and again overcome with misery and doubt.

I looked at my watch: it was still working, but it wasn't quite midnight. I thought I should not despair simply because the time wasn't right. I resolved to hold myself together just a few moments longer.

I thought about the words of the angel again: "At the bridge of tomorrow, over the river of yesterday." I assumed the river was in Israel. I was wrong. I was sure the river meant this river here by my home. But there was no bridge here, and I thought this held a metaphorical meaning, like the future itself. But then it came to me in a flash. The bridge of tomorrow was not a physical bridge or a metaphor: it was a specific time. It was midnight. I was in the right place, just not the right time.

A smile came to my face, and my spirit brightened tenfold. I cast my line into the rushing water and waited. I knew that I was going to catch something. I didn't think about not catching something; I thought about catching something. This is the critical piece. Experience taught me that if I focused on what I didn't have, I would get more of what I didn't want. If I focused on what I wanted, I would get more of what I wanted. Remember this.

Sure enough, I caught a fish.

I was so excited; I was like a kid in a candy store. It wasn't the biggest fish I'd ever caught, but it certainly wasn't the smallest. It was a little mountain whitefish, maybe a foot in length and about a pound in weight. It looked like pure silver in the final afterglow of the sun that was already set. The moon was also out and shedding some light.

After about a minute of staring at the fish, nothing happened. It simply lay upon the rock fighting for air. I felt bad for the fish, so I put it on a stringer and kept it in the water, not exactly knowing what I should do with it.

My mind danced with a million ideas. Do I cut up the fish here? Maybe something is in the stomach of the fish. Would the fish feed five thousand people? I knew I wasn't Jesus, but should I expect a miracle? What should I be looking for, exactly?

It was dark now, and I put my rod and gear away and took out my flashlight. The fish was still alive on the stringer. It was too dark to fish, and even if I could see anything, I doubted that catching any more fish would bring me any closer to solving this puzzle. I thought about using my flashlight to attract the fish, but I knew this was illegal, and it was also very unsportsmanlike. I didn't desire to go about this the wrong way.

This too is an important piece of the puzzle. Even when there is no reason to have faith, even when there is no reason to continue, this is the moment to step up. This is the moment true faith is born and when miracles happen.

I sat down upon the cold rock and prayed straight through midnight. Nothing happened.

I was exhausted. I was no longer angry or sad. I was in this state where I knew I just needed to get home. And so I gathered my things and was about to leave when I realized that I almost forgot the fish. This was an easy thing to do at night and with very little light. When I picked up the fish, I suddenly didn't have the heart to kill it. After all, I didn't come there to get food. I came there for answers.

I opened the stringer and tried to set the fish free. But it was stuck on something. When I reached in, I found something in the fish's mouth. It was a small key.

I was holding this key, completely perplexed. The fish jumped from my hands and landed into the water with a little splash. I saw a momentary flash of silver from my flashlight that hit the water, but it was gone.

Three Days in
the Desert

I WALKED BACK TO MY CAR in a state of euphoria and put my gear in the trunk with such haste I think I broke my rod. I got to my house in a haze. I don't remember driving there or getting ready for bed. It was like I was floating. I couldn't put that key down; I knew it was the most important clue that I had ever found. This was something physical, something tangible that I could hold. I knew it unlocked something, and I was determined to find out what that was.

I was exhausted, and sleep took me, though I still clutched that key tightly in my hand.

That night, I dreamed I was in a vast, open plain with the sun beating down on me and a dry wind upon my cheeks. Looking up showed me a beautiful blue sky without a single cloud. I felt light and free.

An angel of the Lord appeared to me and was hovering over me. It was wearing white and had huge white wings and a glowing halo around its head. It looked mostly masculine, though it had no facial hair, which made it look rather effeminate. It descended from the heavens and hovered over me.

The angel called me by name, and I went down on my knees.

The angel's voice did not sound like the angel Kyle, but rather it sounded as if it were almost singing. "You have come very far. You are very close now. Keep your faith, and follow your feet."

I clasped my hands together and looked up at the angel. "Tell me what I should do."

The angel reached down and touched my head. "You are to go into the desert for three days and three nights. You will find a house there, and your key will open it. Your answers await you there."

"Which desert?" I asked.

The angel smiled and touched my chin. "The desert you know."

I didn't know what that meant, but I wanted to ask more questions before the dream ended. "How will I find this house?"

The angel smiled and spread its arms wide. "Your faith will guide you there."

"What desert do I need to go to?" I asked as my hands turned into fists.

The angel only smiled. "The desert of your mind, of course."

"I'm not sure what that means."

The angel began to fade.

"Wait!" I yelled, getting up to my feet.

I woke up in bed in a kneeling position.

I wrote my dream down on a pad of paper I kept by the bed. This was another clue, I thought, but like always, I didn't know where to begin.

#

I sat in bed for a long time with my lamp on, looking at my notepad and wondering what I should be doing. I had no idea of where to go, and I didn't want to go across the world to Israel again just to find out that I needed to travel to my backyard.

I blinked.

Eastern Washington was very much like a desert in that it was very arid and in the rain shadow of the Cascade Mountains. This was my backyard.

I didn't know where I was going, but I decided that I would go there. The angel said I would be guided by my faith, and so that was what I was planning on doing. I got ready for my day the way I usually did. I fed the cats first, or they would have murdered me. Then I took a shower, got dressed, and ate breakfast. After my meal, I got a backpack, filled it with some food and some water, and grabbed the key that I found in the fish.

I opened my night table drawer and grabbed my 1911 pistol. I pulled it out and looked at it for a moment. Why did I grab my pistol? I was looking for Death, after all, and I didn't think I would need such devices. I put my gun on my night table, and as I let go, I felt like I had finally put away my last sword of my mind. I was ready to accept whatever the Lord had planned for me.

I then called my children. I wanted to hear their voices, and I wanted to let them know that I was well. We mostly made small talk, but that was okay. I wasn't in the mood for a lengthy conversation. I didn't tell them where I was going because I didn't want them to worry about me. It was then that I realized that I would never be coming back. I was nearing the end of my journey, and I knew it. It was a deep-seated understanding and acceptance, and I knew my journey would lead to an end of some sort. I felt that I may never get to talk to my children again, so I made sure to tell them that I loved them, and I made sure that they knew that I was okay.

After I got off the phone, I filled several large bowls full of cat food and water. I gave Skipper and Felix a good scrubbing, and I set a picture of Lorraine near their food so she could watch over them.

I stepped outside. The air was warm already. It was summer, and by midmorning, it was already hot. I started to go for my car, but then I dropped my car keys; I no longer needed to be burdened by them, though I did make sure not to drop the key I found in the fish. I then decided to walk.

I wasn't sure where I was walking to, but I thought I would just walk down the road and out of the city. I followed a dirt road for a time, and when I came to a remote spot, I headed south. Spokane wasn't a desert, but it did get very hot, and it was rather dry in most places. I decided then to walk across country, cutting through farmsteads and old, abandoned roads.

I trespassed many times, but I thought no one would mind an old man wandering around. I kept putting one foot in front of the other, holding the image of a house that I would somehow find three days from now.

I didn't know if I was supposed to walk through the night or not, and I wasn't in the shape that I was once in. I decided to go as long as I could and then camp for the night.

I camped out in open fields or near small trees. About the only thing interesting I found that night was a rattlesnake. I didn't have a gun with me, or I may have just shot it. We often had to shoot snakes that came out to our farm when I was a kid. My father didn't want them stealing eggs. I'm not sure they ever got that far, and maybe my father was just scared of snakes. I don't know. But I distrusted such things, and I usually just stayed clear of them. This snake was no different, and I briefly wondered if it was an evil spirit. But the snake left me alone and wandered off elsewhere and left me to sleep.

When I woke up, I found myself wondering exactly where I was. That first night I thought I was still in Korea, and I woke up with a bit of a fright. I grabbed around on the ground, looking for my rifle, and when I couldn't find it, my heart began to race.

When I realized that I was home and camping out under the stars, I breathed deeply and enjoyed the beautiful sunrise. I ate a small meal, said a prayer, and went about my way. After the second day, I did not see anyone. Of course, I saw a plane overhead, and I heard the noise of cars from time to time, but I didn't interact with a soul. When the third day came, I felt truly alone, and although I wasn't exactly in a desert, the landscape was brown, dusty, and arid, and whatever trees there were looked very thirsty.

I looked up into the sky and asked the Lord to guide me the rest of the way and to grant me the strength to see through this final journey. I held firm in my mind a cabin that this key would unlock. I felt that I was getting closer to it with every step.

In the middle of nowhere, nearing the third night, I came upon a shack. It wasn't exactly a cabin like I pictured, but I was exhausted by now, and any shelter looked more favorable than another night on uneven, cold ground.

When I approached the shack door, I hesitated. I was about to grab my key to try the lock when I first decided to see if the door was open. I turned the handle, and the door opened; it was empty. It looked like some sort of makeshift cabin that might have been mediocre decades ago. But now all that remained were broken windows, rotting wood, empty, rusty tin cans, and broken beer bottles. It looked like it was frequented by roaming teenagers for a great amount of time. My shoulders shrugged, and I closed the door. I stood there for a long time and looked out to the landscape around me. There wasn't another house or shack anywhere to be seen. The sun was getting low, and the air was already cooling off.

I wondered what brought me out here, and I looked down at the key that was in my palm. I wondered why this key from a fish in a river miles away would be opening a shack in the middle of nowhere.

It then occurred to me that my faith was again being tested. So I straightened myself up. I looked toward the sky and the setting sun. Rays of orange and yellow light pierced through the sparse clouds in the sky, and it reminded me of a day on the farm when I watched a sunset with Joe.

I closed my eyes and allowed the fading sunshine to warm my face. I took a deep breath, and I displaced the doubt in my mind and replaced it with faith. I thought about how I would see the angel inside the shack. How I would open the door and how he would be standing there in his black tuxedo and in all of his glory. I pictured Kyle as I remembered him. I imagined his top hat, his cane, his white-and-black shiny shoes, and that boyish grin upon his face.

I said a short prayer, and I used the key in the shack door. The key fit. I tried to calm my breath and calm my heart, but this didn't happen. My heart was knocking at my ribs, and my palms became sweaty. This is no big deal when you are young, but as an old man, I felt like I was having a heart attack. I opened the door.

There was a bright light; I held up a hand to shield my eyes, and I squinted. From behind me, the sun caught something on the far wall and blinded me for a second. I stepped into the shack with my eyes closed and one hand held up to block the light. As my eyes acclimated to my surroundings, I could see a figure standing there.

I blinked.

I blinked again. It was Kyle, the angel.

My mouth flapped for a second without any words coming forth, but then I managed to say, "I've been looking for you for a long time. Where were you?"

The angel smiled and tipped his hat so he could see me better. He looked exactly the same as he did the first time I saw him in Korea all those decades ago. There was not one gray hair on his head, and there was not one wrinkle on his face. His tuxedo was crisp and clean like it had just come from the tailor. He leaned on his cane. "I've been here waiting, of course."

I looked around the shack. It was the same shack with broken windows, rotting wood, and trash scattered about it. "You've been waiting here all along?"

The angel nodded.

I raised both of my hands up. "I don't get it. If this was your hiding place, why not just give me a map to the place?"

The angel yawned. "Don't ask me. You are the one who brought me here."

"I brought you here?" I asked. I was confused and a little upset. "How did I bring you here? You were waiting here when I arrived."

Kyle tilted his head to one side. "Is that what you saw? Or did you summon me?"

I squinted. "I summoned you?"

"Of course you did. Why do you look so surprised?" The angel smiled and poked me once with his cane.

"Well, I'm a bit overwhelmed, to tell you the truth. I've been trying to piece together all of the clues you left me."

The angel wore a quizzical look. "Clues? What clues?"

I raised my hands up for emphasis. "You know. You said that we would meet at the beginning and the ending. You told my brother that you would meet him on the bridge of tomorrow on the river of yesterday. I found your key in the fish. I found the desert. I walked three days to get here. I put together all of those clues."

The angel laughed.

This made me more uncomfortable than upset, as his laugh was not a human one. It was like someone trying to force a laugh that wasn't really meant to be one. Like an alien that learned to laugh by watching humans in the movies.

"What's so funny? Can you tell me what is going on? I'm very confused. I would like to know what is happening. I don't want any riddles, and I don't want any runaround. I want straight answers."

Kyle looked at me and leaned in closer. "I am not laughing at you. I am delighting in your innocence."

"My innocence? What the hell does that mean? I'm almost ninety years old!" I said, shrugging my shoulders.

The angel poked me again with his cane. "You think that I left you clues. You believed in it so much that your faith led you to me. Don't you see? I didn't leave you any clues. Your faith became so strong that you found me. This is how you summoned me. You have pushed away your fears. You have pushed away your doubt, and you won the struggle against what your eyes were telling you to be true. You dared to look past what was perceived to be real. It took you a lifetime to gather this strength. I see it in your eyes. But you did it. And now, here I am."

I nodded. My anger was fading now. I wanted to ask a lot of questions. "I feel as though I am on a mission. I would like to know what the next step is. I would like to know how I can help."

"Help what?"

I shrugged once and then waved my hands for emphasis. "Help. I don't know. Help the heavens."

Kyle shook his head. "Heaven doesn't need help."

I pointed at Kyle because I didn't have a cane to poke him with. "If the heavens don't need help, why do they have angels?"

Rolling his eyes, Kyle said, "What I mean is that the heavens have plenty of help already. What is it that you really want to do?"

I pointed to my left palm as though I were reading off of a card. "I want peace in the world. I want justice. I want everyone to know that there is hope."

Kyle laughed again, this time tilting his head back. "You sound like a beauty pageant participant."

"Well, what should I have said?"

The angel shrugged. "That's entirely up to you. It is your choice. You are the creator of your own destiny." The angel then reached out to my head as if to pull at a long hair, and then he paused to smile at me.

"What are you doing?" I asked.

"I'm admiring your lines of destiny. You have a great many. You have touched many lives, and you have been an inspiration. I hear the voices that tell stories of your triumphs and your pains."

"What are lines of destiny?" I asked. Looking above my head, I saw nothing.

"You won't be able to see them. They look like silver and gold strands that extend out from you. But I can see them, and I can read them. That's why you were able to see me that day on the battlefield."

I eyed one of the chairs in the room and wondered if it could hold my weight. I was exhausted. "So only those with lines of destiny can see angels?"

"No. Only those wishing to see angels can see them. Tell me, what did you expect to see when you opened that door without the key?" the angel asked.

I turned to look at the door briefly. "I don't know. An abandoned shack, maybe."

"What else did you see?"

I shrugged. I didn't see where he was going with this. "Broken table, broken bottles. Some rusty cans."

"And what did you actually see?" Kyle asked.

"Pretty much just that."

"Pretty much or exactly that?" the angel asked.

I sighed. "Exactly, I suppose, but not the details. I couldn't have foreseen green beer-bottle glass, for example."

"So what did you expect to see the second time when you used your key?" Kyle asked.

I smiled. I was beginning to see. "I told myself you would be in here, and here you are."

"So what does that tell you?"

I nodded. "That faith led me to you."

The angel did a brief tap dance with his feet, and he waved his top hat twice before putting it back on his head. "That's right. But not only that. You have the power to create the world around you. You have the power to create the life you want, to control it and to direct it."

I started to point at the angel again and then stopped. "Are you saying that if I'd thought there would be gold and diamonds in this shack that when I opened the door that is what I would have found?"

The angel wobbled his head and looked up for a moment. "Yes and no. You have to expect it. It isn't enough to just think it. Your subconscious mind is the engine of your car, and you are the driver. You have to believe it enough to expect it. And the second time, just now, you believed it enough to expect it. And here I am."

I coughed. "It can't be that easy."

"Why not?" the angel asked. "Knowledge doesn't have to be acquired only through pain and suffering, you know. It can be acquired by acceptance too."

"Well, if it were that easy, everyone would be doing it. If it were that easy to conjure gold and diamonds, everyone would be wealthy," I said, folding my arms.

The angel winked at me and shook a single finger in the air. "Ah, but that is the heart of the matter. Not everyone can believe it enough to expect it. Instead, they choose to conjure a shack. Poverty, disease, misery, a job they hate, a spouse they don't like. This is the easy road, and our experiences may lead us more in one direction than the other. But ultimately, it is choice. You chose to be here. You chose to believe what you believe. And because of that, I am here."

"Okay, so I made the key appear inside of the fish's mouth?" I asked.

The angel nodded. "You saw what you wanted to see. Everything in your life has begun with a thought, given up to spirit, and then expected. You wanted daughters, and you got daughters. You expected to live through the war, and you did."

I scratched my head. "So are you saying that poor people made themselves poor? And people with cancer have given themselves cancer? Why would God do this to people?"

The angel smiled. "This should not concern you, but please know these people may have wished to experience these things."

My face scrunched up. "Why would anyone want to experience poverty and misery, let alone cancer?"

Kyle pointed at me, waving a finger in the air. "You wanted to become a marine, didn't you? You wanted to experience combat like your brother. So why would this be foreign to you? Your soul is eternal. How else do you plan to spend eternity? But enough about that. I am not here to tell you how to live your life, and I have already influenced you enough as it is. I can see that one strand of destiny is now closed to you. This is my fault." The angel sighed deeply, his shoulders slumped somewhat, and he looked down at the floor.

There was a long pause, and the angel just stood there, crossed his arms, and appeared to be lost in thought.

I cleared my throat and was suddenly very conscious of how I was holding my body. I felt awkward or even naked. "Okay. Well, so now what?"

"Now you have a choice. It is a simple choice, but one you must carefully understand before you answer me. You see this?" The angel held out his cane. "This is the sword of Archangel Michael. It has been passed down to me, and I have been its keeper for a great number of years. Exactly how long, I'm not sure. Where I am, time has no meaning, and with this sword, I can go back and forth through time. I had taken up this sword in my youth to save a friend of mine whom I had lost. But as with many things, you must recognize the relationship between gain and loss. I saved my friend from certain doom, only to find doom for myself."

"Doom?" I asked. "I don't understand."

"With this sword, I cannot be slain by any normal earthly means, and I cannot live in the normal world. I am caught between this world and the next."

"Like purgatory or something?" I asked.

Kyle shook his head. "Not exactly. There are not many who can see me. I don't need to eat, sleep, drink, or do any of these earthly things. I've been wandering through time hoping to meet someone like you and carefully reading at lines of destiny of course. And now here you are."

"Here I am. You want me to do something. What is it?" I asked.

Kyle folded his arms, and his face grew serious. "I want you to take this sword from me. With it, you will have the power to save your brother's life. There is a reason you can see me. Your faith is strong enough to wield this sword. You have nothing left to lose. But know that once you take the sword, you will never be able to return to this world as a mortal man. The time is right for you."

"What do you mean?" I asked.

Kyle tilted his head back as if to see me more clearly. "I took up the sword very young. I never had a wife, and I certainly never had children, grandchildren, or great-grandchildren. My parents never knew my fate, as much as I tried to let them know. This was a curse I did not want to bestow upon you."

"So this sword will help me save Joe, but you are saying that I cannot return to my life here?"

Kyle nodded, unfolded his arms, and backed up so that he was leaning upon the table. "That's correct."

I bit my lip. "What will happen to you once I take it?"

Kyle took a deep breath and looked up at the ceiling as though it were made of pure diamonds. "I will disappear from this place without a name, this place without a time, and this place without a purpose."

"How do you know this?" I asked.

"I once took this sword from the man before me as he had taken the sword from a man before him. There is a long list of men and women who have held this sword. All of them had the faith strong enough to wield it."

I looked down at the cane, and my shoulders slumped a little. "It looks like a cane to me. I don't see a sword at all."

"You see what you want to see, and your mind fills in the blanks. A sword would look out of place, but a cane does not. I do not fully understand this artifact even though it has been with me for a great length of time. With this sword, you will have the power to save your brother, though time is a strange thing. We might not have the wisdom to know every end."

I rubbed my hand through my short gray hair. "You could have tricked me. You could have thrust this sword on me."

Kyle poked me with the cane and touched it to my palm. "It doesn't work like that. I must offer it, and you alone have to make the decision. I cannot force anything upon you. Also, while holding this, I cannot utter a falsehood."

My eyes were fixed upon that cane. "How will I know where to go? How will I know what to do?" I asked.

Kyle's face was relaxed and calm. "You will know what to do. There is more wisdom in this artifact than you can possibly imagine."

I didn't realize that I was rubbing my knee up until then. I stopped for a moment. "Give me the sword."

The angel Kyle straightened himself up and appeared taller now, and I looked up at him. "You do know that you will be trapped between worlds as I have been trapped."

I nodded. "Yes, you told me. But like you, I can find someone of great faith to take my place, correct?"

Kyle was silent for a moment. "This might take you thousands of years, though in this place, there is no such thing as time. It is eternity."

I flexed both of my hands by opening them wide and then forming fists. "I know that there were many people in my life who would gladly slip into eternity to save me—my wife, Lorraine, my daughters, my parents, and even Pastor Jacob. I would dishonor all of them if I didn't take this sword."

"Do you willingly take this sword?" Kyle asked.

I stood up straight. "I do."

"Do you understand the consequences of this sword?"

My face grew with determination. "I do."

"Time is a strange and complex thing. The sword will guide you in many ways, but if you are unclear about even one detail, you may destroy things that you never meant to destroy. You may find that you can save Joseph but never meet your wife. Are you sure you wish to take this risk?"

"Yes. I'm sure."

Kyle nodded and put the cane upon the table. "All you have to do is take it."

I reached over and touched the black cane with white tips.

THE ASCENSION AND THE
SWORD OF DESTINY

ANY THINGS HAPPENED IN THE moment when I touched
the cane. The first thing I noticed was that the cane was not
a cane at all but a sword. It wasn't a sword like the Vikings
used or a samurai sword, but rather it resembled something that the
ancient Romans or ancient Greeks used. It was short like a long, broad
dagger and had a small hilt. It felt like a murder weapon, something that
could be used up close and personal, but at the same time, its purpose
was far beyond killing. I could feel the immense power from it, and I
instantly was drawn to it like a moth to flame, but there was something
more urgent at hand.

I looked up, and the entire shack was filled with golden light. It
was like bathing in sunshine upon the beaches of Hawaii but without
sound or judgment, without wind, and without heat or discomfort. I
was surrounded by calmness and peace. It was like watching a flower
spring forth from the ground and blossom into great beauty in front
of my eyes.

The golden light penetrated me, went through me like an x-ray. I
watched Kyle as he transformed from corporeal into ethereal. I could

see through him now like I was looking at him in a reflection of glass. His feet were off the ground, and he floated upward with his arms open like statues of Christ or Mary in churches or cathedrals. Kyle's face was obscured by light that emanated from his head like a halo.

There was a rustling sound of leaves as wings of light extended from Kyle for a brief moment. He said something to me then, but the words I did not understand. I felt like he was speaking to me from a greater place of wisdom and understanding. One of knowledge and peace. I wanted to thank Kyle for all that he had done for me and all that he inspired me to do—I wanted to reach out to him, to shake his hand or to give him a pat on the shoulder or even a hug.

But this was not meant to be. Kyle simply vanished from sight, and I was never again to lay eyes upon him. When he disappeared, I stood there marveling at the light that was produced like a star that died and winked out of existence.

The bright golden light was replaced by the rays of the setting sun, and I was alone in a shack, holding a magical sword. At first, I did nothing but stand in awe of what just transpired, but then I looked down to inspect the blade that was in my hands.

The handle of the sword was not what I expected. I have seen medieval swords before in museums, and this did not look anything like them. Its handle was made out of bone with carved grooves for each finger. The hilt and pommel were made of bronze and appeared to have several pearls imbedded in them. I wondered if some of the brass fixtures were actually gold.

The sword felt alive, speaking to me on many different levels. With each step I took, the blade glowed whiter, and the humming I heard was coming from the sword itself.

Vibrations came up my sword arm, and it felt good, like a massage of the body and soul. The white light filled me, and I felt hope and faith. I felt as though all my prayers could be answered, and I felt as though a conduit was opened up to heaven. All of my doubts that were taking camp in my mind just got up and got out. Never again did I see them take root in my consciousness.

This was just a feeling, however, and I never saw a divine being. I never saw heaven or any such thing. I held up the sword so the tip pointed to the sky, and I gazed at it in wonder.

It was a short blade, probably less than eighteen inches, and it was surprisingly light, perhaps only a pound and a half. When waved in the air, it traced light and made a peculiar vibration. The blade was dark steel with swirls in it that looked like Damascus steel, but this pattern was even more beautiful to behold, and I found myself entranced by this work of art. It was flawless. It had no scratches, no marring, and no rust anywhere. The edge of the sword was not beveled like a cheap kitchen knife. It had a diamond cross section and felt very lethal as if I could cut a lion in two with minimal effort. I made sure not to touch the edge, not knowing what that would do to me. It felt powerful, like a loaded piece of artillery that I could hold in one hand.

Not wanting to scratch the blade, I tapped the sword to the table in that shack, and to my surprise, it cut the table clean in two without a splinter or one speck of dust. The two halves separated and fell to the floor. I bent down and touched the edge of the wood I just cut. It was warm to the touch and smooth like glass. I stood back up and put my fingers to my lips and blew on them.

I looked around for something to contain this weapon. When I found nothing, I muttered, "Where do I put it?"

When I said this, a scabbard appeared by my waist, supported by a red leather baldric. I gingerly placed the sword into the scabbard, making sure my fingers were nowhere near the blade. A quick glance at the scabbard showed that it was made out of gold, diamonds, and what looked like bloodred leather. I touched the scabbard with great care. There were symbols etched in the gold that I could not read.

I could feel a great power around me. I was holding history. I was holding a weapon of massive power … a power I didn't understand and was both in awe and afraid of.

The longer the sword was in my possession, the greater the strength I felt. My breathing was easier, my shoulders and neck relaxed, and even the pain in my knees was subsiding. I felt more capable than I ever had in my entire life. I felt like a two-hundred-year-old man inside the body of a twenty-five-year-old man. I was ready.

#

Erich leaned and wiped his face. His eyes were no longer swollen, and the redness was almost gone. He pointed at the old man's cane. "That is the sword? What is it called? Every magical sword in literature had names, like Excalibur."

The old man shook his head and picked up the cane to inspect it. "I don't know if this sword has a name. You could call it Archangel Michael's sword, I suppose. It has a rich history, something about which I learn a bit more of each day that I am with it."

Erich scrunched his face up and wiped the last bit of snot from his nose. "That doesn't have a good ring to it. It needs to convey a message. It needs to be bold and powerful. How about the Sword of Destiny?"

The old man lowered the cane and looked up at the ceiling. "The Sword of Destiny?" he repeated and then nodded. "Yes, I do believe that would work."

"Why can't I see it? Is my faith not strong enough or something?" Erich asked.

The old man put a finger to his cheek and pulled downward so that more of the white of one of his eyes was exposed. "Your faith is plenty strong, but we still see what we need to see. After all, an old man with a cane makes sense, but an old man with a sword makes little sense."

After taking a deep breath, Erich asked, "What sort of magical properties does the sword have? You said it could travel through time. Does the scabbard have powers too? Like Excalibur? Do you know what they all did? How did you know it was magical at all?"

The old man again looked at the ceiling. His eyebrows were furrowed, and he scratched his chin for a moment. "It's the same way you know a dog is a dog. The same way you know a table is not alive. This was before I touched it, of course. I could tell it was not a normal thing. If a bear walked into this room, you would recognize how deadly and dangerous

it could be, even if it was on a leash with a trainer. It is alive with danger."
The old man paused and picked up the cane and pointed it at Erich.
"What do you feel?"

Erich jumped noticeably backward. "Weird. It felt like you were
pointing a pistol at me there for a second. But now it looks so normal to
me, even though I couldn't pick it up earlier. I don't get it. You said that
there were markings on the blade. Can you remember any of them? Can
you show them to me?"

The old man squinted and looked at the cane and pointed at the
middle of it. "I can't read them. It is some sort of angelic script, I guess.
It doesn't look like anything I've ever seen before. It is a very beautiful
script."

There was a moment of silence, and the two men looked at one
another.

Erich was the one to break the silence. "I'm going to die tomorrow."
The old man nodded. "Yes."

Looking at the rash on his wrists, Erich muttered, "I didn't think
it was going to end like this for me. I wanted to have children one day.
What's going to happen to my wife? She will likely remarry. She hasn't
been in here to see me at all. She can't stand to look at me. I can't say I
blame her. I didn't want to look at me for a long time. I think this is the
first time in a long time that I actually feel free. Even though I'm in a cage
and awaiting slaughter like some farm animal. I chose this fate. I chose
this for myself. I can make all the excuses that I want, but in the end, it
wasn't the booze that killed that family. It was me."

The old man leaned in and touched Erich on the arm, and Erich put
his hand on the old man's. "It is good that you are facing this now. I see
your strength returning to normal."

"My strength? What does that matter now?" Erich asked.

"To everyone else in the world? It doesn't matter even in the slightest.
Tomorrow they will rid the world of a monster, and the world will keep
going. However, you have the choice about how you face that end. What
will you choose then? Fortunes can change, just as they have changed
for me."

Erich grunted. "Will you tell me how it ends?"

The old man tilted his head to one side. "Should I allow you some sleep? It will be morning soon."

Shaking his head and looking at his feet, Erich said, "No. I won't be able to sleep, anyway. Besides, I think I will be able to rest soon enough. Please continue with your story."

\#

I stood in that shack somewhere in Eastern Washington, holding the Sword of Destiny. Exactly how long I was there I cannot be certain, as I no longer had a clear perspective on these things. I prayed to have the strength to carry on and prayed to have the strength to do what I was about to do.

I already knew where I was going long before the angel ever mentioned anything to me. I knew what I must do and where I had to go. I kept these things firm in my mind. My mission was clear to me all my life, even though I may not have admitted it to myself over the long count of years.

I thanked the angel Kyle, even though I did not see him. I felt like he could hear me wherever he was. I thanked Lorraine, Joseph, my family, and my friends. I was thankful to be alive. I was thankful to not only know what my purpose was in life but to be living it to the fullest.

I raised the sword in the air, and the sword communicated to me. It didn't have a voice, and I didn't hear whispers in my head, but it talked to me just the same. I knew that for me to travel through time I would need to fashion a door.

Holding firm in my mind my destination, I swung the sword in an overhand stroke through the air. The air parted like a curtain, but behind that curtain was the blackest night I have ever seen. I poked the glowing angelic sword into that darkness, and I could not see the light coming from it. When I removed the sword, some of the darkness stuck to the blade like the meniscus in a glass of water. It disappeared quickly, but this gave me pause. I touched some of the blackness, and it felt sticky like molasses. It evaporated quickly, and I was left to wonder what exactly this darkness was, and the sword provided me with no answers other than I was to go through it. I took a deep breath. I put the sword back in its scabbard, and I stood tall.

I walked into that darkness like a soldier walking toward his commander in a ceremony. What happened next made my head swirl like I was drunk and falling.

Traveling through time was not an experience that I could ever have anticipated. I'm not sure what I was expecting, but what I got was different from my mental picture. I suppose I imagined a tunnel and churning lights or clouds around me. I imagined an amazing fanfare and obvious signs that I in fact walked back into history. I wanted a thunderous roar, a glorious flash of dazzling lights, and a foreign smell that could only mean that I was in a different place and a different time.

This did not happen.

I knew that this was another test of sorts and that my fear would be tested, so I did not hesitate, though, truthfully, I think that the power from the sword was lending me a great deal of mental fortitude to do this. Without the sword, I wouldn't have the courage, and I may not have stepped through to that blackness at all.

The darkness was cool to the touch but light like water. I held my breath and took a step.

Stepping through this black paste was brief. No more than a step or two, but I felt as though I was completely submerged underwater. For a brief moment, I couldn't hear, see, smell, and taste anything; I forgot who I was, and my worldly concerns did not matter. It was like I was floating on an ocean of time without a body.

My third step was not a physical one, because if I indeed had no more body, how could I have taken a step at all? There was a memory of who I was, and that was what I became, at least for a moment. I don't know how long that third step took. Perhaps it took a second; perhaps it took a lifetime. I don't know.

There was an odd sensation, best described as a mild earthquake but perhaps more like a big truck moving down the road. It was brief, but it was very distinct. Along with this vibration, there was a warping of light as if I were looking through a really old window with wavy glass.

When I looked around, the table and the entire shack were gone. The ground beneath me was sand, the sky above me was blue, and the air about me was warm but not hot.

Looking around, I saw what I thought at first was a desert and rough rock that looked almost Martian in appearance and very few bits of vegetation. But then I heard the sound of gulls above, and the smell of seawater filled my nostrils.

Looking down at myself, I saw that I was now wearing a black tuxedo and a black top hat upon my head. The fabric was the best that my body had ever come in contact with before, and it felt smooth to the skin like silk.

There was something on the beach, which I couldn't make out at first, as my eyes were still adjusting. When things came into focus, I saw barbed wire, iron tank traps, and concrete barriers littering the beach like seaweed. Looking up the bluff, I saw concrete embankments that were alive like giant stationary turtles spitting plumes of smoke and ash. My eye followed what the cannons were shooting at when I saw the dozens of ships in front of me in the water.

As more things came into view, I saw landing craft on the beach. I saw men getting out of their boats and heading inland. I knew where I was now. I was on Omaha Beach, the day was June 6, 1944, and I was witnessing the beachhead assault of Hitler's Atlantic wall. My brother was out here somewhere.

On the Beach, and
in Foxholes

I WATCHED THE BOATS COME in to the shore of the beach like it was a movie, because it seemed so surreal and distant like it wasn't happening at all. There were the sounds of artillery and machine guns and other sounds of war. Men that came ashore were shot, blown up, tossed like rag dolls in the air, drowned, or burned alive. It was a horror that I witnessed before, but now as I stood there holding the Sword of Destiny, I was seeing it from a different perspective. I did not hold the fear of a normal man, and so when I witnessed these things, I would often have to stop and notice the gleam of light from a shiny button on the sand. Or I would see a burst of flame that looked like orange paint on the canvas of the greatest painter on earth. There was so much happening, so much horror mixed with so much beauty, that I simply looked around like a tourist traveling to New York for the first time and staring up at the tall buildings around him.

I strolled among the men and debris. Explosions were to the left of me and to the right. Machine gun fire kicked up sand and water into the air, but none of these things touched me. The anxiety was gone, and I looked out over the water, and it suddenly all looked very beautiful to me. I was surrounded by human misery, death, and chaos, and there I was admiring the water, the clouds in the sky, and the sand at my feet.

There was a rush of understanding. There was a simple peace of knowing that all things end, and it was important for me to see that even though there was suffering, there was still beauty if I chose to look for it.

Before long, there was a lightness to my step and a smile upon my face. I moved around from soldier to soldier. I was looking for Joseph, but I felt overwhelming faith that I would find him, and so I was not in any particular rush. I was soaking in the beauty of that land and seeing colors that looked alive.

Without knowing it, I began to dance. I imagined that I was with Lorraine again. I imagined that first dance we had together and how all my thoughts and cares in the world were only of her. I felt her touch upon my skin, I smelled her heavenly perfume, and I remembered the fondness we had for each other.

I still missed her, of course, but it was as though I were only living happy memories at this time. I clicked my heels like some teenage fool, and there was a lightness to my gait that I have never known before. A weight was lifted off of my shoulders.

And then I saw him. Or more appropriately, *he* saw *me*.

I was dancing in the sand near one of the tank traps that lay scattered upon the beach. There were body parts at my feet, and there were shell holes in the ground. Machine gun fire ripped around me and avoided me like water repels oil. I saw the Sword of Destiny as a cane, and I twirled it about me like a baton.

Joseph's eyes were wide. He was wet, covered with sand, seawater, and other people's blood and tissue. His helmet was askew, and his rifle was half-buried in the sand beside him.

I stood in front of him for a moment, and we both looked at one another. How I missed my brother. Seeing his face, even during this duress for him, was still better than not seeing him at all. I bent down beside him, and his eyes were like saucers. "Hell of a day, isn't it?" I said to him.

Something caught Joseph's eye, and he looked away for a moment. There was a nearby explosion that kicked one of the tank traps into the air. There was a mist of blood that clung to the air like a fine spring shower.

I tried to ignore it and distract Joe by tipping my hat and standing up and doing a little twirl. "You should get up and follow me," I said to Joe.

I stood in front of Joe so that my back was to the machine gun fire. Though Joseph was reluctant at first, he quickly followed me. When Joseph stood up, I could feel the bullets hit my coat like tiny pebbles tossed on an old window. I made sure to block the path of incoming fire, and dancing back and forth seemed like the best way to do this. I felt a sense of the timing for bullets and for the fragmentation from the explosions.

Joe followed me, despite the cries from his fellow soldiers. His shoulders were slumped, and his face was low, but he did not look away from me. I moved him from tank trap to tank trap, and I walked him up that beach. I found a path in the barbed wire that was open, and I crawled up an embankment and stood up. When Joseph came to follow me, the machine guns again ripped around us and tore up the ground.

I kept dancing to distract Joseph. Sometimes he would look this way or that, but every time I moved, his eyes centered back on me. I took him to a concrete barricade, and I looked around. He was out of the line of sight for some machine gunners.

Another soldier crawled up alongside Joseph and me. He was a thin man with blond hair, and his clothes looked two sizes too small on him. His M1 Garand looked like a cannon next to his small frame. The young man pressed his back up against the concrete, and he was panting like a dog out on a fresh run. He poked Joseph with a backhand. "Are you okay? Are you hit?"

Joseph didn't look at the soldier. He just shook his head.

I bent down to get a better look at Joseph. His eyes were wild still, but some of his fear left him, and there was a peace about his face that I remembered seeing on him before whenever we were out on the Little Spokane River to fish.

"You will be all right from here," I said. "Farewell, Joseph. Remember that your brother loves you very much, and he is waiting for you to return. You will be fine as long as you keep your wits about you."

I stood back up intending to leave, but I was momentarily caught off guard by the beauty of the landscape. There was movement by my feet, and I looked down. Joseph's mouth moved a bit before words came out.

"Where are you going?"

I smiled. "To the bridge of tomorrow, over the river of yesterday."

This reply got all sorts of confused looks, but I knew this was the right thing to say. Not for Joseph necessarily but for myself. I was beginning to see that it was I who was leaving clues for myself and not Kyle at all. I was the Angel of Death to some, but I was the Angel of Destiny to myself.

I tipped my hat and raised the Sword of Destiny, and I cut a hole in time and space. The way parted like a curtain at a movie, and I nodded to Joseph before I stepped through to my next stop.

#

The Ardennes was simply beautiful, even with all of the trees in some areas cut in half and splintered from the constant bombardment of shells on both sides of the conflict. I was able to catch glimpses of joy, hope, and prosperity in every living thing that was around me. I stopped several times to touch birds under the chin or to pet a squirrel or rabbit.

When I stepped out of human misery, I really stopped and saw things more clearly. There is an entire world that surrounds that misery that is oblivious to it.

We tend to focus on what is right in front of us, and it dominates our thoughts, and as a result, we attract more of the same in our lives. I believe this to very much be true. We are what we think about.

The Sword of Destiny isn't just a tool to travel through time; is it not an instrument of pure destruction, though I daresay I strongly feel that it could be used in this fashion if necessary. The sword is a symbol of hope, of courage, and of true sight. It illuminated my mind so that all the dark recesses were obliterated from it. I was no longer worrying, doubting, or fearing.

However, there was something I felt that was not what I was expecting. I felt that no matter how hard I tried to change things, it wasn't up to me to change them. It was up to the people I interacted with to change them.

I alone do not have the power to remove, replace, or add a line of destiny to someone. All I can do is influence them to perhaps change their perspective. But ultimately, the decision to change comes from that person and not by my hand and not by the sword, either.

It was then that this thought clung to my mind like a wet blanket. I possessed the faith to know that everything was going to be fine in the overall sense. After all, we are all mortals, and the lives of mankind are fleeting in the cosmic sense of time. But I also had the understanding that no matter what I did, the outcomes may not change the human condition whatsoever.

One might think that this could have made me sad or even depressed to know that even with all the power that I carried, I was powerless to stop people from doing anything to themselves. But I did not feel sadness, sorrow, or melancholy. I was surrounded by beauty and love, and I wanted nothing more than to pass this to others that I encountered, especially those whom I loved.

I had no reason to suspect, of course, that Joseph would be okay from the one encounter I had with him on the beaches of Normandy. He relayed this story to me, in time, when he returned from the war, and he still took his life. I knew that I would have to visit him again should I want to save his life.

It was then fitting that I would visit Joseph again. This time it was winter—and again in the Ardennes forest—in a foxhole dug into the frozen earth with a tarp above it. I came upon a scene.

I first tried to find the two German soldiers who were trying to surrender to my brother. After a time of wandering between the lines of Germans and Americans, I found a pair of Germans who were obviously wandering through no-man's-land toward the Allied lines. I tried to get their attention, tried waving my hands and dancing around them. The younger soldier looked at me briefly, and I thought I made a connection, but he looked away soon after and resumed his conversation with his friend. They both looked miserably cold, and I wanted nothing more than to provide them with a warm place to stay and a hot meal. Perhaps the Sword of Destiny was capable of manufacturing something like this, but I didn't know how to use it. In fact I sensed a great deal I didn't know about the sword, both its powers and its consequences. However, this did not fill me with woe or dread.

I moved swiftly ahead of the soldiers, faster than a normal man could travel, not only because my feet did not sink into the snow but because the sword granted me the power of haste. Maybe I slowed time down for everyone else and I was moving normally, or maybe it was only I who was moving fast. Having no clear point of reference, I have no idea which one it was. The result, however, was the same, and I reached the Allied line very quickly.

I came upon a series of foxholes that were farther apart than they should have been. The Allied line was stretched horribly thin and in fog so dense that one could imagine passing an army through the cracks of such a defense.

I felt Joseph this time before I saw him. I found him like a bloodhound chases prey—not by scent but by lines of destiny, which Joseph now had coming out of him like steam from a kettle on the stove.

I opened the tarp that was atop of his foxhole, and I moved inside and sat next to him. His eyes were open, and he saw me, but he blinked a few more times. There was someone asleep and leaning on him on the other side of him.

"You," Joseph said.

I put my finger to my lips and pointed at his friend that was sleeping. "Don't want to wake him up. He won't be able to see me, but you can."

"Why are you here? Why are you following me? Why are you torturing me? I feel like a mouse that is being played with by a cat. If you want to take me to the hereafter, by all means, just do it," Joseph whispered, pulling a wool blanket closer to him.

I took a deep breath, and I put a hand on Joseph's shoulder. "I'm not here to take you. I'm here to help you. There are two Germans who are heading this way. They mean to surrender, though they both have rifles with them. You don't have to kill them. Besides, you only have one shot in your Garand. Check it," I said, pointing to his rifle that he was cradling like a doll under his blanket.

Joseph grimaced and he paused. "I topped it off." He then opened the action, which revealed that there was only one round left in the chamber. The clip was slightly lodged in the action still, but he pulled it out with his fingers, popped in a fresh eight-round clip that was on his sling, and looked at me. "How did you know?"

I shrugged. "I know many things. I know there are many horrors in this world of yours. But if you look closely, you can see things that are beautiful. You only have to look to see the joy, the happiness, and the laughter. Do not concentrate upon the chaos; concentrate upon the beauty."

Both of us perked up—there were footsteps approaching. Joseph's grip tightened upon his rifle.

I grabbed Joseph by the arm. "One of the soldiers looks like your brother. It would be a shame if that boy didn't return home to his family. Don't you agree?" I let go of his arm. The footsteps were a lot closer.

Joseph scrambled out of his foxhole. Joseph was much stronger and swifter than I ever was, and watching him spring into action was like watching a tiger pounce on prey. It didn't matter that he was scared, tired, and cold. He was bred for war, and his hands were steady like a surgeon's. I came out with him, albeit late, and stood by his side.

At this moment, I felt like a spectator at a sporting event. I could cheer for my team as much as I wanted, but ultimately, I was not on the field. I had no power to influence the game once the ball was in motion. All I could do was watch, hope, and pray.

My brother raised his rifle and aimed it at the Germans, who were now only thirty feet away from us. "Stop!" he yelled.

The Germans were startled and abruptly halted, which caused their slung rifles to swing forward.

Joseph waited; his breath clung to the frigid air. Both Germans raised their hands. Both of the German soldiers were talking frantically.

I stood next to Joseph and said to him, "They said, 'Don't shoot. We surrender.'"

Joseph was shaking, not from the cold but from adrenaline. His rifle was trained on the face of the larger, older German soldier.

I took a step forward so that Joseph could both see me and the men in front of him, though I did not obstruct his view. "Tell them the following: 'Ich werde nicht schießen.'"

"What?" Joseph said, gripping his rifle tighter and not looking at me. I repeated the sentence.

Joseph cleared his throat and said, "Ich werde nicht schießen," with a horrible accent, but it was close enough.

I nodded. "Good. Now say, 'Langsam fallen die Waffen.'"

Joseph repeated what I said, and the two Germans slowly grabbed their rifles and let them slip down to the ground.

The older, larger German had a Spanish Astra pistol in his belt, and I pointed at it. "Now say, 'Die Pistole auch.'"

Joseph said this, and the German grabbed the butt of the pistol between his thumb and forefinger and raised it out of his belt and tossed it into the snow. Joseph smiled.

By this time, there were more Americans roused, and the eyes of the Germans went wild, and they shifted from foot to foot. They fell to their knees, and the youngest one had tears in his eyes. I stood in front of the Germans, thinking that if anyone took a shot, I could still save them.

"Holy shit, Joe. Nice work. I didn't know you could speak Kraut," a sergeant said, pointing his M1 carbine at the Germans. He kicked them both so that they were lying flat on their stomachs. "Your accent sucks, but we can work on that." He then searched them for more weapons with a free hand.

Joe's rifle was still trained on the Germans. His breathing was rough like he had just been out for a jog, and his eyes looked directly into mine. "You were right. He looks like my brother."

A soldier next to Joe said, "What was that?"

Joe pointed his rifle at the smaller German and cleared his throat. "That one there looks like my brother. It's weird."

The sergeant that kicked over the Germans was finished searching them, and he pulled up the younger German. "Holy shit. Maybe he joined the Wehrmacht?"

The man began to laugh, and Joe chuckled too.

I smiled. "You see. There is laughter still. Even out here, Joseph. All you have to do is look for it." I tipped my hat to him and did a twirl. "Happiness, then, is just one thought away."

There were now two lines of destiny coming from Joe, and they were stronger and more brilliant shades of gold.

"What happens now?" Joseph asked.

I put my hand on Joseph's shoulder. "That's up to you, of course. Live a happy life. And let all of this go. There's a lot to look forward to."

"Well, we have to take them to the back lines. They will put them in a camp over there and get them out of our hands," the sergeant said, looking at the Germans.

I felt I should go, and so I took a few backward steps away from Joseph, and he watched me leave. I could tell he wanted to ask me more questions, but he probably kept silent because of the other men around him. "I will always be around for you, Joseph, should you ever need me."

ONWARD THROUGH TIME

I WAS EXCITED TO SEE HOW my actions influenced the timeline. After leaving Joseph there in the Ardennes, I took the Sword of Destiny and cut a path to 1946 in the small town of Spokane, Washington, to my former home with my family.

I walked from one snowy wood to another, and as I was standing at my old family's farm, I couldn't help but feel a wave of nostalgia and love for that place. My father took great care of the house back then, and even though there was a blanket of snow on everything, I could tell that it was nurtured and loved.

I moved over to the driveway, where one of our old cars stood. It was a black four-door 1940 Ford Deluxe sedan. It was the one in which I learned to drive and the one where I had my first kiss with Lorraine. I couldn't help but lean in, wipe the snow from the window, and peer inside. The windows were frosted over, but I could still see the seats and the chrome on the controls. I took a deep breath and admired the craftsmanship.

It wasn't the best car in the world or the fanciest, but the style was gorgeous to me, and I caressed it like it was the finest silk in all of China.

Looking up at the house, there was a plume of smoke coming from the chimney, and the smell of firewood filled the air. I took deep breaths of the stuff and held out my arms to accept the snow that was falling from the sky. It never touched me, it moved around me like I wasn't there, but I still absorbed its joy and its happiness.

I took confident strides toward the home and went to the back door, and to my surprise, it opened. My father stepped out of that door at that exact moment, donned with his hat, mitts, and boots with their laces carefully tied. He passed right by me without notice, and I managed to step through the door before it closed.

I came to the kitchen, and I stopped dead in my tracks. My mother's back was toward me, and her hands were expertly working the kitchen. Meticulously, she gathered all of the things that she needed and placed them on the counter beside the stove. She took out a loaf of bread and cut some slices. She took out the eggs and checked them all by giving them a quick turn. She opened a wax paper bundle to reveal thick slices of bacon, which she placed under her nose and inhaled.

Although I wanted to stay in that moment longer, my heart was yearning to see Joseph again, so I moved past my mother and quietly moved to the hallway. There, in the hall, I saw myself.

I was all of sixteen then, skinny, pimpled, and hair that was out of place. My shirt and pants looked too big on me, and I couldn't help but smile. I wanted to smack the younger me for dragging my feet while walking and slouching. My younger self paused for a moment, and I thought he saw me, but then he continued into the kitchen, passing by me in the process.

I moved farther into the hall and took a step into Joseph's room. I couldn't wait to see him, and I couldn't wait to give him a hug that I'd wanted from him all of those years ago.

Joseph was not in bed like I imagined him to be. I saw movement to my left, but I didn't want to look. In my heart, I knew what was there, and I did not want to witness it. I knew I failed even before my eyes saw Joseph in the closet dangling by the necktie I had given to him as a gift. There were no lines of destiny here.

I moved over to the body of Joseph and waved the sword around him, hoping that the magic from that artifact might have some power to heal his wounds and make him whole again. As great as the powers were for this weapon, Joseph's soul had long since passed, and my mission was a failure.

I sat down on Joseph's bed and contemplated the meaning of things. I visited Joseph twice, and yet this was not enough. I assumed that the killing of the two Germans was the thing that broke his mind, and this is what led to his downfall. But I was wrong. Of course, I thought I would just go to him directly before he had time to kill himself, but I didn't think this would work. I thought that I had to cure the problem and not just the symptom. I felt that if I simply went to the moment of his suicide that I would be too late, anyway.

A normal person might have been stopped by this failure. A normal person might have given up at that moment and accepted that destiny and fate had a mind of their own and that there was nothing a person could do to change that. I, however, was not a normal person any longer, and I wasn't concentrating upon failure; I was concentrating upon possibilities and solutions.

I stood up, I swung the Sword of Destiny, and I cut a hole in space and time.

#

I was standing outside of Pastor Jacob's office in his church. His heavy wooden door was slightly ajar, and I could hear movement coming from inside. I moved through the doorway, and I looked in wonder at everything in the room. There was an old wooden desk, which was cheap then but priceless in the future. It was covered in books that were scattered in a haphazard manner. There were wooden bookshelves also stuffed with books, and the entire place smelled very familiar.

Pastor Jacob was standing behind his desk with his back to me; there was a book in his hand. He slowly raised his head up and closed the book.

"Well, then. I wondered when you would return," Pastor Jacob said as he turned around and faced me. "Please come in and close the door."

I did what he said, and I took a seat in a chair that I had sat in long ago when I first talked to him when I first lost Joseph. I still felt like that same boy. "How did you know I was here?"

Pastor Jacob smiled. "I didn't until now. I've been saying that every day for the past three months, wondering if someone would answer the call. Apparently I was right."

I smiled when I saw that there were twelve lines of destiny above Pastor Jacob, each of them strong, and each of them like willow branches in the wind stretching out above him and into the beyond. "You know why I am here, then?"

Pastor Jacob scratched his beard. "I could venture a guess, but I would rather hear it straight from you."

I nodded. "I have a quandary, and because I have no one in the world to talk to, I came here seeking your guidance. I am glad that you can see me. This brings me a great deal of relief."

"Guidance? From me?" Pastor Jacob let out a good belly laugh, and the fat on his chest and stomach jiggled. I couldn't help but mirror his enthusiastic smile. "I was hoping to get guidance from you!"

I placed both of my hands together and touched my thumbs to my lips as though I were praying. I felt so much joy, love, and happiness that I was almost in tears. "This is an awkward moment, then, isn't it?"

We both enjoyed the laughter together.

Pastor Jacob looked at me from head to toe, a beaming smile still upon his face. "Thank you for giving me such joy and comfort."

I waved away the pastor's words. "Nay. It is I who owe everything to you. You opened my eyes and taught me how to see, to love, and to feel."

"That's perhaps the best gift I have ever received. But you did not come here to congratulate me or for an exchange of gifts. Why, then, have you come?" the pastor asked.

I took a deep breath. "There is a boy in your congregation that will take his life one week from today."

Pastor Jacob sighed, and his face looked heavy. "That is grave news. And you have come asking for my help in this matter?"

I tilted my head to one side. "I tried to save him, but I was not successful. I went back in time and tried to influence him, but it would appear as though my work was in vain. He still chose the darker path."

Pastor Jacob's eyes widened, and he sat back in his chair. "Joseph. You are talking about Joseph."

I nodded. "Indeed I am. The war broke him in ways that I do not understand."

Pastor Jacob opened up both arms like he was conducting a sermon. "I can see it in your eyes that you carry a lot with you. Oh my. You are his brother, aren't you? It appears that you have grown old and wise. I did not know angels were born in this manner."

I smiled. "You are the first to ever recognize me, Pastor. All others see what they want to see. This is curious, don't you think?"

Pastor Jacob shrugged. "I spent the first half of my life running from things, and now I sit in acceptance of things. But look at you. You look great. I would love to hear your story sometime."

"It is a long story and one that I will relate to you, should you care to hear all of it. But right now, this matter is troublesome to me, and I was wondering if you could aid me as you have in the past."

Pastor Jacob put an elbow on the old wooden armrest of his chair and placed his hand upon his chin and scratched the hairs that were nestled there. He thought about it for a moment. "You have a haunted look about you that I did not see until now. I think you might be looking in the wrong place. I don't think the problem lies with Joseph." Pastor Jacob pointed at me. "You look much older, but I see you for who you are. The tuxedo and cane do not fool me. I know you have come to save your brother, but the real person you need to save is you."

It was so simple. It was exactly what I needed to hear. "You are right. I have corrected only part of the problem. I must go back and correct the other half." I stood up. I knew where I needed to go. "Thank you for your time. It was good to see you again after all these years."

Pastor Jacob's face sunk somewhat. "Funny. I just saw you a few days ago. Will I ever see you again?"

I nodded. "Should you desire that, yes."

Pastor Jacob's smile returned. "I would. But how can I find you?"

I winked. "That part is easy. I come when your faith beckons me. I will hear you, and I will come again."

BATTLE OF THE BULGE

I PLANNED ON OPENING A portal to another time, but as I stepped through the darkness behind the curtain, I changed my plans. Instead of taking a step forward into the darkness, I took a step to my right first and then stepped forward. I knew that this would take me where I needed to be, and I stepped out into cold air, and the hardwood floors of the church beneath my feet were replaced with fluffy white snow.

I was in a forest of pine trees in rough and steep terrain that was almost mountainous. The sky was blue, the air frigid, and the scent of pine trees was like freshly baked apple pie to my nostrils. My feet were on the whitest snow I ever saw, and yet I was standing on top of the snow and not sinking into it. I bent down to touch the snow, and I shoveled it into my hands like it was diamonds or gold dust.

I brought the snow to my nose, and I swear I could smell the beauty in it. It was like smelling my wife's pillow or one of the scarves that she used to wear. It was a smell of great comfort, beauty and joy.

I moved around the trees like I was a toddler. I swung around the trunks like they were equipment you might find in a child's backyard. My feet took to dancing again, and I felt the lightness and power of peace from the fresh air around me. My sword was once again a cane, and I used this to tap tree trunks and the heels of my feet as I meandered among the fresh snowscape.

After a time, I noticed a column of German tanks upon the valley floor below me. Filled with childlike wonder, I moved to those tanks swiftly.

There were the usual sounds of war, the screech of the incoming shells in midflight, and the roar of explosions. The tanks around me were maneuvering into better firing positions, and some stopped to take shots.

I looked around. I found the tank that I was looking for. I caressed the side of the armor. It was a Panzer IV, and although it wasn't the best German tank of the war, it was certainly a formidable opponent. This one was modified with a seventy-five-millimeter dual-purpose gun with a longer barrel.

At first, the commander on the tank did not see me, as I approached the tank from the rear. The commander was looking through a pair of binoculars out of the top hatch of the tank. I could hear him talking with the others inside of the tank, and although their voices were muffled by the thick armor, I could still hear what was being said.

Judging by their conversation, I would have to say that this tank column was a part of the Fifth Panzer Army, and judging by the terrain, I would have to say that it was in the Ardennes at the Battle of the Bulge.

As a young man, I looked at many pictures of tanks, and I admired the German tanks the most, because this is where the world had seen a huge leap in technological prowess. However, this was the first time I had actually seen a German tank up close before. It was a marvel to behold.

I admired the thick armor, the roar of its engine, and its mighty gun. When I put my hand on the thing, it felt alive, like a mystical dragon or some other fantastic creature. I stood on the tank, and when it lurched forward for a better position, I didn't have to change my footing much.

I recognized the commander immediately: he was the younger version of the officer I met a long time ago, and if he had a commanding presence when he was old, he possessed much more of that here in this tank. I couldn't help but smile and feel a certain amount of pride for him. He was in his element, and it showed with every movement and every word he spoke.

I moved beside him and looked out to the landscape upon which he was watching with his binoculars. He called out coordinates and gave the order, "Feuer!"

The large gun boomed, and the tank rocked from the recoil. A plume of smoke was at the massive barrel, and the hiss of the round flew through the air. Even without any aid to my vision, I could tell that they hit a tank that they were aiming at. The whole reality of the war was very surreal to me—part of me wanted to clap like a little kid. It was like it was all fake and that everyone would simply stand up once it was all over.

I knew that it wasn't the case, of course, but this was the feeling I was experiencing.

I stood in front of the commander to get his attention.

He put down the binoculars and looked at me. For a moment, I admired his uniform, which looked rather clean and pressed even though his face had dirt on it, especially around his eyes. "Who are you? What the hell are you doing here?" he said to me.

"Don't you just love the air out here? I can't believe how beautiful this all is."

"Get off immediately!"

I heard voices from the tank below, but I ignored them. The sense of impending danger was getting close, and I had to act quickly. I started dancing upon his tank, as I knew that this would infuriate him into action. "What are you going to do? Shoot me?"

The officer gritted his teeth and pulled himself out of that hatch faster than I imagined a man could move. "Get off!"

I shook my head. "Why don't you make me?" I asked. I felt that goading him on was the best way for him to get moving and get off of that tank.

The officer wasted no time and took a swing at me. I dodged this faster than I normally could have, and though his second punch struck me in the chest, it felt as though I had been hit lightly with a comfortable cushion.

"Come now. I thought the Wehrmacht was stronger than that!" I yelled.

This seemed to be the right thing to say, because he tackled me off of that tank and into the snow. I moved with him, and in midair, I made sure to spin so that I was on top of him when the rounds came in.

There were two explosions not too far apart. The first one missed the tank, but the second was a direct hit, and the mighty Panzer was a glowing ball of flame and black smoke. Many chunks of shrapnel hit my back but bounced off like flies on a windowpane.

I stood up and straightened out my tuxedo even though there was no wrinkle or a single stitch out of place. The officer stared at his tank, his eyes bulging from his head.

I smiled and offered to help him up. "Sorry to antagonize you, friend. But I believe that was the only way to get you off of that thing. I do think you will forgive me one day."

The officer refused my help and looked at me from head to toe. "Who are you?"

I shrugged, tipped my hat, and did a twirl. "If I told you that, you wouldn't believe me. However, one day, a man will come knocking on your door long after this war is over, and you will be an old man. Let him into your house, and he will tell you of a fantastic journey. He will tell you who I am." I smiled at the man and turned to leave. I could feel the man's destiny shift, and I knew now what Kyle had been saying about the lines of destiny. This officer had three lines, and one of them grew in great strength above his head, and it waved in wind unfelt.

"So that's it?" the officer asked.

I turned back to him. "The war is over for you now. But it will always be there with you. It can be used to strengthen you or weaken you. That is your choice."

I took a few steps away, and I was preparing my sword.

The officer took several staggering steps toward me. "Wait. Where are you going?"

I turned around and tipped my hat with my cane. "To the bridge of tomorrow, over the river of yesterday."

THE SALVATION

A GREAT DEAL OF NOISE was coming down from the hall, and both Erich and the old man turned their gaze toward it. Lights were coming on in the hall, and Erich's face was now in his hands. Two sets of footfalls were outside in the corridor, the clanging of steel on steel, some chatter, and a few shouts here and there. Footsteps paused at the cell door, and a small tray of food was pushed underneath the metal bars. It was a few pieces of toast with butter and what looked like overcooked scrambled eggs. A small glass of milk was placed beside it. The two guards said nothing to Erich and moved on to the next cell.

Erich harrumphed. "Breakfast. What's the point of feeding me when I will be dead in minutes, anyway? I don't know if I could eat even if I were hungry. What sort of joy that there is left in meals has already been forgotten."

The old man's eyes lingered at the food on the floor for a moment, and then he looked back at Erich. "I can't help but feel as though I have usurped your last moments here. If you would like to be left alone, please say so."

Erich shook his head. "I'm glad you stayed the night. I would not be able to bear this alone. What sleep would I find in these final hours? You are my solace. You are my last sense of dignity. And I don't even know if you are real or not. Maybe I've just traded one delusion for another. Maybe I've concocted this entire fantasy here." Erich pointed at his head.

The old man shrugged. "That is certainly one way you could choose to view it. But it is clear that you have come to terms with your faith and that you are attracting good things to you, despite the harsh conditions you are faced with here. Also, I am quite real."

Erich laughed. "Well, maybe my mind would make you say that."

"Or maybe your prayers were answered."

Rocking himself back and forth in his chair, Erich stretched his neck from side to side. There were more noises from the hallways: shouts of men, clanging of steel, and footsteps on stone. "Tell me more of your story. It is keeping my mind occupied. I'd rather listen to you than that prattle outside. It's unbearable."

The old man took a deep breath. "Where was I?"

"You had just saved that tank commander from death."

Raising a finger, the old man said, "Ah, yes. I knew then that my mission was to aid my own faith by intervening where it was necessary. So, of course, the tank commander came to mind because this was a powerful story that stuck with me and encouraged me to continue my pursuit.

"Then, of course, there were the two instances in Korea and in Vietnam. However, the Sword of Destiny made me aware that Kyle already went to those places, and so, by me going, it would be unnecessary. Despite knowing this, I went anyway."

Erich rubbed his head. "Sorry to interrupt, but I don't get it. Why did you have to do all of these things that Kyle already did? Kyle intervened on the beaches with Joe. He intervened with you in Korea and Vietnam. Why go back and do all of that over? That work was already done. Are you saying that when you took up that sword that you somehow erased what Kyle had done? Wouldn't that then mean that you would also erase all of the good things he had done?"

The old man leaned forward, and his eyebrows rose. "You are now following the mysteries that I was following. You are now questioning the fabric of time and what it means to interfere and influence. I did not know if I became Kyle by taking up the Sword of Destiny. Perhaps I am Kyle. I still don't know. And so I did choose to go back to Korea and Vietnam, but I don't think it was necessary. I chose to go back to these places because I thought maybe I could add something. But when I got there, the lines of destiny were the same. And so I knew that adding more sugar to the cake would not make it any sweeter. I was simply following the wrong lead."

Erich took a deep breath. "Why not just go to Joseph again? Why not try to stop him the moment he tried to hang himself?"

The old man raised a finger. "You are close to a solution. But I don't think just going there would have worked, either, because Joe's decision was already made. His mind was made up, and my influence may have postponed it, but it may never have changed it. But Pastor Jacob was not wrong. I was just looking at the problem from the wrong direction ..."

#

I returned to my childhood farmhouse in my old living room. It was the night of Joseph's suicide, and all the family was still asleep except, of course, for Joe. It was eerily quiet, and I was very conscious of each step and each breath I was taking. I walked through that house like a ghost. The memory of that day was so vivid in my mind that it was like I was walking through memory. Although I was not afraid and although I had no fear, I still had no idea if my plan would at all work.

I walked into Joseph's room. He was sitting on the edge of his bed and held his head in his hands. He was rocking himself back and forth, and on occasion, he would mutter something to himself. He pulled at his short hair hard enough to pull some hairs out, and he dropped them to the floor. I watched him for a while, hoping he would look up to see me, but when he didn't, I decided to say something.

I crossed my arms. "Hello, Joseph," I said.

My brother looked up, and his face was red and his eyes swollen, and he was shaking as though he were cold. "You? Get out of my mind."

I shook my head. "I'm not in your mind. I'm standing with you in this room."

Joseph let out a low whistle. "Okay, then." He looked away and put his fingers in his ears and continued to rock himself back and forth.

Joseph did not appear to be receptive to any placation. This was also my expectation, and so I am left to wonder if it was I who created this moment.

I sat down on the bed beside Joe, and when I did so, he immediately got up. I took this opportunity to tap the wall with my cane. Joseph took several angry steps in one direction and spun to take a few angry steps another direction. He was muttering something to himself, which sounded like a low growl that a cat might make. He took to pulling at the hairs of his eyebrows, and although he didn't have his fingers in his ears, I knew he wasn't really listening.

I changed my position on the bed and tapped the wall again with my cane.

Joseph took to leaning up against the wall now, and his face was in his hands. I tapped the wall again with my cane.

"Stop that," Joseph said.

"Why?"

"It's annoying. Don't you have some battlefield to pick through? Some corpses to dance on? Or are you waiting to finish me off right now?" Joseph's eyes finally met mine.

I tapped the wall again. "Joseph, I'm here to help you."

Joseph's teeth were clenched, and he pointed a bony finger at me. "I don't need your help."

I nodded. "I know *you* don't need my help, but I can show you someone who does."

Joseph gave me a quizzical look. "You are talking nonsense."

The door swung slowly open with a creak, and my younger self dressed in pajamas stood in the doorway. "You okay, Joseph? I heard you tapping on my wall."

Joseph looked to my younger self and then to me. "Yeah, I'm fine. Go back to bed."

The younger me shifted from side to side. "You don't look fine. Why don't we go outside for a drink or something?"

Joseph shook his head. "Nah. You should go before you wake up Mom and Dad."

My younger self moved into the room and closed the door. I noticed now that my younger self had a line of destiny waving like a willow branch from the top of his head. It was thin, dull silver, and yet it was there.

I cleared my throat so that Joseph would look at me. "Why don't you tell your brother how you plan to hang yourself with the necktie he gave to you as a gift for Christmas? Have you ever thought what damaging effect that would have on such a young mind? He will live out his life wondering why you never loved him."

Joseph took a step backward and fell into the wall.

My younger self took a baby step toward Joseph and whispered, "You can tell me anything. I know what happened to you fighting the Germans was rough. I know I will never know what that is like." With every word that my younger self spoke, I saw and felt lines of destiny change. I knew now that I was in unchartered waters. I was coming to the crescendo. Whatever would be said or done at this moment would completely change my world forever.

"Tell him, Joe," I said as I stood up. I wielded the Sword of Destiny, holding it over his head.

"A sword?" Joseph said in almost a whisper, and I knew that he could see it for what it was.

"If you want to die tonight and leave this boy to wallow in misery for all of his life, please let me slay you so you can have that dying wish granted."

Joseph's hands were raised in the air. "I didn't say anything about that."

The younger me stepped in front of Joseph. "What are you looking at?" The younger me turned to face me, but I ignored him.

"You know," I said, "I could just cut his head off and be done with it. All of his pain and suffering would end. All of your selfishness will never be known. He will die knowing that his brother was a hero. His brother was a man of honor, and his brother was there for him when he needed him. He would never know of your suicide. Choose now, Joseph. Choose to live, or choose otherwise."

Joseph pushed the younger me so that he was behind him. "Don't you hurt him," he said, frothing through gritted teeth. There was a spark of life and of anger in his eyes that I had only seen when Joe was pushed over the edge. "You get away from him. You understand me?"

"I have come to slay the boy. Get out of my way," I said.

"You will have to cut me down. No one gets to my brother," Joseph said.

"Joe, you are scaring me," my younger self said, but Joseph made sure to keep between us.

"Stand aside, Joseph. I'm here for the boy's head, not yours," I said.

Joseph pushed me, and his hands became fists. "I don't know what you are, but you are not going to hurt him."

The lines of destiny over Joseph's head grew in number and in strength. I saw two new lines form and even intertwine with my own younger self. I smiled and took a step back. I lowered my sword, and it became a cane, and I leaned on it.

I looked Joseph in the eye. "You can only protect your brother when you are around."

"I'll manage," Joseph said through a sneer.

I nodded. "Listen to your brother. He needs you more than you can possibly fathom. He would go to the ends of the earth to make sure that you were okay. He would fight the devil if that is what it would take to make sure that you come back from whatever hell that you are in. You can only protect him as long as you are alive to do so."

I turned to walk out of the room. I could feel everything change.

\#

The gift came to me not as a big explosion of fire or holy light. There were no angels coming down from the heavens, and there were no sounds of trumpets, but what I received was far more precious than the largest diamond or the purest gold. The gift was far better than the finest wine and the best steak in the world.

Memories. I was granted a new life by the Lord, God, the Creator, or the Universe, whatever it might be called. I was given all the things my heart ever wanted. Memories are the things that really matter and the only possessions we can ever own, because they are the only things that we can take with us to the afterlife. We may fool ourselves for a time with fancy cars, mansions, or even endless vacations. But really the only things that matter are our connections to others we care about. I knew this before that moment, of course, so this wasn't the revelation that I felt.

Joseph never killed himself. He did not break. He suffered the sorrow that plagued him and endured it one day at a time. He grew up and grew old. He married, albeit twice, but he fathered two children of his own and even had three grandchildren.

Having these memories bombard me instantly was a shock to my system, and so I went outside of the farmhouse and sat in the snow. It was an epiphany, like suddenly remembering a word or song that I had forgotten. I sat there in the cold and replayed my memories over in my mind. I remembered each Christmas, each Thanksgiving I spent with Joseph and our large family, how close we were, and how close our children were. I remember how happy my mother was to host large family gatherings. Children running around all over the place, the smell of pork roast in the oven, and these little dinner rolls my mother would make. They were like candy to everyone with a little bit of butter. She was forced to make three times the normal amount, because inevitably, everyone would steal them before dinner. When I say everyone, I mean everyone. My father, my brother, and all of our kids would come in to the kitchen one by one and take one of those dinner rolls and a bit of butter.

My mother always put on a good show of shooing us away and trying to discourage us from eating them. But deep down, I think she liked the attention, and I think she liked that everyone adored her cooking so much. It was all in good fun, of course. Good times, happy times. And the years of depression in my family that once followed Joseph's suicide simply never happened. All of that evil and all of that sorrow were washed away. It wasn't perfect; we still fought, still bickered over little things. But that's normal family life. That's each human trying to manifest his or her creative power over everything. Sometimes those lines of destiny bump up against one another. But it certainly was much better than what I originally experienced.

I remembered going to church with Joseph, baptizing our children, and every football game we went to. I remembered the great talks we used to have and how he helped me with my own marriage and my own personal problems throughout the years.

Joseph encouraged me to go to both Korea as a soldier and to Vietnam as a journalist; he never told me why, but I listened to him because I trusted him.

Joseph went on to become an entrepreneur, creating a chain of hardware stores aimed at the common homeowner. His business was so successful that he even hired me when my career wavered after my short stint in Vietnam. We worked well together, and a true mastermind formed between us. Our brains actually became a third brain, and we dreamed up new ideas of how to provide better service to others. If we didn't have expertise in a certain critical area, we hired skilled professionals to help. We were constantly dreaming, constantly inventing new ideas. It was a very rewarding career for me, not only because I was with my brother but because I truly enjoyed the work. It made my family very secure financially, and the brotherly bond I shared with Joseph only grew stronger over time. We became pioneers in this field, and by the time we were in our fifties, we were already retired. We passed the business on to very capable hands and remained on staff for consultation purposes. We gave ourselves handsome retirement bonuses, and we helped the business out whenever they needed it.

We had long and prosperous lives. My devotion to angels endured because Joseph had seen them, and I had seen them. We talked about our angel experiences with each other but kept it secret from the others. However, we used these experiences to strengthen our faith and to lead others to live healthy and happy lives.

We walked in the light and led good lives, not out of chance or luck. I don't believe in fate or destiny as something that is outside of us, but rather as something we create for ourselves. We were successful because we had a vision, a plan, and we acted on that plan. We had faith that it would work out, and it simply worked out. But that's how the world works if you stop to think about it.

Think back to anything in your life that you had a single-minded purpose to achieve—you probably achieved it. Anything you were wishy-washy about you probably forgot about, and consequently, it never happened for you.

And so, my story both begins and ends with my brother. My brother was back in my life and in a greater capacity than tragedy. He raised a family, and I had nieces and nephews.

So this story ends with a question that I ask of you. Do you believe in angels?

THE CHOICE

E RICH LOOKED FROM SIDE TO side as the old man stared at him in silence. "Um, you are sitting right there. And either I must accept that I am insane or I must accept that you exist."

"You didn't answer my question," the old man said.

Erich rolled his eyes. "I believe in God, and I believe I could be forgiven for the horrible things I have done. I have prayed every day since I've been in here. I've prayed when my family abandoned me and when my wife left me. I know that I am a good man despite the evil I did. I know it was wrong, and my punishment is just. I'm just afraid is all. I feel as though I'm about to step off into the darkness."

The old man cocked an eyebrow. "That still hasn't answered my question."

Erich threw up both arms. "What would you have me say? I suspect that there is something else that you want to ask me."

The old man shrugged. "Of course."

Erich stood up and rubbed his head and face. "You want me to take the sword. You want me to take the binding oath that you took, and you want me to take your place."

The old man nodded. "With the sword, you will be given the power to change history. You will be given the instrument to cleanse your life.

234

You will be given the chance to right every wrong you have done, and you will have the opportunity to walk in the light."

"Your story doesn't even make sense. If Joseph didn't die, why would you have gone back in time in the first place? Why would you have been seeking out Kyle in your old age? Why not just be happy?" Erich asked.

The old man shrugged. "I had already gone back through time and became what I am now. Nothing could have changed that since I took up the sword. With the Sword of Destiny, you could undo the things you did in your life."

Erich began to pace about the room. "But I would be trapped in time like you are. I would be unable to live like a normal person. Or die like a normal person. I would be a wanderer, a loner. I have all of that right now. But at least I know it is ending. How long have you been like this?"

The old man shrugged. "I don't know. A very long time."

"What's a long time? Five years? A hundred?"

The old man wiped his face. "I can't be certain. Time doesn't work the same way for me. And so it could be an hour, or it could be a thousand years."

Erich continued to pace. "A thousand years? You might have been alone for a thousand years?"

Raising both hands, the old man said, "I am far from alone. I talk to people every day. I inspire people. I help people see the joy, the beauty, and the laughter. Even those who cannot directly see me still benefit from my being present. Happiness and joy follow me."

Erich harrumphed and waved his hands around the room, pointing to all the walls. "You call this joy?"

"We all see what we wish to see."

Erich stopped pacing and put his hands on his hips. "But you can never hug your granddaughters again, can you?"

"Not exactly. I do visit them often, and even though they cannot see me, knowing that they are well and thriving fills me with a sense of pride, hope, and love."

Erich bit his thumbnail and spit out to his left. "The sword can cut through time, yes? Why not just cut a hole here so that I can escape?"

The old man smiled and shook his head. "It doesn't work like that. To go through the tear in time, you would have to be the master of this artifact. You would have to take my place the way I took Kyle's place," the old man said.

Erich sat down. His shoulders slumped forward, and his neck drooped downward. "So my choices are to face death here or wallow in misery for eternity? Those are the only options? Surely you must have a better plan than that."

The old man moved to the edge of the bed and put on his shoes, which were now fancy, shining black shoes. "I didn't say it was an easy choice. But it is a choice. Before I came along, you had no choice. You have the faith strong enough to summon me, strong enough to see me, and strong enough to wield the Sword of Destiny … should you want it."

Erich's face was becoming red, and he clenched his teeth together. "I feel so weak. There is nothing left for me. No one in the world cares about me."

When the old man stood, he was suddenly wearing a black tuxedo with a top hat and holding a black-and-white cane. He adjusted the buttons on his coat and put a hand on Erich's shoulder. "I care about you. And I am here with you when it matters the most. I am here when everyone else has abandoned you."

There were the sounds of heavy chains rattling and the footsteps of several men far before there were guards standing outside of the cell. There was a clack of a metal key, and the cell door creaked open like the front door of a haunted house.

The lead guard threw down some chains near Erich's feet. "Stand up and hold out your hands."

Erich's eyes caught the old man's. "I don't suppose you could cut us out of here?" he whispered.

"What are you muttering?" a shorter guard with a furrowed brow asked.

Shaking his head while he stood, Erich said, "Nothing." He extended out both of his hands and looked away so he wouldn't have to look any of the guards in the eye.

The shorter guard placed irons on Erich's wrists, right at the same point he had his rash. Erich winced but otherwise didn't move. When the guard was finished, he put the heavier irons upon Erich's ankles. When he was done, he pulled them once for good measure, which almost pulled Erich off balance. The shorter guard stood up and gave Erich a small shove. "Don't try anything stupid."

Erich shrugged and didn't answer.

The three guards moved Erich out of the cell and led him down a long corridor, which was lined with other iron-bound cages for men.

The old man walked beside Erich, and he was smiling, breathing deeply, and looking at the walls around him as though they were painted with the most beautiful frescoes or adorned with gorgeous tapestries. Erich looked around at the walls and could not see what the old man was looking at.

The old man continued to survey the drab walls. Sounds from other cells filled the hallway. Several hands reached out through bars toward the guards.

One guard smacked away a pair of hands that were groping outward. "Knock it off, or we'll come in there and give you a beating."

Erich looked into each cell as they passed. Blank stares with sunken eyes looked back at him. The prisoners were shrunken, hunched, and dried-up-looking, as though they had all the moisture sucked out of them. Most of them stood in silence as the hallway group passed by. One, however, made eye contact with Erich.

"Courage," he said.

"Excuse me?" Erich asked, leaning toward the cell.

The man was dirty, as though he had rolled around in filth. "I said, 'Have courage.'"

Erich nodded and swallowed some spit; he was wearing a bewildered look now, and he gazed over his shoulder twice to watch the man with whom he had just spoken. The man smiled back at him and saluted.

The group continued down the corridor for a few minutes until the guards stopped at a series of heavy doors, and when the final door was opened, a great amount of light poured into the dark corridor—so much so that everyone squinted and averted their eyes. All except the old man, who looked skyward, beaming with joy as tears came down his face.

Erich sneezed twice.

Once outside and in the courtyard of the prison, the guards moved Erich toward a wooden staircase that led to a platform where a man in a black hood and a priest were waiting. In front of the platform, about twenty people stood in a roped-off area. Erich stopped when he saw this.

"You will be with me, right?" Erich whispered.

"I will stay with you until your last breath. But my offer still stands." The old man held out his cane toward Erich.

Erich looked at the cane but made no attempt to touch it. He lurched forward as he was struck from behind by a guard. "Keep moving."

The small group of people behind the rope barrier began to shout when they saw Erich and the guards. Fists were raised in the air amid ugly words and shouts.

The guards continued on and led Erich up an old wooden structure where the noose had been prepared. The man with the black hood was slightly overweight; his belly stuck out from his shirt, and his breathing was audible. He stood by a large wooden lever. The old man walked next to Erich in his tuxedo and with his sword that appeared as a cane. When the guards pushed Erich over a trapdoor, the fat man with the black hood came close and wrapped the noose about Erich's neck. He gave it a tug to make sure it was secure, which made Erich stumble somewhat.

The priest came forward in front of Erich, facing the crowd. He wore a strange conical white hat and held a Bible in his left hand. The crowd began to hush when the priest held up both hands.

"We are here to see justice done today. We are here to witness the ending of Erich Kunze's life."

This inspired cheers from the crowd. The priest said a few words about the family that Erich had slain, but his words were drowned out by shouts and foul language. The priest gave up, turned to Erich and asked, "Do you have any last words?"

Erich coughed and swallowed. There were slight tears in his eyes, and his gaze met with the old man's; he nodded to him. The crowd began to settle down as the length of silence grew. "I am sorry to have caused so much grief and catastrophic harm. Nothing except today can erase that."

"Lick me crosswise on the ass!" someone shouted.

"Go to the devil, demon!" shouted another. Spit and other trash flew near Erich, but he wasn't hit by anything.

"God will not see you here today!" cried out an angry and bitter-looking woman whose fists were clenched so tightly that they were white.

A greasy-looking man held his hands to his mouth, and he yelled, "String him up!"

The priest nodded, his face devoid of emotion. The priest then splashed a bit of holy water upon the Erich and said a prayer, albeit rather quickly and insincerely.

Erich's face drained of color, and he was shaking; even his breathing was erratic. The fat man in the black hood put a black hood over Erich's head.

"I'm still with you," the old man said.

"I'm sorry," Erich's voice wavered.

The fat man in the hood muttered as he patted Erich twice on the shoulder. "Too late for that, son."

Ignoring the fat man, Erich said, "I'm sorry I can't help you. I don't even know your name."

The old man embraced Erich and put his forehead on Erich's. "I don't need a name."

Erich coughed and let out a nervous laugh. "You could be anyone."

The old man smiled. "Yes, I could be anyone. I will be fine. There will be others. Be at peace." He kissed Erich on the forehead.

Erich's breathing became like a dog panting. "Don't let go of me."

"I'm right here with you."

Erich grunted, "I believe in angels, but I don't want to be lost in time."

The old man held Erich in an embrace and held his breath.

The order was given, the fat man pulled the lever, and Erich Kunze dropped through the hole in the trapdoor with the old man holding on to him.

Time slowed. The sounds of the shouting crowd faded for a breath. Erich's descent was captured in time, and the old man's eyes caught a bird that was flying above, its wings spread wide and its head held high. Its beak caught the angle of the morning sun just right and twinkled like morning dew. The old man smiled.

The old man exhaled, and time resumed its normal pace. There was a terrible sound of cracking of bone, and the body of Erich dangled from the end of the rope; his legs twitched several times and then stopped. The old man glided down to the ground, looked up at Erich, and let go of his embrace. He tipped his hat with his cane and did a short bow from his head.

Turning his back to the angry shouts from the crowd, the old man adjusted the collar on his tuxedo and swung the Sword of Destiny, making a vertical cut through the air. Reality parted, rippling open as the curtains of time appeared. The old man paused for a moment as he looked briefly over his shoulder toward the swinging body of Erich and then stood up straight and took a deep breath; he stepped through the blackness and beyond.